Editing by Amy Gamache @ Rose David Editing

Cover Design by Melissa Gill Designs

Table of Contents

Chapter One
Abel

"Abel." Her voice is so clear, like an angel calling to me from the darkness. "Abel." I follow the sweet sound. "Abel."

My eyes shoot open and I blink rapidly, taking in the blackness of the room, my chest rising and falling in quick succession.

I squeeze my eyes shut, trying to fall back into the dream. It's one I've had hundreds of times before. I'm standing in a hallway. Everything is white. The floors, the walls, the ceiling. There's white everywhere I look. And then she calls to me. I chase the voice, desperate to find her, but I always wake up before I can. It never changes. Over and over I search for her in my dreams.

"You okay?" Moments later, a hand slides across my stomach.

I flinch at the contact.

"Fine," I grumble, quickly rolling out of bed.

I don't know how I fell asleep here. I'm usually up and out within minutes of finding my release, but tonight, too little sleep and too much whiskey seems to have gotten the better of me.

"Where are you going?" Melanie whines. Or maybe it's Michelle. Fuck, I can't even remember her name.

"Home," I say flatly, fumbling around the dark room in search of my clothes.

"You don't have to leave." She shifts in the bed, light flooding the room seconds later.

I squint at the brightness, snagging my jeans off the floor before stepping into them.

"Come back to bed," she coos. I look at her just long enough to see her propped up on her elbows, her breasts spilling out over the top of the blanket.

She's an attractive enough woman. Long red hair, blue eyes, a body that would make even the most committed of men take notice. But she's not the person I want to see. That person is gone, and she took my heart and a piece of my soul with her when she left.

"I can't." I slip on my shirt and grab my shoes off the floor.

"Can I see you again?" I feel her eyes follow me toward the door.

"I told you earlier. I'm moving back to Chicago in two days." The thought alone has my insides turning in on themselves. It's time, I know that. California is beautiful and has offered me an escape when I needed it the most, but it's not my home.

While I'm ready, a part of me knows how hard being back there is going to be. It's been three years, yet those three years have done nothing to lessen the tremendous amount of loss I feel. I'm starting to wonder if the pain will ever go away.

But I've gotten good at hiding it. At burying it down deep and pretending like everything is okay. Only it isn't okay. I don't think it ever will be again.

"But that's in two days. What are you doing later today? Do you want to meet up for dinner or something?"

"I can't." I don't try to hide the irritation in my voice.

It's nothing she's done, of course, and I feel mildly bad for being so short with her, but this is what it means to get involved with someone like me. *Emotionally unavailable. Closed off. Here for only one thing.* I made it clear what this was from the beginning. She's the one who chose to bring me home. I guess you could say she brought it on herself.

"Can I at least get your phone number?" Her voice stops me right as I've stepped out into the hallway.

"Thanks for a good night," I tell her, not answering her question.

This feels wrong. It always feels wrong. And yet randomly hooking up with strangers is the only thing that makes me feel even remotely better. So I keep doing it, even though in the long run it usually makes me feel worse.

I don't wait around to hear her response. Slipping on my shoes, I make a bee line for the door, not able to get out of here fast enough.

It isn't until I step out into the cool night air that I feel like I can take a real breath. I cross the parking lot toward my car and quickly slip inside and shut the door, letting my head fall back against the headrest.

Trying to ward off the wave of nausea making its way through my gut, I take a deep breath in, letting it out slowly.

I know better than to drink so much. When I do it puts me in situations like this and I don't like being in situations like this.

Lifting my head, I press the ignition button and listen to my car as it rumbles to life. Checking the time, I see it's just after five in the morning.

Even though I feel completely sober, a part of me is tempted to shut the car back off and sleep off the remaining alcohol still flowing through my veins. And even though that's the smarter option, I find myself popping the car into gear and slowly backing out of the parking spot.

"You got all your stuff?" My brother Adam steps around the back of the car where I'm shoving the last of my things into the trunk.

While it would be much quicker to fly back to Chicago, it's easier to drive. That way I don't have to worry about shipping all of my stuff. Plus, being in the car for two days alone will give me time to mentally prepare myself for how I'm going to feel being back in Chicago for the first time in three years.

"Yep, this is the last of it," I say, stepping back to close the trunk.

"You got everything you need for the road?"

"I think so. I packed some drinks and snacks. Anything else I can get along the way."

"I can't believe I'm saying this, but I think I'm gonna miss having your moody ass around."

I chuckle, my gaze going to my oldest brother. Adam and I had never been extremely close while I was growing up. Being eight years apart, Adam left for college when I was still in grade school. It's been nice having this time with him. Don't get me wrong, he's no peach to live with, but I was surprised by how similar we are even though our lives are polar opposite.

He's a doctor and one of the most promising ones in his field. I'm a musician who spends the majority of his nights jamming out at whatever dive bar I'm able to land a gig at. He's clean shaven and nicely dressed. I've got a sleeve of tattoos down one arm, sport a permanent week-old scruff, and wear whatever shit is laying around that smells relatively clean, which usually equates to a wrinkled t-shirt and jeans.

But for all of our differences, when you take away the superficial shit, we're more alike than I ever realized.

"My moody ass?" I finally comment. "I hate to tell you, big brother, but you're not one to talk."

"I blame that on sleep deprivation." He chuckles.

"Maybe you shouldn't work so hard."

"The harder I work, the more lives I save."

"You should trademark that shit and stick it on a business card."

"That's not a bad idea." He shoves my shoulder.

"You won't have to miss me for long. I'll see you at Aaron's wedding in what, three weeks?"

"I can't believe it took him and Sam this long to finally tie the knot. They've been engaged forever it feels like."

"Probably because they have."

"Good that you're going home now. It'll give you a couple weeks to get settled before the wedding madness begins."

"Yeah, and it will give everyone something to focus on other than my return."

"So you *did* strategically plan it this way." He gives me a knowing look.

"What can I say? You know I hate being the center of attention."

"*You*?" He blanches. "Since when?"

"Fuck you, dude." I laugh, crossing toward the driver's side of the car. "I guess I should get going. I want to try to make it to Wyoming before stopping for the night."

"Well, good luck with that. That's nearly half of your thirty some hour trip. You'll be lucky if you get there by the middle of the night."

"I may stop earlier if I get tired."

"Make sure you let me know when you hit your first stop."

"Yes, Mom," I tease.

"Shut up." He shakes his head at me as he makes his way to the sidewalk.

"Hey, Adam." I pull open the door and pause, my gaze sliding to a few feet in front of my car where my brother is

11

standing. "Thanks for everything," I say, knowing I don't need to elaborate what *everything* means. I think we both know I'd be in a hell of a lot worse of a place if it weren't for him letting me stay.

"Keep your head up, little brother," he tells me, an unspoken moment passing between us.

I nod, not feeling like any more words are needed, before silently slipping into my car.

Chapter Two
Peyton

"Please tell me you have my shoes." My roommate, Henna, bursts into my room, completely unannounced. Her slender body is clad in a fluffy white robe and her long black hair is hidden underneath a towel twisted on top of her head.

"You'll need to be more specific," I tell her, buttoning the last two buttons of my cream-colored blouse.

"You know, the red strappy ones with the black heels." She purses her lips.

"You're planning on wearing *those* to work?" I give her a questioning look. "I can't imagine old Mrs. Jenkins would approve," I say, referring to the uptight marketing executive she works for.

"No, to Sam's bachelorette party tonight. I need to buy a new dress, but I want to wear those shoes. I need to take them shopping with me on my lunch break to make sure whatever I buy matches."

"I'm going to go ahead and keep what I'm thinking to myself." I bite my bottom lip to contain my smile.

"Oh screw you, Peyton." She sticks her tongue out at me. "Have you seen my shoes or not?"

"I'm pretty sure they're in the hall closet," I tell her, pointing in that vicinity.

"Of course they would be in the one place I haven't looked." She sighs dramatically.

"You know, you wouldn't have this problem if you kept all your shoes in the same place."

"Have you seen how many shoes I have?" She gives me a knowing look.

"Good point." I laugh.

"Don't forget, we're meeting at Rain's at six for pregame drinks."

"I might be a little late. I don't get off work until five."

"So tell John to let you leave early."

"That's not how it works. I can't just tell my boss what to do."

"Oh please." She waves her hand at me. "You have the most laid-back job in the world, with quite possibly the coolest boss ever. You can do whatever you want."

She's not wrong there. I really do have the best job with the best boss, who also happens to own the company. At just thirty-three years old, he operates one of the largest video game testing firms in the country. Not that I actually get to play video games for a living. I handle the scheduling and working with the developers, but that doesn't make it any less enjoyable.

"Not to mention, he totally thinks you're hot. That never hurts."

"He does not," I disagree.

"Yeah, okay." She snorts sarcastically.

"Speaking of work, you're going to make me late," I tell her, stepping into my nude pumps.

"Fine. But your ass better be at Rain's by six."

"I'll do my best," I tell her, garnering myself a pointed look before she spins around and quickly exits my room.

As much as I love living with Henna, I'm starting to think I would have been better off getting my own place. At least then I would be able to get dressed for work without her barging in anytime she wants. Privacy is not something she respects. I guess you could say she doesn't have a very good grasp on how boundaries work.

Then again, I'd never be able to afford this apartment on my own. The rent alone would take half of my monthly pay and that doesn't count utilities or any of the other expenses I have.

I honestly don't know how people afford to live on their own, especially in a city like Chicago. Even at twenty-six, with a good paying job, I don't think I could manage. Hence why when Henna, whom I've known since middle school, suggested we get a place together, I jumped at the opportunity. I was dying to get out of my father's house, not to mention living downtown is extremely convenient. Now, instead of driving forty-five minutes to the city every day, I'm less than ten minutes from the office.

Despite Henna's insistence that I be on time, I fire off a quick text to Sam to let her know I might be a little late tonight, before stuffing the device into my wristlet and heading for the door.

"Hey, you got a minute." I look up to see John leaning against the doorframe of my office.

His button-down shirt is untucked, the top two buttons are open revealing the smallest sliver of tanned skin. He gives me an easy smile, his brown eyes locked on me as he steps further into my office before he closes the door.

"Yeah, what's up?" I close my laptop, watching him slide into the chair on the opposite side of the desk from where I'm sitting.

"I wanted to see if you'd be able to join me at the upcoming video game convention in New York. There will be a lot of developers there and I could really use someone with your talents." He swipes a hand through his messy dark blonde locks.

"My talents?" I cock my head to the side, a small smile playing on my lips.

"You know more about this company than some of the people who were here when I started it. Not to mention you have a way with people. Besides, I think it would be a good learning experience for you. Give you a chance to see how the other side of the business works. You'd have your own hotel room for the weekend and the company will cover all your travelling expenses."

"When is it again? My friend, Sam is getting married the first weekend in May. That would be the only thing that may conflict."

"It's not until the end of June, so that won't be a problem."

"Would it be just me and you?" I ask, not sure why the thought makes me a little uncomfortable.

Don't get me wrong, John is a good-looking guy who is very successful, and while he's never given me a reason to feel uncomfortable around him, I'm not sure how I feel about a weekend in New York alone together. Not that I think anything would happen.

"Diego will be going as well." He stretches out his legs and crosses his ankles. "So, what do you say? You'd really be helping me out."

"Okay. Yeah, I should be able to make that work."

"Perfect." He clasps his hands together. "I'll have Bev make all the arrangements and send you the itinerary once it's confirmed." He pushes to a stand.

"Hey, really quick," I say to his back right as he turns. I wait until he's facing me again before continuing, "Would it be okay if I head out about an hour early today? I'm supposed to be meeting the *bride-to-be* at six and I have a few things to take care of first."

"Bachelorette party?" he guesses.

I nod, feeling mildly embarrassed by the way he smirks at me. It's like he knows a ton of alcohol and male genitalia will likely be involved.

"Yeah, no problem. You could use a night out."

"What's that supposed to mean?" I arch a brow at him.

"It means you work too much." He grins.

"You're my boss. You're supposed to like that I work too much."

"And I do. But I also know that everyone needs to let off a little steam from time to time. Have fun tonight." He moves closer to the door.

"Thanks, John."

"And if you find yourself in any trouble and need a ride or a bail out, you have my number," he says before pulling open the door.

"Pretty sure it would be highly inappropriate to call my boss to bail me out of jail."

"Wouldn't be anything I haven't done myself." He winks, disappearing into the hallway moments later.

I laugh to myself, oddly enough not having a hard time envisioning John behind bars. Something tells me while he may work hard, he plays even harder.

Refocusing, I open my laptop and pull my email back up, needing to get some things taken care of before I leave.

Chapter Three
Abel

"I can't get over how tan you are." Claire smiles at me from across the table.

"I spent a lot of time on the beach." I shrug, fiddling with the straw wrapper in front of me.

"You look good."

"You just saw me a week ago," I remind her.

"Yeah, but that was Facetime. Seeing you here, in person, after nearly three years. I don't know, you just seem better."

I resist the urge to tell her that getting out of bed every day feels like a chore. Or that since I arrived in Chicago three days ago, I've felt this overwhelming weight pressing down on my chest that makes me feel like I'm suffocating. Instead, I smile and nod. I know that if anyone understands my pain, it's Claire. Finley was her sister after all. Maybe in a way I feel like I'm protecting her by making her believe that I'm okay. I'm not even sure I know what okay looks like anymore.

While we've talked nearly every week since I left three years ago, recently most of our conversations have been pretty light. In the beginning, we talked about Finley a lot, but after a while there wasn't much to say that we hadn't already said.

"How are you? Still seeing that guy from work?"

"Hell no." She crinkles her nose.

"What happened? I thought you really liked him."

"So did I. That was until I caught him making out with Bethany in the break room."

"In the break room?" I arch a brow.

"Oh yeah. I'm not sure if the soda machine has ever seen such action before."

"That sucks. I'm sorry."

"Don't be. I'm glad I found out what a slime ball he was before things went too far." She forces a smile. "What about you? You seeing anyone?"

"You already know the answer to that. You ask me every time we talk."

"Maybe now that you're home you can open yourself up to the possibility of an actual relationship."

"I'm not interested in a relationship."

"Just emotionless fucking then?"

I choke out a laugh at her bluntness. "There's something to be said for emotionless sex."

"I beg to differ. What is sex without emotion? It's empty and meaningless."

"That's kind of the point."

"Abel," she starts but I quickly cut her off.

"I'm not ready." I don't leave any room for argument with my tone.

"It's been three years. Don't you think…"

"I said I'm not ready, Claire," I grind out. She falls silent, blowing out a slow breath. "I'm sorry." I shake my head.

"Don't be." She holds her hand up to stop me. "I shouldn't push." She pauses before changing the subject. "I talked to your mom the other day. She seems to be doing well. Still cancer free."

"Yeah, she is. She's focused on Andrew's wedding right now. I swear, if she asks me if I've made it to the tailor to get my measurements for my tux one more time I'm going to lose my mind."

"She just wants to make sure everything is perfect for his big day. You should cut her some slack."

"I'm trying." I sigh. "It's just harder than I thought… Being back here."

"Give it time. It's only been three days."

"I see her everywhere," I admit in a moment of vulnerability.

"I know the feeling." She reaches across the table and pats my hand.

"How do you handle it?"

"When I see something that reminds me of her, or I hear a song on the radio, or I pass her favorite restaurant, I try to remember her smile and her laugh. I try to focus on how lucky I was to have her in my life for the time I got her and not be angry that I didn't get more."

"But I wanted more. So much fucking more." I blow out a defeated breath.

"I know you did. And you *deserved* more. But you can't torture yourself over what you lost. You have to remember what you had. Remember her, the way she wanted to be remembered. And remember what she asked of you." She falls silent for a long moment. "All she wanted was for you to find happiness again."

"I don't know if I can," I admit.

"You can. And you will. You can't force it, but you also can't push it away."

"You remind me so much of her." I look into Claire's eyes and sometimes I swear I see Finley staring back at me. I'm not sure if it brings me comfort or deepens the pain.

"I'm glad."

"You are?"

"Of course I am. She was my sister."

"You're strong, just like she was."

"I like to think I am, but most days I'm not so sure." Claire shrugs, relaxing back into her chair. "So, how's the work prospects coming along?" she asks, and I'm relieved for the change in topic.

"Not too bad. A lot of the bars I used to play at were happy to welcome me back. I've got my first gig lined up for next week."

"Are you nervous to be back on the scene?"

"A little. This will be the first time I've played a show in Chicago since…"

"Since before Finley died."

I nod slowly.

"You'll be great," she reassures me. "Tell you what, text me the details and maybe I can make it out to see you play."

"You'd do that?"

"You're family. Of course I would. Besides, it'll do you good to look into the crowd and see a familiar face."

"You're probably right. For all the years I've played I don't think I've ever felt as uncertain of myself as I do right now."

"It's just being back home. You'll get up on that stage and it won't matter where you are. Illinois, California; it's all the same as long as you're on a stage. No matter how big or how small, you've always belonged there. Finley knew it and I know it too."

"Thank you. I know it probably seems juvenile but sometimes it helps to hear someone say that."

"We all need a little reassurance from time to time."

"I think I need more than a little these days." I chuckle, turning my gaze to the right when our waitress appears with our order.

"Chicken wings for the gentleman." She sets my food in front of me. "Salad for the lady." She smiles, her eyes lingering on me for longer than I like.

"So typical," Claire whines. "Men always get to eat the good food."

"Technically, you could have gotten wings," I remind her.

"Yeah, right. I'll gain five pounds just looking at yours."

"Is there anything else I can do for you right now?" the young waitress interrupts.

"I think we're good," I tell her, my eyes not leaving Claire. "You want a wing?"

"Are you trying to torture me right now?" She laughs, shaking her head.

"Come on, live a little."

"By live a little you mean get fat."

"One, you are nowhere near fat. Two, one wing isn't going to change that. Now shut the fuck up and take a wing." I pick one up off my plate and shove it in her face.

"God." She sighs loudly before taking the wing from my hand. "Way to peer pressure me." She tries to fight the smile on her lips but fails miserably.

Seconds pass before she tears off a bite and pops it into her mouth, moaning dramatically as she does.

"I forgot how good wings are." She takes another bite.

"See, sometimes it *is* worth it."

"Tell me that in sixty seconds when I'm mad at myself for being so weak."

"I'll just shove another wing at you to keep you quiet." I laugh.

"Remind me again what my sister saw in you."

"Well, my obvious charm and good looks, of course." The smile on my face feels more natural than it has in a very long time.

"Good to see California hasn't weakened your sense of humor."

"I wasn't being funny," I deadpan, able to hold a straight face for all of five seconds before we both start laughing.

"Remind me again why I agreed to this," I grumble, following my brother Aaron through the thick wood doors of Ripley's Tavern.

"Well, for one, he's your brother. And for two, you're in the wedding party, and as such it is customary to attend the bachelor party."

"Don't they usually do these things right before the wedding? Why the hell are they doing it two weeks prior?"

"People do them whenever the hell they want. Besides, this was the only weekend before the wedding that they were free." He crosses the crowded room toward the back where a private party room is located.

"I should have stayed in California a week longer. Adam had the right idea not flying in until the weekend of the wedding."

"Are you going to moan and groan all night or are you going to shut the fuck up and try to have a little fun? I know it's a foreign concept to you, bro, but how about you put on a happy face for Andrew's sake."

I'm seconds away from smarting off an asshole comment but somehow, I manage to refrain. Aaron's right, tonight isn't about me. It's about Andrew. And while I'd like to strangle him more times than not, he's still my brother and I owe it to him to not ruin his good time.

"There you fuckers are!" Our mutual friend, Nick spots us the moment we enter the room. "'Bout time you showed up." He closes the distance between us, shaking Aaron's hand first before reaching for mine. "Abel." He pulls me into a half hug. "Long time no see, brother."

"How's it going, Nick?" I pat his shoulder once before stepping back.

"Oh you know, living the life." He raises his rocks glass that's filled with an amber liquid.

"Starting early I see," Aaron comments next to me. "What are you drinking?"

"Scotch. You want one?"

"I think I'm gonna stick with beer tonight." Aaron shakes his head.

"Suit yourself. Abel?" Nick turns his attention to me.

"Actually, scotch sounds perfect." I nod, following Nick when he turns and heads toward the small bar along the far back wall, while Aaron joins the other guys sitting around a long rectangular table in the center of the room. Most of them I know, some I don't recognize. Based on how a few of them are dressed, I'd venture to say they're colleagues of Andrew's from the law firm he works at.

Sliding up on a barstool next to Nick, I order a double shot on the rocks from the middle-aged man working the bar.

"So where is my brother?" I ask, looking around for Andrew. "Isn't this his party?"

"Sam's bachelorette party is tonight, too. I guess he wanted to see her beforehand. Probably wanted to pound one out really quick." He chuckles.

"Not a visual I want." I crinkle my nose and shake my head, nodding when the bartender sets my drink in front of me.

"So, listen, not to bring the party down before it has even begun, but I wanted to tell you how sorry I was to hear about your girl." The moment the condolence leaves his lips, the familiar ache in my chest returns full force. Not that it ever leaves; I've just gotten somewhat used to it.

Lifting my rocks glass, I take a long drink before setting it back on the bar.

"Thanks, man." I nod, keeping my gaze forward.

"I just…" He stops midsentence due to a commotion on the other side of the room. We both turn in unison to see my brothers Andrew and Alex enter the room.

"Gentleman." Andrew holds out his arms and I instantly hear the slur in his voice.

"Fuck me. Is he already drunk?" Nick asks, clearly thinking the same thing as me.

"This is going to be a long night." I knock back the rest of my scotch and gesture to the bartender for another.

"I'm getting married," Andrew announces, as if we didn't already know.

"Because the bachelor party didn't make that apparent," I mutter under my breath.

"Stop talking and start drinking," Aaron yells at Andrew and the other guys all start laughing.

I turn back around, not interested in whatever else my brother has to say.

"You ready for this?" Nick chuckles, sensing my aggravation.

"Not in the least." I grab my second scotch when the bartender takes my empty and replaces it with a full one.

I'm happy for my brother, truly I am. But it's hard to join in on his happiness when I feel like my only chance at true happiness died the same day *she* did. Maybe that makes me selfish, that I can't see past my own pain to celebrate for my brother. Or maybe it's easier to be pissed off than to give in to what I'm really feeling.

"I say we get so hammered that we have fun no matter what bullshit we end up doing."

"I'm game with that." I clink my glass against Nick's and dump the contents down my throat, the liquid burning a warm path all the way to my stomach.

"I thought we were dropping you off at your place?" I ask, my gaze going from the window of the SUV to Andrew, who's so drunk at this point he can barely hold his head up.

Andrew has never been much of a drinker, so being able to handle his liquor is not something he ever mastered. I'd be lying if I said I wasn't finding a little humor in seeing him this wasted just three hours after his party began.

"This is where Sam is," Alex answers my question.

"So why are *we* here, then?" I ask, looking back out the window to the bright neon sign that reads *Pulsations.* "Are we picking her up?"

"No, we're going in?"

"In there?" I ask, gesturing to the dance club.

"Relax, little brother. Hot girls dancing on tables and stiff drinks. What more could you ask for?"

"My fucking bed for starters."

"You know, you used to be a lot more fun." He crinkles his forehead.

"And you used to be less of a dick," I point out.

"I may be a dick, brother, but at least I know how to enjoy myself from time to time. Trust me, when you get married and have a raging two-year-old running your household, you'll live for nights like this."

I resist the urge to remind him that I've already been married, and instead push open the door and quickly climb out.

Andrew's party started with about twenty people and has since dwindled to half that. If I had known this is where we were heading, I would have dipped out early, especially after Nick bailed, leaving me to fend for myself.

"Come on," Alex says from behind me. I turn just in time to see him hoist Andrew from the back of the vehicle.

"You sure it's a good idea to take him in there?" I ask.

"He'll be fine. He just needs a water and some time to sober up a little."

"What he needs is two Tylenol and a pillow." I snort.

"Where's my girl?" Andrew slurs, completely oblivious to the conversation taking place right in front of him.

"Hey, Aaron," Alex calls, waiting until our other brother steps up next to us. "Here." He playfully shoves Andrew in his direction. Aaron barely catches him before he would have likely hit the ground.

"Seriously, asshole?" Aaron grinds out, helping Andrew stand upright.

"What? I've been on babysitting duty all night. It's your job now." He gives Aaron a knowing smirk and then takes off toward the front entrance of the club.

"Let's just stick his ass back in the car and take him home," I suggest.

"I'm not going home." Andrew chooses this moment to actually listen. Shaking off Aaron's grasp, he follows Alex inside, impressively able to walk a semi-straight line as he does.

"Last stop. Might as well make the best of it." Aaron shrugs.

"Fuck me," I mutter under my breath before following my three brothers into the club.

Loud, pulsating music instantly surrounds me the moment I step inside. I squint, having trouble seeing through the dark room lit only by rotating colored lights that dance across the floor.

The place is packed. The dance floor is crammed with people. The bar is surrounded and the two stages on either side of the room are both overflowing with drunk girls trying to show off their dance moves.

Andrew and a few others make their way onto the dance floor, no doubt in search of Sam, while I veer straight toward the bar.

The music is so loud I have to scream my drink order at the bartender and that's after waiting nearly fifteen minutes just to reach the bar. I order a double, knowing there's no way I'm going to wait in that line again anytime soon.

Throwing a twenty on the bar, I snag my drink and turn, running straight into a girl standing entirely too close behind me. Some of the amber liquid in my glass sloshes out, dripping over my hand, down the front of my shirt, and onto the floor.

"Oh shoot, I'm so sorry," she says seconds before my fiery gaze shoots up from the floor and lands on a petite blonde with big blue eyes and full lips painted bright red.

"Ever hear of personal space?" I lash out, ignoring how attractive she is. My eyes rack down the length of her. Ample chest, small waist, curvy hips. All accented by a little black number.

"Ever hear of an accident?" she immediately bites back, pretending to ignore the fact that I was very clearly checking her out.

"It was an accident that you were standing so close?" I raise my voice to be heard over the music.

"It's not like I had much of a choice." She gestures to the space behind her, or rather the lack thereof.

"You did actually. You could have chosen not to stand so close," I tell her, stepping further into *her* space. She instinctively takes a step back, running into the girl standing directly behind her.

"Sorry." She turns her head and apologizes before her gaze snaps back to mine. "Are you done now or are you going to stand here the rest of the night glaring at me?"

"Something tells me you'd like that too much," I sneer, pushing past her without another word.

I have no idea where that came from. I'm usually a pretty friendly guy but something about her put me on edge and I have no idea why.

Chapter Four
Peyton

"What the hell took you so long?" Henna stands, snagging her drink from my hand.

"I just ran into the biggest asshole I've ever met." I look back toward the bar already knowing that he's no longer there. "He yelled at me for standing too close to him in line." I exhale quickly. "Can you believe that?"

I don't know why I'm so bothered. It's not like this is the first time I've come face to face with a jerk before.

"Was he hot?" Henna asks, taking a drink of her Cosmo.

"What the hell does that matter?"

"Because if he was hot and an asshole then that's a win. If he was ugly and an asshole then that's a pass."

"Since when is being an asshole a win?"

"Since nice guys are relationship material and tonight that's not what we want. But a hot asshole? That we can work with." She twirls her tongue around the rim of her glass. "So, was he hot?"

"Unbelievably." I sigh out, pissed that I can even think that after how rude he behaved toward me.

Then again, I can't deny it either. His messy dark hair, scruffy jaw, and crisp blue eyes were enough to make me a little weak kneed. My reaction having nothing to do with the way he was glaring at me and everything to do with where I was picturing those perfect lips of his.

"Speaking of hot," Henna purrs, pulling my attention to where her gaze slides to the group of guys standing next to our table. Among them is Sam's fiancé, Andrew, whose face Sam's currently swallowing.

"What is he doing here?" I ask, confused why her soon to be husband would be randomly showing up at her bachelorette party.

"She called him earlier. Told him to meet us here." Henna rolls her eyes. "Typical Sam. She can't go more than a few hours away from him."

"He makes her happy." I shrug, feeling the familiar pang of jealousy in my gut. What girl doesn't want a guy she can't get enough of? I'd give anything to have that in my life.

Unfortunately, I'm cursed when it comes to love. Every guy I date either turns out being a complete douche bag or a cheating liar. Either way, it never ends well for me. Which is why I've sworn off relationships for a while. I need a break from the constant disappointment.

"Well, all his hot friends make me happy." She winks at me, taking a sip from her glass.

I let my eyes travel back to the group of guys. I recognize two of them as Andrew's brothers, Alex and Aaron. I've met them both a few times at social gatherings. A couple others look familiar but there's a few that I've never seen before.

"You may want to wait until after the wedding before screwing one of Andrew's friends." I laugh, shaking my head at her.

"I don't know. That one right there might be too delicious to resist." I follow her line of sight, pulling in a sharp breath when my eyes land on the asshole from the bar right as he steps up next to Alex.

"That's him," I whisper, more to myself than to Henna.

"That's who?" she asks, clearly not following.

"The jerk from the bar. The one who got pissed at me for standing too close."

"And you didn't pull him into the bathroom why?"

"Because I don't screw random guys in the bathroom, Henna." I give her a look I know she'll understand.

"Oh come on! That was one time." She laughs.

"One time too many."

"How was I supposed to know he was married?"

"The wedding ring on his finger should have been a dead giveaway."

"I was twenty-one and drunk out of my mind. I wasn't looking at his fingers." She throws her hand up. "You're never going to let me live that down, are you?"

"Not when you keep suggesting I take random strangers into the bathroom to have sex with them."

"Okay, so maybe not the bathroom. But that still doesn't change the fact that you need to get laid."

"You act like I'm a pubescent boy who can't keep it in his pants. We're not all sex crazed lunatics. Some people are perfectly okay going without."

"And some people are living in denial," she quips. "Go talk to him." Her eyes slide back to the group of guys.

"Who, him?" I discreetly gesture to Mr. Asshole himself.

"Duh."

"Why would I do that?"

"Because he's sexy as sin."

"And?"

"Do you really need more reason than that?"

"I mean, I do. But if you don't, then by all means, *you* go talk to him."

"Fine." She sets her drink on the small round table. "But don't be jealous when I'm the girl leaving on his arm tonight."

"I'm sure I'll live," I say flatly, watching her saunter off.

Seconds later, she slides up in front of the man who looks down at her with a hell of a lot less disdain than he looked at me with. I ignore how irritated this makes me, not really sure why I care in the first place. I'm used to seeing Henna get this type of reaction from guys. It's like all she has to do is smile and they're eating out of the palm of her hand.

Deciding I have better things to do with my time, I kill off the remainder of my drink and join Mariah and Chelle on the dance floor. We only get through a couple of songs before Sam comes to inform us that Andrew has had too much to drink and they're taking him home.

I resist the urge to tell her he's old enough to take care of himself, and instead tell her to be safe and text me once their home, before I go in search of Henna to see if she's ready to call it a night.

When I finally manage to make it back to the table, after weaving through the thick crowd of people cluttering the dance floor, the only person still at the table is Andrew's brother, Aaron.

"Hey." I smile when I reach him. "Where'd everyone go?"

"Most of the girls are leaving with Sam and Andrew. Tim's taking them home in his car. I volunteered to stay back with everyone who wanted to stay. Make sure everyone makes it home safely."

"That's awfully sweet of you," I tell him, slipping onto the stool next to him.

"It was the only way I could get Sam to take Andrew home. Needless to say, my brother cannot handle his liquor."

"And he's how old?" I arch a brow.

"Twenty-nine." He snorts out a laugh. "To be fair, he didn't drink like the rest of us did in college. He's a bit of a late bloomer."

Before I have a chance to say anything, I feel someone slide up next to us, pulling my gaze to the side. My eyes lock with *his* for a split second, causing my skin to prickle slightly, before they dart back to Aaron.

"Sam said you're staying to make sure all the girls get home," he speaks directly to Aaron.

"Yeah, figured it was the least I could do."

"Okay, well I'm going to head out. I've had about as much of this as I can take."

"You got a ride?"

"I'm gonna walk. It's not that far and I could use the fresh air."

"Alright, man." I watch the pair do some weird handshake thing before he spins around and quickly walks away.

"No offense, but your friend is an asshole," I tell Aaron once the guy is out of earshot.

"Brother," he corrects, laughing when my eyes go wide. "And yes, he is an asshole."

"I'm sorry, I didn't know," I start.

"It's all good. I call him an asshole at least once a day." He smiles, and I'm forced to acknowledge the similarities between the two now that I know they are brothers.

And while yes, Aaron is a good-looking guy, his brother is something else entirely. And those eyes. God, I don't think I've ever seen such an intense blue before.

"How is it that I've never seen him around before?" I ask, having to lean in closer when the music kicks up a notch.

"He's been living in California the last few years with our oldest brother, Adam. Even before that, Abel never really hung in the same circles as Andrew. It's not surprising you've never seen him."

Abel...

"So he lives in California?"

"He did. He just moved back a few days ago."

"Oh, gotcha." I try to play it off like I'm just making casual conversation and really don't care. But the truth is I'm very intrigued by the man.

"He's actually a pretty good dude. He's had a rough go the last few years. You'll have to cut him some slack." He lifts the beer bottle to his lips and takes a long pull.

"It's all good. We all have our moments."

"Hey!" Aaron and I pull apart at the sound of Henna's voice. "Where the hell did you go?" she hollers over the music.

"I was dancing, why?" I ask, watching her slip into the seat next to me.

"You weren't lying. That guy kind of is an asshole," she tells me. "Hot as hell, though."

"That's Aaron's brother, Abel," I tell her, giving her a look that tells her to cut it on the asshole remarks.

"Oh." She looks as surprised as I was by the news, her eyes going to Aaron. "Yeah, I guess I can totally see that." She smiles. "What's his deal? Has he always been such a stick in the mud?"

"Actually no, he used to be the nicest guy in the room. Got along with everyone. A real people person."

"Then what happened?" my blunt friend doesn't hesitate to ask.

"His wife died."

The instant the words leave his lips my heart sinks in my chest.

"What?" The word falls from my lips before I can stop it.

"Cancer." He nods, taking another pull of beer. "They weren't together that long, but man was he crazy about her. He hasn't been the same since she died."

"Now I feel bad for calling him an asshole." Henna frowns.

"Don't be. He's still an asshole." Aaron brushes it off with an easy smile.

"I need another drink," Henna announces, pushing to a stand. "Anyone else?"

"Yeah, I'll come with you." Aaron slides off his stool. "You need anything, Peyton?"

"No, I'm good." I shake my head, knowing I probably shouldn't. I feel pretty good right now, but one more and I very well may end the night hugging the toilet.

"Water?" he asks.

"Yeah, water would be awesome. Thank you." I smile, watching him follow Henna toward the bar.

Once I lose them in the crowd, my eyes scan the room. I'm not looking for anything in particular, just people watching. Or at least that's how I justify looking for Abel, even though I know he's already gone.

After what Aaron just told me, I have this overwhelming urge to talk to him. To tell him I understand what it's like to lose someone to cancer. I was only fifteen when I watched it take my mom in a matter of months. It was like one day she was completely healthy and the next she was slipping away. Nothing can prepare you for what that feels like. Nothing can make it better when it's all said and done. Death is permanent. There's no bringing back the people we love once they're gone and we quickly find that we're different people in their absence.

Not that Abel would care to hear any of that from me. I'm just some silly girl who crowded his space and caused him to spill his drink.

I don't know why I care so much. I don't know why he seems to be the only thing I can think about since the first moment he looked at me, or rather *glared* at me. There's just something about him.

"One water." I jump when Aaron and Henna reappear seemingly out of nowhere, interrupting my thoughts.

"Thank you." I take the glass Aaron extends to me, taking a long drink of the cold liquid. It feels incredible on my throat and I immediately take another gulp.

"So, Aaron suggested that maybe we get out of here. Go somewhere a little less crowded." Henna leans in toward me.

"I thought you were responsible for making sure everyone got home okay?" I question.

"We're the only ones left. Apparently everyone else left when Sam did."

"Seriously?" I bark out a laugh. "Some friends they are."

"What do you say?" she asks, giving me a look I understand all too well.

"Why don't you two drop me off at home and then go? I'm honestly not feeling all that great."

"You sure? I don't want to leave you home alone if you aren't feeling well." She pouts. What she's really saying is she doesn't want to seem like a bad friend in front of Aaron who she is suddenly interested in spending more time with.

Henna has always been a fly by the seat of her pants kind of girl. She lives in the moment—always—and does whatever feels right to her. I've always envied that about her.

"Yeah, I'm sure. I'll probably be asleep within thirty seconds of my head hitting the pillow," I tell her, forcing out a yawn for show.

"What do you say?" She looks to Aaron with hopeful eyes. "Do you wanna drop her at home and then go have a drink with *me*?"

"Sounds good to me." He grins, clearly just as taken by her.

Oh lord… here we go.

Chapter Five
Abel

"House of Blues. I don't know, man. I've only played one show since I've been back. I'm not sure I'm ready for that."

I shift my cell phone to my other ear just in time to hear Rob's reply. "You'd really be helping me out. I've got a sold-out show booked and no opening act."

I hesitate. Even if I did feel like I was up to it, I haven't been back to House of Blues since the night I met Finley. It's where we shared our first kiss. Where we laughed and danced and sang the night away. I don't know if I'll ever be ready to walk into that place again.

"I can double what we usually pay for the night. I'm that desperate."

"Rob, I just…"

"Please just say yes."

"I don't think I can, man." I pace around my living room still lined with boxes. I've been back in Chicago for nearly a week, yet the only things I've really unpacked are clothes, towels, and a few bedroom items. Everything else is still piled throughout my new apartment.

"Tell you what, you do this for me and not only will I double your pay, but you can drink for free the entire night."

"It's not about the money, or the booze."

"Abel, you're just coming back onto the scene. Don't turn down an opportunity to put your name back in people's mouths. It'll help you gain momentum and you know it."

He has a point. A very good point in fact. I mull it over. Every fiber of my being screams *no* while the logical side of me knows I can't refuse.

"Okay," I cave.

"You'll do it?"

"I will. But I'm not coming in until last sound check and I'm leaving as soon as my set is over." There's no way in hell I'm going to hang out there any longer than I absolutely have to.

"Sounds good. Be here by six. Set starts at seven-thirty. And thank you. I owe you one."

"No problem. I'll see you tonight." I end the call before sinking back onto the couch I retrieved from storage yesterday.

To say I've been dragging my feet is the understatement of the year. I don't know why I'm doing it. I don't know why I don't unpack and get it over with already. I've made the decision to stay so there's no need to prolong it. I want to be here. I want to be close to my family, my friends, and Claire.

I look around the sparse space. It's not as nice as my old apartment but it's still one of the nicer complexes in the area and is only a couple blocks away from where I used to live so I'm familiar with my surroundings.

"Tomorrow," I mutter to myself.

Tomorrow I will unpack and resettle. Tonight I have a show to play. And while I feel nauseous as hell about the thought of going back there, a part of me, a very small part, is a little excited. House of Blues is one of the best stages to play on. Not to mention the exposure.

It's never been my goal to chase fame. I don't want it, nor do I need it. But playing? That I *do* need. And playing at House of Blues ensures I can land other gigs around the city. While most people still know me from *before*, there have been a lot of changes. New management, new staff. Nearly every place I went to this past week was manned by someone I had never met. Walking into a place you've been to a hundred times before and feeling like a complete outsider. It's weird.

I guess that's what happens when you up and disappear for three years.

Letting out a deep sigh, I peel myself off the couch and head toward the bathroom. If I want any hope of getting there on time, I better get my ass in the shower and get a move on.

Everything is exactly as I remember it. From the gold fixtures to the eclectic art, not one single thing has changed. I look around the room from my place on the stage. The crowd is electric tonight. Deafening. I pull and thrive on their energy.

I manage to make it through my forty-five-minute set without any hiccups. I won't lie and say that I didn't look out into the crowd several times and see Finley's face on every single person looking back at me because I did. But I used it to push me, not hinder me.

I thought being here would be painful, but in reality, I feel closer to her tonight than I have in a very long time. Maybe that's been my mistake all along. Running from the memories instead of embracing them.

After talking to some of the guys backstage, I decide to stay and have one drink. I haven't had one since the shit show that was my brother's bachelor party and honestly, I could use something to take the edge off.

Exiting out the side doors, I slip into the main hall and head directly for the bar. A few people stop me to congratulate me on a great show, while a few others insist I get a picture with them. I smile and nod as graciously as I can, and while they seem to buy every second of it, it feels so fake I can barely stand myself.

I've almost reached the bar when a familiar voice washes over me from behind.

"What the fuck?" I turn just in time to see Aaron close in on me. "I didn't know you were playing here tonight." He shoves at my shoulder.

"It was a last-minute thing. What the hell are you doing here?" I ask, knowing this isn't his usual scene.

"I came with Henna and one of her friends."

"Who?" I question.

"Henna. You know, the girl with the long black hair. The one you were talking to last week at *Pulsations*?"

"The one who was trying to get me to fuck her friend?" I question. "Yeah, I remember."

"She what?" He chokes out a laugh.

"Never mind. I didn't know you liked Alternative music."

"It's okay. I'm not really here for the music." He smirks.

"I see." I bite back a laugh.

"You sounded amazing up there, by the way. I can't remember how long it's been since I've seen you play."

"Probably since I was a teenager."

"Probably. Maybe you should tell me when you have a gig and I can come see you more often. You're pretty fucking talented."

"Thanks." I nod, thinking this might be the first time any of my brothers have actually acknowledged my talent. Normally, it's them lecturing me on getting a *real* job and doing something with my life. It's hard to explain to someone who is blind to the arts, what it does for a person. Music is my outlet. Music is the one thing that sets me free. Music is about the only thing keeping me standing upright and still functioning most days.

"Abel," a female voice says seconds before Henna steps up next to my brother. "Oh my god, you were incredible up there. I had no idea you were a musician." She addresses me like we're old friends.

"Yep." I rock back on my heels.

"Wasn't he amazing, Peyton?" I turn to see who she's speaking to. It's the girl who spilled my drink at the bar last weekend.

"Really good," she agrees, sliding up next to her friend. "Hi." She waves awkwardly at me. "Remember me? We weren't formally introduced but I'm Peyton."

"Peyton, how could I forget? Thanks to you I went to bed smelling like scotch." I manage to keep a straight face even though I'm totally just messing with her.

"Yeah, um, I'm sorry about that…again." She laughs, much more timid than the last time I saw her. Hell, if I had to guess I'd say she's downright nervous. The thought ignites a tiny fire in the pit of my stomach, but I quickly extinguish it.

Even though I try to keep my eyes on hers, I can't stop myself from taking a moment to drink her in. Her blue eyes, her small nose, her full lips covered in a light layer of clear gloss. Her blonde hair is wavy, falling just past her shoulders, and she's wearing a black, sleeveless tank, tight ripped jeans, and black heels. The entire look suits her well.

She really is a beautiful girl. Someone I definitely would have went for *before…*

I quickly shake the thought away.

"No, I'm sorry. I shouldn't have snapped at you like that. It was a… rough night," I offer her a smile which she instantly returns.

"Yeah, it was kind of a hot mess."

"I think shit show is the phrase you're looking for." I turn my gaze back to my brother. "I was just heading to the bar to grab a drink. You guys wanna join me? Rob owes me some free drinks."

"Free drinks?" Henna is the first to respond. "You don't have to twist my arm." She grabs my brother's hand and pulls him toward the bar.

"When did that happen?" I ask Peyton, gesturing to Aaron and Henna's joined hands as we follow behind them.

"The night of the parties, I guess. They dropped me off and went out for a drink. The next morning he was at our place and I've seen him every day since then. Henna even paid double for another ticket on a reseller site just so he could come with us tonight." She rolls her eyes.

"You don't approve?" I question.

"Oh no, I really like Aaron. He seems like a great guy."

"He really is."

"It's just Henna." She shakes her head. "She's an all or nothing kind of girl. Zero to sixty in three seconds flat. So far it hasn't really worked in her favor."

"Is that your way of telling me she'll break my brother's heart?"

"More like I'm afraid he'll break hers. She falls hard and fast. I've seen the aftermath of that scenario more times than I care to admit."

"Want me to warn him that I'll break his face if he hurts her?" I keep my eyes trained forward, not sure why I don't want to look at her.

It's not like I haven't hooked up with my fair share of women over the last three years. I'm not proud of it, but it is what it is. We all grieve in our own ways. But this girl... I don't know. There's something about her that doesn't sit right with me and I'm not sure why that is.

"I'll let you know if I'll require your services." She giggles and the sound makes my chest tighten.

What the fuck?

"You do that." I slide up to the bar next to my brother. "What's everyone drinking?"

"Apple martini for me." Henna is the first to answer.

"I'll take a beer." Aaron taps the bar.

"Peyton?" I turn to see her eyes locked on me; an expression I can't read etched onto her pretty face.

I shake away how that look makes me feel and try to ignore the uneasiness that settles in my stomach.

"Just water for me," she finally answers. "I'm the designated."

"Water it is. Apple Martini." I point to Henna. "And beer for this one." I bump my shoulder into Aaron's.

Once I have everyone's drinks ordered, I hand them out one by one as Rose sets them on the bar. Rob must have told her not to charge me because she walks away without asking for any money.

"You staying to see Hollow Hound play?" Henna asks as we make our way back toward the main hall.

"I was thinking I might catch part of their set. I haven't seen them play in a while."

"This is going to sound bad, but do you think you could maybe introduce us to them after the show?" She sips her Apple Martini.

"I wish I could. But they're actually leaving right after the show. They have another gig tomorrow night in Cleveland, so they aren't hanging around."

"Bummer." She pouts out her bottom lip.

I open my mouth to respond, but quickly snap it closed when my phone begins to vibrate. Snagging it out of my back pocket, I smile when I see Claire's name flash across the screen.

"Hey," I answer, clicking the volume up so I can hear her over the noise of the crowd.

"Well, how'd it goes? Did you rock their socks off?"

"It went really well." I turn to the side when I feel Peyton's eyes on me. "Better than I expected."

"See, I knew you'd be fine." She pauses. "What are you doing now? Based on the noise in the background I'm assuming you're still there."

"Yeah. Actually my brother and a couple of his friends showed up." I throw a quick glance at Aaron whose focus is solely on Henna, not paying one bit of attention to me.

"Boyfriends or girlfriends?"

"Girl."

"Is that so?" I can hear the smile in her voice.

"It's not like that, Claire," I quickly correct her.

"Look, all I'm saying is if it *were* like that, I'd be happy for you."

"Well it's not, so you can keep your happiness," I say teasingly.

"Okay, well, you never know."

"Claire." I cut her off before she can say more.

"Okay. Okay." She laughs. "I'll let you get back to your friends. We still on for dinner tomorrow?"

"I wouldn't miss it."

"K. See you then."

"Bye, Claire." I disconnect the call.

"Who was that?" Aaron asks as I shove my phone back into my pocket. Okay, so maybe he was listening.

"Claire." I lift the beer bottle to my lips and take a pull.

"How's she doing? I haven't seen her since…" he trails off, clearly rethinking what he was going to say. Even though I already know. He hasn't seen her since the funeral.

"She's good." I take another drink of beer, purposely not looking at Peyton.

It bothers me that I feel so off kilter around her. I don't even know the girl, yet she's made me feel more emotion in five minutes than I've felt in the last year combined. Albeit, mixed emotions, but emotions just the same.

You think she's pretty. I can almost hear Finley as if she were standing right next to me.

Pretty, yes. But she's not you.

"I think the band is getting ready to come out." Henna offers the distraction we need, and I glance up to the stage right as the lights dim.

The band filters onto the stage within seconds and a heavy guitar riff fills the space. I try to keep my focus on them, but I have this gnawing feeling in my gut and I can't keep myself from glancing down at Peyton who's standing a couple feet to my right.

Her face is turned toward the stage, but something tells me she senses my eyes on her, because I no more than look at her and she's looking back at me.

Finley's face instantly flashes across hers and guilt slices through me. I quickly look away, taking another long drink.

I shouldn't be here. It all feels wrong. I shouldn't be exchanging stolen glances with another girl in *our* spot. I shouldn't be standing here thinking how beautiful she is or how it would be so easy to suggest we get out of here. It would be effortless. Taking her back to my apartment, letting her make me forget for a while. But I know what comes after, and while I could stomach it halfway across the country, I don't know if I can here. Not when so many memories of Finley are swimming around me.

It all feels like too much, too real. Like it happened yesterday. My chest begins to tighten and a hard-lump forms in the back of my throat. The urge to escape becomes impossible to ignore.

I should say goodbye. Tell my brother I'm heading out. But I'm too deep into the oncoming panic attack to even attempt it. So instead, without a word, I turn and head for the exit, my feet not able to carry me away fast enough.

Chapter Six
Peyton

"Can you believe how snazzy this place is?" Henna slides up next to me in the bridal dressing room. Tonight is our dry run of the ceremony, or rehearsal as I guess it's typically called.

I've been somewhat dreading this day. But I'm not really sure why. Maybe it's because I'm not a huge fan of weddings or being in them more specifically. Or maybe it's because I know *he* will be here.

Abel.

I haven't been able to shake him from my mind since watching him run out of House of Blues without so much as a backward glance.

I tried not to be offended, but honestly, it's kind of impossible not to be. I've run it over in my head a hundred times, trying to figure out what I could have done to send him sprinting toward the door.

The only thing I've been able to come up with is that it didn't have anything to do with me at all. And yet deep down I still feel like, in some weird way, it did.

"Earth to Peyton." Henna pulls me back to the conversation, making me realize that she's been waiting on me to respond.

"Sorry, what?" I shake my head, refocusing on my friend.

"I was just saying how nice this place is." She gestures around the room.

She's not wrong. The church is beautiful. I can't say I've ever seen one quite so elaborate, or big for that matter.

"We've known Sam for years. It really shouldn't surprise you that she would find the nicest church in Chicago to get married in."

"True. She's making it really difficult for the day that one of us gets married. There's no way we're going to be able to top this."

"That's what you're worried about?" I arch a questioning brow at her. "You two have always been way too competitive for your own good." I pause. "I wouldn't want to match this. To me, it's all a bit much. The reception hall, the over the top church, the dresses." I give her a knowing look.

Our bridesmaid dresses are beautiful, but far too elaborate if you ask me. Dark blue, off the shoulder, floor length gowns, with two-foot-long lace trains. When we went in for our fittings, I couldn't believe that she picked out bridesmaids' dresses with trains. For one, I thought only the bride had a train on her dress, and secondly, they aren't very practical. I'm already taking bets in my head on how many times mine will get stepped on over the course of the night.

"I'm with you on the dresses. But then again, it's Sam." She laughs to herself. "How would you do it?"

"How would I do what?" I question, not following.

"Your wedding. What would you do differently?"

"Everything," I admit. "For starters, I'd rather have a small intimate ceremony. I wouldn't have a large wedding party either. Too much work."

"Is that your way of telling me that I won't be in your wedding?" She looks at me expectantly.

"Guess we will see," I tease. "Besides, I think this conversation is a bit premature considering I'm not even dating anyone. At this rate I'll never get married."

"You're twenty-six, Peyton. I think what's premature is saying you'll never get married. You could meet the love of your life tomorrow. You never know." She shrugs. "Sometimes we find love in the most unexpected places."

"Uh oh." I lift my hand to stifle a laugh.

"What?" She seems confused.

"I know that look," I tell her. "It's only been two weeks."

"And?" She crosses her arms over her chest.

"Refer to my previous statement."

"You're always such a buzz kill." She pouts.

"I'm not trying to be. I'm just worried."

"Well there's no reason to. I'm a big girl. I know what I'm doing."

"And what about Aaron?"

"What about him?"

"Do you think he's taking this as serious as you are?"

"I mean, I think so…" She trails off, seeming suddenly uncertain.

"Well, given that he has barely left your side in two weeks, I'd say it's a safe bet. I swear I've never seen two people so consumed by each other." I decide to throw her a bone and stop giving her such a hard time.

I try to convince myself that I'm not raining on her parade out of jealousy, but deep down I think that might be part of my problem.

Don't get me wrong, I'm happy she's happy. But sometimes it's hard to watch everyone around you find someone while I feel destined to spend my life alone.

You're the one that swore off relationships, a tiny voice in my head reminds me.

"I don't know how to describe it." Henna's eyes glaze over like she's lost in a daydream. "The way he looks at me sometimes. It's like I'm the only person he sees. It's exhilarating."

"You really do have it bad." I chuckle.

"Speaking of having it bad, Abel's here. I saw him a couple minutes ago when I was out in the hall on my phone."

"And I care *why*?" I feign disinterest.

"Oh please. You can play cool and collected all you want, but I see through you, Peyton Rivers."

"And what is it that you think you see?" My eyebrows knit together.

"You're totally taken with him. Not that I can blame you. He's gorgeous. And my god can that man sing. Every female in that place was in love with him from the moment he opened his mouth. And maybe some of the men too."

My mind jumps back to when I was standing in the crowd watching him on stage. He was incredible. I had goose bumps by the time the first word left his mouth. And while I've always found musicians attractive, it's usually their talent I'm attracted to. But in Abel's case it's everything. He is the entire package in every sense of the word.

"I am *not* taken with him," I disagree. "I don't even know him."

"Please. I saw the way you two were looking at each other at the concert. There's some serious chemistry between you two."

"You're delusional." I roll my eyes.

"If I'm so delusional, then why did Aaron notice it too?"

"In case you missed it, the last time we were in the same room together he bolted like he couldn't get away from me fast enough."

"That had nothing to do with you."

"And you know this how."

"Aaron told me that House of Blues is where Abel and his wife had their first date. He thinks he took off because it was too painful for him to be there."

"Oh." I suck in a sharp breath. "I didn't know that."

"Of course you didn't. How could you have?"

"Why didn't you tell me sooner?"

"I didn't think you cared."

"I don't, but at least it would have explained his sudden disappearance."

"Aaron said that she was sick when they met. I guess Abel didn't know, but once he found out he didn't leave her side. He invested his heart fully even though he knew she was dying. They eloped in Vegas a couple weeks after she received a terminal diagnosis."

"That's so sad." I have trouble ignoring the swell of emotion this information brings to the surface. "Did he say how old she was?"

"He didn't, but she couldn't have been very old considering Abel's only twenty-nine and she died three years ago."

"God, I can't even imagine."

"Yeah, me either." She shakes her head, a frown turning down her lips.

"Alright, ladies." Sam's mom, Lilith, stands next to the double doors that lead into the hallway. "Samantha should be arriving any moment. Her and Andrew got stuck in traffic on the way here. As soon as they arrive, we are going to get started. Let's go ahead and take our places." All eight bridesmaids shuffle toward the door.

"Delilah, you'll be walking with Alex. Trina with Dan. Kate, you're with Adam. Henna is with Aaron." I watch my friend beam at the news, like she didn't already know she'd be walking down the aisle with him. "Peyton, you're with Abel." I stop listening to her after that.

Wait…
What?

"I thought I was walking with Josh?" I whisper to Henna, referring to one of Andrew's lawyer friends.

"No idea." Henna shrugs.

I try to squash the nervous energy forming in my chest, but it doesn't do me a bit of good. I don't know why I'm so anxious. It's just a quick walk down the aisle. *And a dance at the reception*, my lovely inner voice pitches in, adding a slow simmer of excitement to the mix.

Taking a slow breath in, I let it out even slower. No matter how attractive Abel is, he's not someone I want to get mixed up with. If there's anything worse than a bad boy, it's a broken one. And there's no doubt in my mind that Abel is most definitely a broken man. You don't suffer the kind of loss he has and come out on the other side still intact.

"Finally," Henna grumbles next to me and I snap out of my fog long enough to see Sam enter the room.

"Sorry, ladies." She seems winded and a bit out of sorts. "Is everyone ready?"

"Heather has the guys lined up in order down the hall, as are the girls here," her mom answers, gesturing to the row of us.

"Perfect." She claps her hands together excitedly. "All right, ladies. Let's do this."

Moments later we are all filing into the hallway. Because the bride and groom's dressing rooms are on opposite sides of the church, we are all meeting in the middle, at the large double doors that lead into the great room.

I spot Abel immediately. His messy hair hanging across his forehead, his ocean blue eyes trained on the ground, his large hands shoved into the front pockets of his faded blue jeans.

I knead my bottom lip between my teeth, the butterflies in my stomach so prominent it's a wonder I can even keep my feet on the ground.

I can't help it. He's *that* good looking.

One by one, Heather, the wedding planner, lines us up next to each other. When she takes my arm and positions me next to Abel, I'm not sure what to do. Do I say hello and act like we're old friends? Do I stay quiet and keep to myself, on the very likely chance he doesn't want to speak to me? God, I've never felt so much uncertainty standing next to a man before.

"You seem about as excited as I am to be here." He speaks low so only I can hear him.

Relief floods through me and I turn my gaze up to his, my heart rate picking up a few notches when my eyes land on his.

"I am excited." I try to seem relaxed even though I feel anything but.

"You sure?" He smiles at me and for the first time I notice the solitary dimple on his left cheek.

Swoon.

"I'm excited for Sam."

"Not a big fan of weddings?"

"I'm just not really a fan of being a part of them."

This causes him to smile wider and I swear my stomach does a full flip at the sight.

"Me either. At least not big spectacles like this." He gestures around us.

"Yeah, I'm with you there."

"Well, at least we can be miserable together." He chuckles, falling silent when the double doors swing open and the first couple makes their way inside.

Abel and I are the fourth couple to walk. When it's our turn he offers me his arm. "Let's get this over with, shall we?"

"Let's." I smile, looping my arm through his.

"Thank god that's over." I jump at the sound of Abel's voice next to me.

I stepped outside to get some fresh air for a minute, not realizing he must have followed.

"Yeah," I agree, sliding down onto the bottom step of the stone staircase that leads up to the front entrance of the church.

Abel's feet shuffle against the concrete seconds before he takes a seat next to me.

"One more day, then this spectacle will be over. Thank fuck." He half sighs, half laughs.

"You are nothing like your brother." *Did I say that out loud?*

"I have four. You'll have to be more specific." He pulls his knees up and rests his elbows on top of them before turning his face toward me.

"I was referring to Andrew."

"You mean he's an uptight, self-righteous tool and I'm not?" He chuckles.

"Yeah, let's go with that." I can't stop the smile from spreading across my face.

"Product of being the youngest," he explains. "I think you'll find I'm not like any of my brothers."

"I don't know, you and Aaron seem kind of similar. Then again, I don't really know you, or him very well, for that matter. Maybe I have no idea what I'm talking about."

"Aaron is the most like me. He's just better at pretending than I am."

"Pretending?" I question.

"Aaron has this innate ability to fit in no matter who he's with or what he's doing. He conforms to his audience and plays whatever role he has to. So while to some he may seem like a judgmental asshole like the rest of my family, to others he's the most laid-back guy in the world."

"You think your family are judgmental assholes?"

"Have you met my family?" He hitches his thumb back toward the church, already knowing that I have. In fact, I spent a good ten minutes after the rehearsal talking to his mom, who went on and on about how incredible Sam's taste is.

She seemed nice enough, but there was definitely an uppity quality to her personality. Honestly, she was kind of intimidating to be around.

"Fair point," I manage to say, looking down to where my hands are knotted in my lap.

"About last weekend," Abel starts after several long moments of silence. "Sorry I disappeared like that."

"Don't be." I play it off like I didn't think anything of it.

"I realize how strange it probably seemed at the time."

"It's fine, really. You weren't there with us. You don't owe me an explanation."

"I know I don't. I just don't want you to think I make it a habit of behaving that way."

"Why do you care what I think?" I glance back toward him, having to physically restrain myself from reaching up to push away a chunk of hair that's fallen in front of one of his eyes.

"Truthfully?" He waits until I nod before continuing. "I don't know."

A small laugh makes its way past my lips. "Well, at least you're honest."

He opens his mouth to say something else, but snaps it closed when the heavy doors behind us jar open.

"There you are," Henna says right as I turn to see her coming down the stairs toward us. Her gaze slides from me to the man sitting next to me. "Oh, hey." She smiles at Abel.

"Hey." He nods.

"Sorry to interrupt." She pauses two steps up from where we are. "Everyone is getting ready to go to dinner."

"Okay." I push to a stand, Abel following suit.

"Aaron's going to drive us there and then bring us back here to pick up my car later."

"Okay." Turning toward Abel, I say, "Guess I'll see you at the restaurant."

"Actually, I'm coming with you. I hitched a ride here with Aaron, so I kind of don't have a choice."

"I call shotgun," Henna announces loudly, and both of our gazes go to her.

"Funny." Abel grins. "I didn't realize people still did that."

"Typically they don't." I snort. "At least not adults anyway."

"Are you judging me right now?" Henna's hands drop dramatically to her hips.

"Maybe a little." Abel shrugs, a smile on his gorgeous mouth. "But it's okay. You can have shotgun. I'd rather sit in the back with Peyton, anyway."

It's such an innocent statement, and one that he likely says to reassure Henna he won't be fighting her for the front seat, but it still sends a zing of excitement through my stomach.

"Hey!" I jump at the sound of Aaron's voice, all three of us looking to the top of the stairs where half of his body is peeking out the door. "You guys coming or what? Everyone else has already left."

"We're coming." Abel takes off up the stairs, leaving Henna and I to follow.

Henna knocks her arm into mine and gives me an excited look, gesturing to Abel. "What the hell?" she mouths.

"What?" I mouth back, playing casual. I mean, what other way could I play it? What she walked out on was casual. Just two semi-strangers making small talk.

"You know what," she whisper hisses.

I shake my head at her and turn my gaze forward, not willing to get into this with her right now. One conversation with

Abel and Henna is probably planning our wedding. When I say she goes zero to sixty in three seconds, that doesn't just mean when it comes to her life. She tends to jump the gun in *all* aspects.

We head back through the church and out the rear doors to where Aaron's Jeep is parked in the back lot. Crossing to the passenger side, I climb in the backseat and settle in directly behind Henna.

"I forgot to ask." Aaron looks at Abel in the rearview mirror as he pulls out of the church parking lot. "Is Claire coming with you tomorrow?"

My excitement evaporates a little at the mention of Claire's name. I have no idea who she is, only that Abel received a phone call from her last Saturday which caused his whole face to light up.

"Yeah, I'm picking her up on my way to the church," he confirms, his gaze going out the window.

"Who's Claire?" Henna turns slightly in her seat. "Is she your girlfriend?"

I bite back the urge to tell my friend to shut up.

"No," he answers simply, not giving her any other information.

Her lips turn into a frown and even though I can tell she wants to push, for once her nosy side doesn't win out and she turns back around in her seat.

The rest of the drive is relatively quiet. It only takes about five minutes to get where we're going, but for some reason it feels like it takes so much longer. There's this weird energy pinging around the back seat and I can't tell if it's just me or if Abel feels it too.

I look down to where his hand is on his leg, his thumb twirling a silver band on his ring finger that I hadn't noticed before.

He's still wearing his wedding band. My chest tightens.

I refocus my gaze out the window.

It would be so easy to let myself get caught up in a man like Abel. Too easy. But I'm not interested in starting anything. And considering he's still wearing his wedding ring; I'd venture to say neither is he. The last thing I need to do is obsess over a man I have no chance of having. It only further solidifies that I need to keep my distance from him.

When I don't listen to my gut, bad things happen, and people get hurt. Mainly me. And right now warning bells are pinging in my head, one after another.

I know I'm getting ahead of myself. I'm overthinking a situation that isn't even a factor. We've had all of two conversations, both of which only lasted a couple minutes and neither of which implied he was the least bit interested in me. But when you're in the presence of someone as captivating as Abel, you immediately start adding some bricks to your wall. Because even if he has no interest in me, it's becoming increasingly more difficult to ignore *my* interest in him.

Chapter Seven
Peyton

"Hey, Dad." I press my cell phone to my ear as I readjust the purse strap on my shoulder. "I'll be right in," I tell Henna, covering the receiver with my hand.

She nods, following Aaron and Abel into the restaurant.

"What's up?" I lean against the brick wall a couple of feet from the door.

"Just calling to see how you are. You know, it wouldn't kill you to pick up the phone and call your old man every once in a while."

"I know, I'm sorry." I immediately feel guilty. "I've been so busy between work and Sam's upcoming wedding. I swear I haven't had time to breathe."

"That's right. I forgot your friend is getting married," he says distantly, like he's saying it to himself and not me. "When is the wedding again?"

"Tomorrow. I'm actually at the rehearsal dinner now."

"Oh." He pauses. "I didn't realize it was so soon. I won't keep you, but I wanted to invite you over for dinner next Saturday. Tina is making pot roast." He knows I can't resist my stepmother's famous pot roast.

"Um, yeah, I should be able to make it. What time?"

"Six?"

"Six works for me." I shuffle my feet. "I really should get going, Dad," I say, nervously peeking through the glass doors of the restaurant to see that our party has already been seated.

"Okay, sweetie. Have fun."

"Thanks, Dad."

"I love you."

"Love you too."

I wait until the call disconnects before dropping my cell back into my purse and quickly making my way inside.

I step into the lobby and scan the open room. When I spot Sam and the rest of the wedding party standing next to the far-right windows, I head in that direction.

By the time I make it to the table everyone has already begun to claim their seats. I scan the long line of chairs, finally spotting an empty one at the end across from Henna.

It isn't until I reach the empty seat that I realize who's sitting in the chair directly next to it. I look for another option, but unfortunately, there isn't one.

It would figure. Out of the twenty some people in attendance, I would get stuck next to the one person I promised myself I would stay away from. The heavens really are against me right now.

"Everything okay with your dad?" Henna asks as I slide down into the chair, draping my purse across the back of it.

"Yeah, he wanted to invite me to dinner next weekend."

"He probably misses having you around."

"It's been nearly a year and a half since I moved out," I remind her. "I'm sure he's used to it by now."

"Even still, I bet it gets lonely in that big house, only him and Tina."

"Who's Tina?" Abel chimes into the conversation, and even though I tell myself not to look at him, I can't stop my eyes from swinging in his direction.

"Step-mom," I answer shortly.

"They live close by?" he asks. And even though I'm not sure why he wants to know, I answer him anyway. He's probably trying to be polite and make conversation.

"About forty-five minutes outside of the city."

"And what about your mom?" My heart sputters slightly in my chest. Most everyone I know already knows about my mom. I can't remember the last time someone asked me about her.

"She passed away when I was fifteen." I turn my gaze down to the unopened menu laying on the table in front of me.

"I'm sorry to hear that." The sincerity in his voice is unmistakable.

"Thanks," I murmur, flipping open the menu. "It was a long time ago."

Thankfully the waitress chooses this moment to appear to take our drink orders and I get out of having to say more. It's not that I mind talking about my mom. I don't. I just don't think now is the time for such a heavy conversation.

Even though I had no intention of drinking when I arrived, when the waitress's attention falls to me, I order a glass of wine. If I have to sit next to Abel for the next hour or two, I'm going to need it.

"So Abel, Aaron tells me you're recently back from California," Henna chimes in the moment the waitress's focus shifts to the other end of the table. "How was that?"

"It was okay." He shrugs, turning his attention from his menu to Henna.

"If I lived in California I would probably be on the beach every single day. Did you live close to the ocean?"

"I was actually staying with our brother, Alex." He gestures to the dark-haired man a couple seats down from him. "He only lives a few miles from the beach."

"And you came back to the windy city, why? If I ever had the courage to go, I don't think I'd ever come back."

"I knew it was temporary when I went. I had a few things to, um, work out." He chooses his words carefully, clearly having no idea that we already know about his wife. "Chicago's my home. It was never a question of *if* I came back, simply *when*."

"And we're glad to have you home," Aaron chimes into the conversation.

I glance at Abel out of the corner of my eye, not missing the silent exchange that happens between the two brothers.

"So," Henna continues when silence falls over our side of the table. "What's everyone getting? Everything looks so good."

"They have the best lobster here," Aaron tells her, leaning in unnecessarily close to show her where the lobster is on the menu.

Little does he know, Henna hates seafood.

"What else?" she asks, choosing not to tell him of her dislike.

"Well, the filet is pretty spot on. And the garlic mashed potatoes it comes with are killer."

"Do you eat here often?" I ask Aaron, not missing how well versed he seems to be with the menu.

"This is one of our parent's favorite restaurants," Abel answers. "We used to eat here at least once a month growing up."

"So then, what do *you* suggest?" Henna asks Abel, leaning forward slightly in her seat.

"I personally prefer the Porterhouse Steak. And Aaron's not wrong about the mashed potatoes. They are pretty amazing."

"What about something that won't clog my arteries and didn't come from the sea?" she asks.

"I think the word you're looking for is salad," Abel says, causing me to bark out a laugh.

I lift my hand to my mouth to stifle the noise, not missing the glare Henna throws my way.

"I'm sorry." I push out through my subsiding giggles. "That was pretty funny." My gaze slides to Abel and the moment my eyes meet his crisp blue ones my chest tightens.

God, he's so good looking it almost hurts.

"What about you, Peyton?" he asks, leaning toward me the smallest fraction.

"What about me?" I try to contain the sudden rush of nervous energy that hits me like an ocean wave, knocking me backward from the force.

"Seafood and steak?"

"I love them both."

"Then get the surf and turf. Trust me, you won't be sorry."

"You know what," I glance down at the menu, locating the item he's talking about, "I think I might try it."

"I think that's what I'll have, too." He gives me a soft grin and I swear my heart melts a little further.

Dear lord, what is this man doing to me? I can't remember a time when discussing a menu has ever felt so overwhelming. It's like he has some magical spell over me that's growing stronger by the minute, and try as I may, I can't seem to shake it.

The four of us make small talk in between our drinks arriving and ordering our food, but I do my best not to look at Abel again. As if keeping my eyes off him will somehow dull this intense energy I feel buzzing between us.

I don't know how to describe it. It's unlike anything I've ever felt. And I certainly can't seem to make sense of it. So instead of trying to understand what this is, I do what I do best. Push it down and hope it goes away.

Various conversations float around the table over the course of dinner. Because I'm on the very end I miss a lot of what is happening on the opposite side of the table, but I catch little pieces of what people are talking about as I eat.

The food is incredible but coupled with my nerves and the three glasses of wine I've managed to suck down, I find that I'm not very hungry. As such, I spend most of the time picking at my food and nibbling rather than actually consuming much of it.

"Do you not like it?" Abel asks, watching me shuffle my food around the plate with my fork.

"No, it's actually really good," I say, chancing a glance at him. Of course I regret it the moment I do. I can't remember a time that I've ever been so attracted to someone that I wasn't able to function normally. I feel flustered and off kilter and I'm not quite sure how to fix it.

It's exhilarating and terrifying all at once.

"I'm just not very hungry," I continue after a long pause.

"Yeah, I wasn't either," he says, my gaze going to his empty plate.

"Oh yeah, you weren't hungry at all." I smile, reaching for my wine glass before taking a long gulp. "So, you ready for this tomorrow?" I ask.

"Define *ready*." He relaxes back into his chair, crossing his arms in front of his broad chest. "Ready to get it over with maybe." He speaks softly so only I can hear him.

"You and me both," I admit. "I've got so much going on at work and this wedding has been a massive time drain. Not that I mind. I love Sam and I'm honored to be a part of her wedding, but I'm ready for things to go back to normal."

"So what do you do?" he asks. "For work, I mean."

"I work for a video game testing firm."

"A what?"

"A video game testing firm," I repeat.

"Like a company that tests video games? Is that really a thing?" He quirks a brow.

"It is," I confirm, not able to contain the smile that slides across my face.

"So what is it exactly that you do there? You don't strike me as a gamer?"

"Probably because I'm not. I work with the developers mainly. I handle all the scheduling and managing the deadlines. It's not the most exciting job in the world, but I love the company and the people I work with."

"You been there long?"

"About four years. John hired me right out of college after I interned there during my senior year. Back then my job consisted more of fetching coffee and running errands, but I've moved up pretty quick. That's one of the great things about working there. There's a lot of growth if you're willing to put in the work."

"Which clearly you have."

"I guess you could say that."

"She's a workaholic," Henna interjects. I glance up to realize that Aaron and her are watching the interaction between us.

"I wouldn't say that," I disagree.

"She's a workaholic," she addresses Abel directly. "Though she probably wouldn't focus so much on work if she had *other* things going on in her life."

Heat instantly creeps up my neck and across my cheeks. I have to forcefully resist the urge to kick Henna under the table.

I love my friend dearly, but sometimes she doesn't know when to keep her mouth shut. I give her a look that tells her that, but her only response is a sweet smile as her gaze goes back to Abel.

"So, what about you, Abel? We know you play music. Anything else?"

"Nope."

"And you make a living doing that?"

"For the last decade anyway." He nods, taking a pull from the beer bottle in front of him.

"Before he left for California, he was playing six or seven nights a week," Aaron chimes in.

"I'll get there again." Abel takes another long drink.

"I'm sure you will," Aaron agrees. "I know I used to give you hell about not getting a *real* job," —He makes quote marks with his fingers— "but after seeing you up on-stage last weekend, I don't know, man. I feel like I finally get it."

"Took you long enough."

"I guess I can agree with that." Aaron chuckles.

"We should totally go see him play again," Henna tells Aaron. "Where are you playing next?"

"Mulligan's on Thursday night."

"Mulligan's?" she asks Aaron, who nods, sliding an arm around her shoulder.

"Sounds good to me," he confirms.

"What about you, Peyton? You in?" Henna pulls her bottom lip into her mouth to keep herself from smiling, as if I don't know her game.

"I'm not sure. I have a lot going on next week."

"Shut up." Henna swipes her hand through the air in my direction. "You'll come."

"So I can play the third wheel?" I gesture between her and Aaron. "I think I'll pass." I drink the remainder of my wine, ignoring the feeling of Abel's gaze hot on the side of my face.

The truth is, I want nothing more than to go. To see Abel up on that stage, to exist in his presence. Which are the exact reasons why I shouldn't go.

"Mulligan's is a pretty incredible place," Aaron tells me.

"Just promise you'll think about it," Henna concedes when she realizes I'm not budging.

"I promise I'll think about it." But I only say it so she will shut up.

"You should come." It's the last thing I expect out of Abel and the one thing that has the power to melt my resolve in an instant. "Mulligan's is a good time. You'd have fun."

A clinking of glass grabs my attention, and I've never been more thankful for an interruption in my life. "Can I have everyone's attention?" Sam's dad stands at the head of the table, a wine glass in his hand.

We spend the next five minutes listening to the father of the bride make what has to be the longest toast I've ever witnessed, yet I don't hear a single thing he says.

I'm too busy tracing the side of Abel's face with my eyes. Taking in his sharp, scruff covered jaw and the way his eyes crinkle slightly at the corners. It's like I'm a woman obsessed.

Yeah, I've been attracted to men before, but never like this. Never where it felt I was going to spontaneously combust just by looking at a person.

Maybe it's because it's been so long since I've been intimate with a man. Maybe it's because I know he's hurting, and I want to be the one who takes away his pain. Or maybe he has this power over every woman and I'm too weak to resist his pull. Whatever it is, the longer I look at him the more bothered I become.

So much so, that by the time Sam's dad finally finishes, I have to wipe my mouth with the back of my hand out of fear that I might be drooling.

It's the wine, I tell myself. I'm a little intoxicated which always makes every situation feel more intense. But then what's my excuse for earlier? What's my reasoning for practically undressing the man with my eyes every time we are near each other?

I shake my head, trying to clear the cluttered thoughts.

"You okay?" Abel asks and I quickly flatten my expression, not sure what he may have seen on my face that would make him think I wasn't okay.

"Yeah, fine." I throw on an easy smile, not sure how much longer I can keep this up.

Chapter Eight
Abel

I don't know what it is about this girl, but she has made what I assumed would be a really shitty night halfway enjoyable.

I can't remember the last time I enjoyed watching a woman squirm the way she did for most of the night.

Peyton blows out a slow breath next to me, resting further into the backseat of my brother's car.

"You okay over there?" My eyes slide to where her hands are splayed out across her slender stomach.

"I feel like I'm about to bust," she admits.

"How? You barely ate anything."

"It's the wine. Always makes me blow up. That's why I don't drink it often."

"I see." I nod slowly, not sure how to fill the lull in conversation when she falls silent next to me.

"Abel, do you want me to swing you by your place since it's on the way back to the church?" Aaron asks from the front seat.

"Yeah, that's fine." I let my gaze drift out the window.

Tonight has been unexpected. It's been so long since I've talked to someone outside of Claire. Nothing earth shattering or groundbreaking, but just talked. Every day normal small talk. It made me feel normal for the first time in a long time. Not that I forgot about the hollow void in my chest for even a moment, but it seemed easier to live with.

It isn't long before Aaron is pulling up in front of my apartment building. I look at Peyton whose focus is anywhere but on me.

I open my mouth to say something, *anything*, but for the life of me I can't think of anything to say.

"You want me to pick you up tomorrow or are you going to meet us at the church?" Aaron asks as I unlatch my seatbelt and prepare to exit the car.

"I'll just meet you there." That way I can sneak out of the reception the moment it's socially acceptable to do so.

"Okay, man. I'll see you tomorrow."

"Sounds good." I open the door, pausing for a split second to look at Peyton. "I'll see you later," I tell her, watching her gaze slide to mine.

"Yeah." She smiles. "See you tomorrow."

With that, I climb out of the car, resisting the urge to look back at Peyton one last time.

"Look at Andrew up there." Alex slides up next to me, gesturing through the open doors to where our brother is standing at the alter looking like he's about to puke.

My mind flashes back to my own wedding day. It was nothing like this. Finley and I got married in a tiny chapel in Vegas. There was a total of four people in the room, including the two of us. I wasn't nervous or uneasy. In fact, I had never felt surer of anything in my entire life. I wanted her to be my wife. It was that simple.

I still remember how she looked. The smile she wore as we stood at the alter and exchanged vows, the way her green eyes filled with tears as I promised to love her until death, and every moment of existence that would follow.

That was when she was still well enough to be Finley. Before the illness stripped away the girl I loved and robbed her from my life.

I'll always remember that day as one of the happiest of my life, because it was. A day when the world existed for just the two of us.

"Yeah, he looks nervous as hell," I finally comment, forcing myself back to the present.

"I know I was when Tanya and I got married. Of course, that was nothing compared to the day Malory was born. There's nothing like looking down at this tiny person you created and realizing there isn't one thing you wouldn't do to protect them. I was filled with so much happiness and so much fear at the same time."

"You're a good dad," I tell him, clasping him on the shoulder. It's rare that I see Alex show even a sliver of vulnerability, and while it would be easy to give him shit, the way he would likely do me, I don't have it in me to do so.

"Thanks, man." His gaze goes back to Andrew who keeps fidgeting with the cuffs of his tuxedo jacket. "Wonder how long it will be before Sam starts popping out little Andrews."

"You really think they'll have kids? Neither strike me as the parenting type."

"I think they will. At least I hope they will. My kids are going to need cousins to play with. Considering Adam is married to his job and you and Aaron aren't seeing anyone, Andrew is my only hope."

"Aaron's seeing someone."

"Yeah, for all of two weeks. You know Aaron. How long do you think that will actually last?"

"He seems to really like this one."

"What are you two talking about?" Aaron chooses this moment to step into the conversation.

"How I need Andrew to pop out some babies since none of you fuckers are on your way to giving Malory cousins anytime soon."

"Yeah, they can have fun with that. I don't want kids." He crinkles his nose.

"You say that now. Wait until you meet the right girl," Alex disagrees.

I'd met the right girl. Someone I saw myself having children with. Someone I wanted to grow old with. Unfortunately, fate had other plans.

I swallow past the hard knot that forms at the base of my throat. Today is already so much harder than I'd anticipated.

"Speaking of the right girl." Aaron's gaze goes off into the distance and a wide smile pulls up the corners of his lips.

Alex and I follow his line of sight to see the bridesmaids making their way toward us. My eyes hone in on Peyton and it's like everyone else disappears.

She looks incredible. The elegant blue dress she's wearing clings to her slender frame in all the right places, accented by the way her hair is pulled up off her shoulders with little tendrils falling around her face. Her lips are painted a soft pink and she's holding a bouquet of white flowers wrapped in ribbon that matches her dress.

I suck in a breath through my nose, trying to rationalize the way my heart picks up speed at the sight of her.

"Hey." She smiles, stopping directly in front of me.

"Hey." It comes out funny and I immediately clear my throat. "You look beautiful," I tell her, gesturing to the dress.

"Thank you." Her cheeks turn scarlet and she looks away for a long moment before her eyes come back to mine. "You look handsome," she returns.

"Thanks. Just something I had lying around," I joke, sliding my hands down the front of my tuxedo jacket. "You ready for this?" I add, offering her my arm as the first couple enters the church and begins making their way down the aisle.

"As ready as I'll ever be, I guess." She slides her arm through mine and turns her focus forward.

"You seem nervous," I whisper, leaning my lips close to her ear.

I don't miss the way she shivers when my breath dances across the side of her neck.

"I *am* nervous," she whispers back, not looking at me.

"Don't worry. I've got you," I tell her, straightening my posture as we move toward the door.

"Just don't let me fall." She looks up at me for a brief moment.

"Never." I smile.

"Abel. Peyton. Go," Heather cues us and side by side we step through the doors.

Peyton's arm tightens around mine and I have to resist the urge to laugh at how nervous she is. But I get it. Most people don't like having hundreds of eyes on them. Me on the other hand, I'm used to it. It kind of comes with the territory when you play music for a living.

We manage to make it to the end of the aisle without any hiccups. I release her arm so that she can take her place with the other bridesmaids while I head to the opposite side and position myself next to Adam. When I spot Claire sitting in the third row back, I smile, instantly feeling more at ease.

Claire has become somewhat of a security blanket for me. I don't have any explanation for it other than her connection to Finley. Don't get me wrong, that's not the only reason. Claire is an incredible person and over the last three years has become like a sister to me, but I don't think we'd be nearly as close if it weren't for our shared loss.

I turn my attention to the back of the church as those in attendance stand and Sam enters the room with her father.

While I know it's customary to watch the bride walk down the aisle, I can't stop my gaze from sliding to Peyton instead.

I watch her expression shift from anxious to smiling to tearing up all in the matter of thirty seconds and I'm so enthralled in watching her that I don't realize Sam has reached us until the minister begins to speak.

Snapping out of my fog, I turn my attention to my brother and his bride. And even though I try like hell to keep it there, I can't stop myself from stealing glances at Peyton every chance I get.

"Well, we survived." I nudge my arm against Peyton's as we sit side by side in the limousine on our way to the reception hall.

"We did." She smiles, her gaze locked on Sam and Andrew who are snuggled together in the back of the car, sharing a private conversation. "They look so happy."

"They do," I agree, trying to keep my thoughts from straying to the past.

It's hard to do. I find myself comparing every single moment to those I shared with Finley. If I close my eyes I can still see her lying beneath me as we spent our first night together as husband and wife. Hear her giggles as we wrestled beneath the sheets. Feel her touch slide against my skin.

It all feels so real.

"Your date looked very pretty," she comments, and it takes me a moment to realize she must be talking about Claire.

"Yeah," I murmur.

"If you don't mind me asking, who is she to you?"

"My best friend." I avoid telling her she's also my sister-in-law.

I'm not ready to talk about Finley with her. I'm not ready to talk about Finley with anyone. Not yet. Not when I still feel the pain of her loss like a knife stabbing me in the chest over and over.

"So you two…" she leaves the question hanging without finishing it.

"Are not dating," I confirm, already knowing what she's asking without her having to say the words.

Her eyes go down to the wedding band on my hand before moving back up to my face, her expression softening.

I don't pretend that her reaction doesn't confuse me. She's clearly seen my ring and yet she hasn't asked me about it even once.

It suddenly dawns on me that Aaron must have told her, and I don't know why, but the thought is almost a relief. If she knows the truth then it spares me from having to tell her.

She opens her mouth like she wants to say something but snaps it closed without uttering a single word.

I'm thankful for that. Now is not the time or the place to discuss such things. Not when there's so many people stuffed inside the limo to bear witness.

Even still, a part of me feels the overwhelming *need* to tell her. As if telling her will somehow lift the burden. As if it will set me free.

Whatever the reason, I *want* to tell her. For the first time since losing Finley, I want to share that loss with someone who never knew her.

I don't know why though. I think that's the part that bothers me the most. The not knowing why I feel this way.

I barely know this girl. I can't pinpoint one *real* thing I know about her. Yet I'm drawn to her. And in some weird way I feel like Finley is behind the scenes, orchestrating the entire thing. Like she's telling me it's time. Time to move on. Time to let go. Time to heal.

And a part of me wants to. A part of me wants it so desperately that I feel like I can't breathe. But then the other part of me, the larger part, is terrified of what it means once I do.

Could I love someone again? Would anyone ever compare to the woman I lost? And while I already know the answer to that question, I also can't deny the tremor of excitement I get every single time I look at Peyton.

I have caught myself thinking about her several times since that night at *Pulsations*. Even though our interaction was short, and I was a complete asshole to her, I knew there was something there.

The limo hits a massive pothole, jarring everyone in the car and sending Peyton into my side. She grips my leg to steady herself, both of our gazes falling to where the contact is being made.

Okay, Fin. Message received.

Chapter Nine
Peyton

The reception dinner goes by in a blur. One minute we're walking into the hall, followed by Andrew and Sam who are introduced as Mr. and Mrs. Collins. The next toasts are being made and the cake is cut.

I've been kind of dreading this part of the night all day. The part where I have to stand up in front of a room full of people and dance with Abel. I know there's going to be fourteen other people on the floor with us, but it does nothing to quell the swirl of nervousness in my stomach.

I try to tell myself it's only the dancing in front of people part I'm nervous about, but if I'm being honest with myself it also has to do with who I'll be dancing with.

It's fruitless to pretend like I'm not incredibly attracted to Abel. You'd have to be blind not to be. But I can't approach Abel the way I would any other guy, because he's not like any other guy.

I can't just say 'hey, I'm attracted to you' or even flirt with him the way I would normally do with a guy I'm interested in. Not knowing what I know. Even if he is interested in me, and this chemistry between us actually blossoms into something, I don't think I'll ever be able to look at him and feel fully content. Not when I know I was the second choice.

Maybe that seems selfish, but I want that for myself. I want to be the one that hangs the moon and the stars. The one a person's world revolves around, not living in the shadow of his dead wife.

The problem is, if Abel were to express interest in me, I don't think I could turn him away, no matter how much I know I should. I'm too drawn to him. I can't help it. Every time I look at him, I get this weird nervous swirl in my stomach and I feel like my heart has been injected with a shot of adrenaline. There's this incredible chemistry between us. Almost like the air zings whenever we're close.

I've never felt that kind of connection with anyone before, let alone a person I barely know. And as much as it confuses me, it excites me just the same.

I'm not an overly confident person in my everyday life. Where I am comfortable in my own skin, and happy with who I am, I'll never be one to assume a guy likes me.

But with Abel, despite everything I know, when he looks at me, I swear he feels it too.

I take a sip of champagne, my gaze sliding to Abel right as he stands. It takes me a moment to realize that everyone at the wedding party table is standing, except me.

Scrambling to my feet, I look over at Henna who gives me a confused look.

"You okay?" she whispers.

I nod, finishing off the rest of my champagne in one long gulp before turning to follow her and the other bridesmaids to the dance floor.

I feel Abel next to me before I even turn, like his presence bears this weight that I can physically feel in the air as it settles around me.

It's not long before I'm forced to face him, and when I do a familiar quiver runs through my chest.

Why does he have to be so handsome?

"So, we meet again." He smiles down at me, our height difference not as pronounced with my four-inch heels in play.

"So, we do." I force myself to relax a little as I slide one hand into his and the other on his shoulder, doing my best to avoid his gaze.

Seconds pass before *At Last* by Etta James fills the space and we slowly begin to move. Abel rests his face against the side of my head, and I shudder at his nearness.

"Leave it to my brother and his wife to pick possibly the most overplayed wedding song in the world for us to dance to," he whispers into my ear.

I smile and nod, trying to ignore the way my skin erupts in goosebumps.

Closing my eyes, I focus on my breathing, on the sound of the music, on making sure my feet move when they're supposed to. Anything I can to take the focus away from how it feels to be pressed up against Abel. From his hand on my back, his thumb tracing lazy circles against my spine, something I'm not sure he even realizes he's doing.

Each second ticks by so slowly, like time has slowed down around us. I was so nervous about dancing in front of everyone, but with Abel it's like there isn't a single other person in the room. It's just me and him and the steady strum of our hearts that seem to be beating in time.

When the music stops, Abel doesn't release me right away. It's like he also drifted off somewhere else and has lost himself to the moment.

I'm the first to shift, pulling back slightly so that our faces are a few inches apart.

A flash of sadness washes over his face and I swear it hits me straight in the stomach. It takes a second for me to realize what that means.

When I closed my eyes all I felt was him, but it wasn't me he was feeling at all. I can read his emotion in every line of his beautiful face. When he'd pulled back, he wanted to see *her*, not me.

The thought has me taking a full step back. Somehow, I muster the ability to plaster on a smile before thanking him for the dance and making my way back to the table.

"Thank you, girls, so much. Seriously." Sam releases me from her hug and moves to embrace Henna. "This day wouldn't have been what it was without you."

"It was our pleasure," I tell her. "We're so happy for you."

"I can't believe I'm actually married," she sings, releasing Henna.

"Truthfully, neither can I," Henna teases. "I thought you two were never going to tie the knot."

"They say couples with longer engagements usually have stronger marriages," I interject.

"Do they?" Henna cocks a brow at me.

"I read it in Cosmo," I tell her matter of fact.

"Well then I guess it must be true." She rolls her eyes.

We all laugh.

"Well, I guess I should get going." Sam bounces on the balls of her feet. "Fiji is calling my name."

"You two be safe. Text one of us as soon as you land," I tell her.

"And take lots of pictures," Henna adds. "Lord knows I'll probably never make it somewhere so exotic. I need a way to live vicariously through you.

"Love you girls." Sam turns just as Andrew approaches.

"Love you too," we say in unison, waving at the happy couple as they make their way into the hallway where their families are waiting to say goodbye.

"You hanging out with Aaron tonight?" I ask Henna once they're gone.

"He's taking Andrew and Sam to the airport. He said if he gets back early enough, he might swing by." She gives me a casual shrug.

"Next thing you know I'm going to have two friends married to Collins' brothers."

"I would be okay with that." She smiles and I swear it nearly splits her face in two. "Or maybe all three of us will end up with one."

"All three?" I question, not hiding my confusion.

"You and Abel seem to be getting awfully cozy with one another."

"What?" I blurt, nearly choking.

"Oh, don't act so surprised. You two were staring at each other all night."

"We were not," I argue, already knowing she's right. At least on my end.

While I successfully avoided him after our dance together, that didn't stop me from scanning the room for him every chance I got. I couldn't help it. Like a moth to a flame, as the saying goes.

"You so were," Henna disagrees.

"He's very attractive, I'll give you that. But we're not getting *cozy*, as you put it. He's still wearing his wedding ring for heaven's sake. Does that strike you as a man who's even the least bit interested in moving on?"

"Okay, so maybe not marriage, but what's the harm in having a little fun, if you know what I mean." Her eyebrows slide up and down suggestively.

"How long have you known me?" I give her a knowing look. "I don't do casual hookups, you know that."

"And look how great that's worked out for you." She sighs. "I'm just saying, maybe you should try switching things up a little. If nothing else, it could be a fun distraction until the real thing comes along."

"I'm not going to randomly start sleeping with someone like it's some kind of game."

"You need to learn to relax. Ever heard the phrase 'it's just sex'?" She makes air quotes with her fingers.

"I'm going to walk away now." Shaking my head, I turn to leave.

"Where are you going?" she calls after me.

"Home," I say, continuing to walk.

"You can't go home without me. You're my ride," she objects, her voice getting louder.

"Well then, I guess you better hurry up," I call back right as I round the corner, my feet faltering slightly when I see Abel and Claire standing next to the door talking.

Taking a deep breath, I force myself onward as if seeing him has zero effect on me.

"Hi, you're Peyton, right?" Claire steps directly in front of me before I can reach the door. Holding her hand out to me, she smiles. "I'm Claire."

"Hi." I take her hand and give it an awkward shake, releasing it moments later.

"I've been meaning to come introduce myself all night, but kept getting distracted," she tells me, her gaze sliding to Abel who seems painfully uncomfortable.

"No problem. It's been a whirlwind." I twirl my finger in the air.

"So, Abel and I were just talking about heading over to Holliday's and having a drink. Would you want to join us?"

"Claire," Abel grumbles, wiping a hand down his face.

Even if I wanted to say yes, his reaction has me shaking my head without a second thought.

"Thanks, but I'm pretty tired. I think I'm gonna head home."

"Okay, maybe another time then." She smiles softly, and even though I don't know a thing about her, I immediately like her.

I'm a firm believer that if you look hard enough you can tell within the first few seconds what kind of person you're dealing with. And it's pretty clear to me that Claire is one of those genuinely nice people. Someone everyone likes. And of course, she's beautiful too. I have a really hard time believing that people as attractive as the two of them have never had any sort of relationship beyond friendship. Then again, I'm a skeptic when it comes to platonic friendships. In my experience they always start as something more and fizzle out or they turn into something more over time.

"Seriously, Peyton," Henna groans loudly as she turns the corner, having removed her heels which are dangling from her hand by the straps. "Oh." She stops talking when she spots Claire and Abel. "Hi, guys." She half waves as she closes the distance between us.

"Well, I guess we should be going." I direct my attention to Claire, knowing if I give Henna time, she will be signing us up to join them for drinks and then some. "It was nice meeting you, Claire," I tell her with a friendly smile.

"It was nice meeting you as well, Peyton." She side steps to let Henna and I pass.

As much as I tell myself to keep my eyes forward and *not* look at Abel, my gaze still slides to him. He's looking anywhere but at me, and while I know I shouldn't, I can't help but feel a little disappointed.

"Would you slow down?" Henna whines as she tries to keep my pace through the parking lot. "What was going on back there?" She waits until she reaches me to ask.

"Nothing. Claire was just introducing herself."

"Claire." Henna looks at me like an explanation is in order.

"Yes, Claire, Abel's friend."

"I knew it!" Henna announces, smacking the top of the car. "He totally has a thing for you."

"How does his friend saying hello equate to him having a thing for me?" I look at Henna like she has five heads.

"Don't you get it? He's been talking to her about you. Either that or she's picked up on the chemistry between you two and was curious to meet you. Either way, my statement still stands true."

"I swear, you can find a way to spin anything." I shake my head, unlocking the car before peeling open the driver's door and sliding inside.

"You know I'm right," she tells me, hopping into the passenger seat.

"Actually, no, I don't. Did it ever occur to you that maybe we just ran into each other in the hallway and she thought it was polite to say hello?"

"You're such a Debbie Downer." She pouts, snapping her seatbelt in place.

"No, I'm a realist."

"Well, realistically you're a Debbie Downer."

"I like him, okay? But Hen, he just lost his wife and I am not the person that can follow some epic love story that ended in tragedy. Even if he was interested in me, which I'm not saying he is, I don't think I could go there with him."

"It's been three years, Peyton."

"It doesn't matter how long it's been. Some wounds don't heal."

"You're referring to your mom." She gives me a sympathetic look. "Listen, I know losing her is still anguish for you but, Peyton, this is different. She was your mom. You can't assume everyone feels the same as you do or handles their grief the same way. For all you know he's ready to put himself out there and find love again."

"Trust me, he's not," I tell her bluntly. "Five minutes with that man and you'll know he's not."

"That doesn't mean he doesn't want to," she argues. "Maybe he just doesn't know how to."

"I'm not talking about this anymore." I start the car and quickly shift it in reverse.

"You know the only reason you're getting all cranky on me is because you really like him."

"I already told you I like him. And I also told you the reasons why it doesn't matter."

"One of these days, Peyton." She sighs. "One of these days you're going to get out of your own way and let yourself try to be happy."

"I am happy."

"Yeah, but you're also lonely. You may not admit it, but I know you are. I know you, Peyton Rivers. You are a hopeless romantic at heart. And you keep waiting for the right guy to stroll in and sweep you off your feet. You expect it to be effortless and that's not how relationships work."

"I'm not a child, Henna. I know how relationships work." I can't help the irritation that comes out in my voice.

"Then act like it," she snaps back. "Stop sitting around waiting for Mr. Perfect when Mr. Right could be standing in front of you."

"Why are you doing this?" I look in her direction for a brief moment before my gaze goes back to the road. "Why are you pressing this so hard?"

"Because I see how you look at him. I don't think I've ever seen you clam up around a guy the way you do Abel. I guess I figure it has to mean something, and I don't want to watch it slip through your fingers because you're scared."

"So, what if I am? I have a right to protect my own heart."

"I know that, of course I do, but would it really be so bad for you to keep an open mind and let things play out rather than fighting yourself every step of the way."

"Play out? Who knows when I'll see him again, if ever." I ignore how the thought of never seeing Abel again makes me feel because it's too unsettling to face.

"Come to Mulligan's on Thursday. Aaron and I are going to see Abel play. Come with us."

"Why? So I can play the third wheel?"

"No, so you can feel out this Abel situation a little more and see if maybe something is there."

"I don't want to *see* if something's there."

"Bullshit. Bullshit. Bullshit." Henna smacks her leg.

"Are you done now?" I laugh at her ridiculous behavior.

"Not until you agree to come with us on Thursday."

"Henna." I shake my head.

"Please, Peyton. Just come with us and if by the end of the night you're convinced there's nothing to explore then I won't say another word on the matter. You have my word."

"Why is this so important to you?"

"Because I want to see you happy."

"And?"

"And because Aaron wants to see Abel happy."

"Please don't tell me Aaron is in on this too," I grumble.

"Just say yes, Peyton. It's one night of your life. What's it gonna hurt?"

I resist the urge to tell her just how much it might hurt and instead consider my options. I can either sit at home on Thursday and obsess over not going to see Abel or I can go see Abel and obsess over him while I watch him play. Either way I'm obsessing over a man that I can't have.

"You promise you'll get off my ass if I go?"

"Cross my heart." She makes an X over her heart with her pointer finger.

"If I tell you I'll think about it, will that be an acceptable answer for the time being."

"As long as I'll think about it equates to a yes, then yes, I'll accept it."

"You're impossible, you realize this, right?"

"And that's what makes me so damn lovable."

"Yeah, let's go with that." I give her a knowing look, laughter filling the car moments later.

Chapter Ten
Abel

"So, Peyton seems nice." Claire grins at me over the rim of her cocktail glass.

"She is," I agree, not taking the bait she's so clearly trying to reel me in with.

"And pretty," she adds, setting her glass on the round bar top table we're sitting at.

"She's okay." I shrug, knowing she's a hell of a lot more than *just* okay, but I'm not about to admit that to Claire.

"Oh, come on. You don't really expect me to believe that, do you?" She gives me a knowing look. "You forget, I was there tonight. I saw the way you looked at her. You're clearly attracted to her."

"So, she's attractive." Again, I shrug.

"Abel." She sighs, shaking her head.

"Why are you looking at me like that?"

"Because you like this girl. I'm just trying to figure out why you're fighting it."

"You know why."

"Don't do that. Don't blame your inability to pursue this girl on Finley."

"I'm not blaming anything on Finley."

"Maybe not, but you're using her as your excuse."

"So what if I am?"

"What did she ask you?"

"Huh?" I question, not sure what she means.

"What did Finley ask you to do before she died?" She waits a long beat before she continues when I don't respond. "She asked you to embrace it. When you found someone that made you *feel* again, to not push it away. She asked you to not close yourself off to loving again."

"I'm not closing myself off."

"Yes, you are. I'm not saying this girl is *the* girl, but she could be. How will you know unless you're willing to explore the obvious chemistry the two of you share?"

"I don't know what you're talking about." I take a pull of my beer, completely content giving her vague responses all night rather than being honest with her, and myself.

"Yes, you do. I can feel it so I know you sure as hell can. Don't make Finley the reason you don't get to know her. Make her the reason you do. Because you know it's what she wanted for you. To live, to love, to find happiness... again."

"It's not that easy."

"I know that. And I know how hard this is for you. I know it's easier for you to take a random girl to bed you feel nothing for than to share a real conversation with a girl you actually might like. But Abel, that's part of moving on. You have to give yourself a chance. It may turn into nothing. You may find that she's not what you're looking for. But how will you know if you don't try?"

"Is this going to be all you talk about tonight?" I give her an irritated stare.

"Until you give me a straight answer, yes." She challenges me in the same way Finley would have.

"I see her, Claire. Everywhere, in everyone, I see *her*. Did it ever occur to you that maybe the reason I'm trying to ignore my attraction to Peyton is because when I touch her, I feel Finley? When I hear her laugh, I hear Finley. When I close my eyes and open them the first thing I feel is disappointment that it's not Finley staring back at me. How is that fair to anyone? I don't know Peyton well, but something tells me she's a woman who wants more than that."

"Give it time. Right now, you associate Peyton with Finley because she's the first girl that's actually ignited a spark in you since Finley died. That doesn't mean those feelings will always be there."

"And what if they are? What if they never go away?"

"They will," she reassures me, reaching across the table to rest her hand on my forearm. "You just have to be willing to open yourself up to the possibility. You have to be willing to look at another woman and not see Finley. To touch another woman and not feel her, and not feel guilty when you finally do."

"But I do feel guilty. Every fucking day I feel it."

"Why?"

"Because I'm alive and she's not."

"But that's not your fault. You can't feel guilty for something you had no control over. Finley died because she was sick. She would have died whether you loved her or not. Be grateful for the time you got with her and not angry for the time you didn't."

"I'm not programmed that way, Claire. I can't see the positive in everything. Not when it all hurts so fucking much. It's not like some switch I can turn on or off."

"I know that. And as your friend I want to tell you to do things in your own time and when you're ready. But as Finley's sister, as the person who promised her she'd make sure you'd be okay, I can't help myself. I want you to be happy, Abel. More than I want it for myself. Because until you are, I don't feel like I can let her truly rest."

"It's not your job to look after me."

"No, but I'm going to keep doing it until I feel like I don't have to any longer. Because that's what we do for the people we love. And I do love you, Abel. You are my brother, maybe not in blood but in all the ways that matter."

"I love you too, ya know?"

"I know." She gives me a sly grin. "I mean, how could you not? I'm pretty fantastic." She giggles and the sound reminds me so much of Finley's laugh it almost takes my breath away.

"If you weren't, there's no way I would let you get away with making a comment like that." I chuckle, pushing past the tight knot in my throat.

"So, Peyton." She jumps right back into it without skipping a beat.

"What about her?"

"You going to call her or what?"

"No," I answer flatly.

"Have I achieved nothing?" She throws her hands up to the sky dramatically.

"Sorry to disappoint." I grin.

"Abel Collins, so help me god. If you don't open those pretty blue eyes of yours and look around, I'm going to be forced to remove them from your head and make you."

"Did you just threaten to rip my eyes out?" I give her a humorous look.

"Desperate times call for desperate measures." She waves a finger at me.

"Hold that thought." I raise my hand as the waitress passes and signal for another round. "If we're going to keep talking about this, I'm gonna need a hell of a lot more than just one beer."

"Dealing with your stubborn ass I'm going to need more alcohol as well," she shoots back, picking up her glass before killing off the remainder of her drink in one long gulp.

"Maybe we should save ourselves the headache and call it a night," I suggest playfully.

"Nope. If I have to get you shit faced drunk for you to open up to me then that's what I'm going to do."

"I am being open."

"No, you're not. I just can't figure out if you're purposely downplaying your feelings or if you're so blind you can't see them yet."

"I really don't know what you're talking about at this point." I scratch my head and laugh.

"We're talking about you liking a girl."

"I don't even know her." I sigh. "How can I know if I like her if I don't even know her?"

"How long did you know Finley before you realized you were in love with her?"

"If I'm being honest, less than an hour," I admit, knowing she had me hook, line, and sinker before we ever left the bar that night.

"Exactly. Is it so farfetched that you could *like* someone after a few short interactions?"

"Peyton is not Finley."

"Of course she isn't. I'm just trying to make a point that if it happened once it can happen again."

"Lightning doesn't strike the same place twice."

"Says who?"

"I don't know, people."

"Technically speaking, lightning can absolutely strike the same place twice. It may take millions of years, but the inevitability is that it *will* happen again."

"Millions of years is a lot longer than one lifetime."

"Shut up." She swats at my hand. "You know what I'm saying."

"Do I?" I cock my head to the side and lift my eyebrow.

Claire bites back whatever it is she was going to say when the waitress reappears with our drinks, setting my beer in front of me before placing Claire's pink drink in front of her.

Emptying the remainder of my existing beer, I hand the waitress the empty bottle as she turns to leave.

"What I'm saying," Claire pauses to take a drink, "is that your logic that what has happened can't happen again is flawed."

"Is that so?" The corner of my mouth hitches upward.

"It is. And I'm going to prove you wrong, even if it's the last thing I do."

"And how exactly are you going to do that?"

"I'll let you know once I figure that part out." She laughs, going in for another drink. "Do you still have her ashes?" The abrupt switch in conversation sends my mind into a spin. It takes me a full minute to gather my thoughts enough to answer.

"I do." I take a long pull of my beer.

"Abel." She gives me a sad smile.

"I went to the beach, the one where I proposed. The one where she asked me to leave her ashes, but I couldn't do it. I wasn't ready to let her go. I'm not sure I'll ever be ready." The last part comes out as a murmur, meant more for me than Claire.

"You will be. One of these days. It may not feel like it now but one day, Abel, one day you will find someone that fills the void she left behind. And when you do, you'll know the time is right."

"I don't think I've ever thanked you," I think aloud.

"Thanked me for what?"

"For being my friend. For understanding when no one else could. For your patience and your kindness. I honestly don't know where I'd be without you, Claire."

"You know, that goes both ways."

"I find that hard to believe."

"Well you shouldn't. You gave me a piece of my sister to hang onto when I needed it the most and because of that, because of her, I have you. And you, Abel Collins, mean the world to me. That's why I push you so hard. Why I'm always up in your business. Because I want the world for you and I fear that while you're still holding onto her, you're never going to get it."

"She was the world to me."

"I know, but you can't spend your entire life chasing after a ghost."

"I know that," I grumble.

"Do you?"

"Of course I do."

"Then prove it. Ask Peyton out on a date."

"What?" I choke out a laugh.

"You heard me. Ask her out. What do you have to lose?"

"I'm not asking her on a date."

"Why not?"

"Because I can barely talk to her when we don't have a choice but to be around each other. What makes you think I could carry on a conversation for an entire evening when it's just her and I?"

"You're a pretty charming guy. I think you'll figure it out."

"Still, not happening. At least not yet."

"Not yet." She smiles. "That's not a no."

"Can we please talk about something else?"

"Fine." She crinkles her nose. "But this isn't over," she warns.

"Like I didn't already know that much." I chuckle, lifting my beer bottle to my lips.

Chapter Eleven
Peyton

"I can't believe I let you talk me into this." I tug at the hem of my shirt nervously as I follow Aaron and Henna into Mulligan's.

"Just relax," Henna hisses back at me, snagging my hand to pull me through the thick crowd as Aaron leads us toward the bar.

"This place is packed," I state the obvious, looking around the large space that appears to be standing room only. "You think they're all here to see Abel?" I ask when we stop in a long line of patrons waiting to place their order at the bar.

"Must be." Aaron shrugs. "I don't think I've ever seen this place this busy on a Thursday night. I haven't been to a show like this in years, but from what I gather from some of the guys, Abel always pulls in a good crowd."

"Probably because he's ridiculously talented." Again, I state the obvious.

"He really is," Henna agrees. "Too bad you didn't get some of his musical genes, babe."

"Are you saying you think my brother is hot?" He gives her a questioning look.

"I mean, yeah, he is, but that's not the point. I just think you'd be even sexier if you could sing like he does."

"I'm going to pretend like you're not comparing me to my brother right now." He can't seem to decide if he should be offended or find her behavior humorous.

"Oh hush. You know I think you're the sexiest Collins brother out there."

"You better say that." He wraps an arm around her waist and tugs her to his chest seconds before his mouth crashes down on hers.

I look away, feeling even more awkward than I did on the drive over. These two have trouble keeping their hands to themselves, which is cute, but a little uncomfortable when you're forced to bear witness to their affections.

"Get a room," someone yells seconds before Abel appears through the sea of people standing around us.

Henna and Aaron break apart, Aaron offering his brother a humor filled "fuck you" before securely tucking Henna into his side.

I try to avoid Abel's gaze but find it impossible to do so.

"You came." He smiles at me, and if I didn't know any better, I'd think he was happy about this fact.

"Henna didn't really give me a choice." I hitch my thumb in the direction of my friend.

He nods, something unreadable passing over his face. "Well, for the record, I'm glad you're here," he says directly to me before turning his attention to Aaron and Henna. "All of you. Means a lot," he says directly to his brother.

"Happy we could make it. Hell of a crowd you got here." Aaron gestures around the room.

"Not too bad considering I haven't played here in like three and a half years."

"Guess people remember talent."

"Can I get you guys a drink?" Abel redirects, not commenting on his brothers' statement.

"We can wait," Henna speaks up.

"What about you?" He turns to me. "I can grab you a drink if you want one."

"That's okay. I can wait with them."

"Okay." He nods rapidly. "Well, I guess I should head up there and make sure we're all ready to go." He gestures toward the vicinity of the stage. "I'll come have a drink with you after my first set," he says to the group, not honing in on one specific person.

"Sounds good." Aaron claps his brother on the shoulder. "Knock 'em dead."

"I'll do my best." Abel smiles, offering me the briefest glimpse of his dimple before he turns to walk away.

By the time Abel finishes his first set, I'm as good as gone. If I wasn't ready to admit my ever-growing desire for him, there's no denying it now. Not when I've spent the last forty-five minutes practically drooling over the man. I can't help it. When he took the stage, I became transfixed by his incredible voice and the way his fingers move so effortlessly along the strings of his guitar.

Where this isn't the first time I've seen him play, it is the first time I've seen him on stage since getting to know him a little. Knowing him only intensifies how incredible I think his talent is. Because now it's not some stranger up on stage. It's a man who has consumed my thoughts for days on end. A man that I can't seem to shake no matter how hard I try.

Every song he sang I imagined he was singing directly to me. Every time his eyes swept to me, I felt like it was intentional. As if he was trying to portray something to me in the song. Of course, it's probably all in my head, but damn if it didn't feel good to pretend it was all true.

I don't know if it's my attraction to him winning out or the nice buzz of alcohol swimming in my veins, but suddenly I feel less concerned with protecting my heart and more concerned with making this man mine.

Abel hops off the stage and makes a bee line to where we're standing, huddled against the far wall a few feet from the stage. My eyes trace his broad shoulders and the width of his chest before coming back up to his face. I have to bite down on my bottom lip to keep myself from moaning.

Maybe that's a sign that I've been kicking back my Long Island ice teas a little too quickly tonight, but I'm past the point of really caring.

I didn't come here intending to drink much. In fact, I rarely drink past a slight buzz, but the instant I saw Abel I knew I was going to need something strong tonight.

He puts me so on edge that I feel almost nauseous from the knots sitting in my stomach like heavy rocks. He makes me nervous, so off kilter. So much so that when he stops directly in front of us and his eyes come to mine, my knees wobble beneath me.

"You are so amazing," Henna coos over Abel, clearly feeling her alcohol as well.

"Thank you." He offers her an easy smile. "I'm going to go get a drink. Does anyone need anything?"

I look down at my near empty drink. "I do. I'll come with you."

"Okay." He nods once. "Anyone else?"

"I'm good." Henna leans into Aaron.

"I wouldn't mind another beer if you're going that way." Aaron holds up his empty bottle.

"You got it." Abel cocks his head, gesturing for me to follow him.

"Be right back," I tell Henna before quickly setting off after Abel.

Instead of getting in the line at the bar that's at least twenty people deep, Abel heads around to the side and flags down one of the bartenders who immediately heads in our direction.

"Two Bud Lights and…" he pauses, turning to point at my drink.

"Long Island," I semi-shout over the crowd.

The bartender nods in acknowledgment before walking away to retrieve our drinks.

"Hitting the hard stuff tonight, I see," Abel observes, pointing at my glass.

"Needed something to take the edge off," I explain, sucking the remaining liquid through the straw before setting the empty glass on the bar behind Abel.

"Is it working?" He cocks a brow.

"Maybe a little," I admit, feeling calmer around him than I normally do.

"Are you having fun?"

"Surprisingly, yes." I giggle at my bluntness.

"Surprisingly?" he questions.

"I wasn't sure how I would feel with those two." I point in the vicinity of where I know Aaron and Henna are. "Third wheel and all."

"Well for the record, I'm glad you're here."

"You are?" My thoughts come out in the form of actual words.

"I am," he confirms, turning when the bartender reappears with our drinks. "Here." He hands me my Long Island before grabbing his and Aaron's beers off the counter.

"Don't I need to pay?" I ask, preparing to grab some cash from my wristlet.

"Bands drink free." He waves me off.

"But I'm not in the band," I object.

"Close enough." He smiles, that damn dimple sending my heart into a frenzy.

"Okay then." I lift the straw to my lips and take a long drink, humming when the taste hits my tongue.

"Good?" He chuckles, watching me with a narrowed gaze.

"So good." I nod enthusiastically, offering him my drink. "Try it."

To my surprise he leans in, wraps his lips around *my* straw, and takes a drink. The whole thing lasts less than ten seconds but it's enough to make me feel like my entire world shifted on its side. My face feels flush and tiny droplets of sweat form at the back of my neck.

My god, what is wrong with me?

"That is good," he agrees after he's swallowed his drink. "Maybe I should have ordered me one of those."

"Nah, beer suits you better," I say, once again voicing my thoughts instead of keeping them in my head where they belong.

"It does?" His lips quirk up.

"Yeah, you know, hot musician and beer just go together. Like PB and J."

"So, you think I'm hot?" His smile widens and I know he's just messing with me.

"Have you looked at yourself?" I blurt. Stupid word vomit. "I mean…" I stutter over my words. "Crap." I laugh and admit defeat. "Yes, I think you are extremely hot. There, are you happy?"

"I actually am, so thanks for that." He laughs. "For the record, you're not so bad yourself." His eyes do one long sweep over my body and I swear every surface of my skin prickles.

"Is it hot in here?" I fan my face with my hand, suddenly feeling severely overheated.

"It's a little warm," he says, thankfully not adding further to my increasing mortification.

"We should get back to Henna and Aaron."

"Yeah," he agrees, but he doesn't move.

"Um..." I hesitate, not sure what to do.

Abel seems to find humor in my indecision.

"Come on." He chuckles. Holding both beers by the neck in one hand, he grabs mine with his other and pulls me through the crowd.

I try to pay attention to where I'm going and not run into anyone, but truth be told I'm finding it difficult to focus on anything other than Abel's fingers wrapped around mine.

If I didn't know it before, I sure as heck know it now. I'm in serious trouble...

Chapter Twelve
Peyton

"Killer set tonight, bro." Aaron raises his beer bottle to Abel when he slides up next to the table we were able to secure after the crowd started to clear out.

It's nearing midnight and they announced last call about ten minutes ago so we, of course, rushed to the bar and ordered another round.

Aaron is more intoxicated than I've seen him before, not that I've been around him that much to begin with. Henna has slid off her stool twice since we sat down. And me, well I'm a happy drunk. Which means I've been sitting here staring at Abel for nearly the entire night with a wide smile across my face. Because while all of the concerns I had earlier are still there, the buzz running through my veins has made it easy for me to forget all the reasons why I can't have Abel and remind me of all the reasons I want to.

"Thanks." Abel runs a hand through his messy hair before snagging Aaron's beer from his hand. He takes a long drink and my eyes are immediately drawn to his neck, throat bobbing as he drinks.

It's such an average everyday motion and yet something about the way he does it makes it so incredibly sexy I can barely contain myself.

"Hey!" Aaron's delayed reaction causes us all to laugh.

"I was thirsty." Abel gives him a shit eating smile and takes another drink.

"If you want a beer, I'm sure the bartenders will get you one."

"Can't. Gotta drive. Just wanted a drink." He shoves the beer bottle back into his brother's hand. "Speaking of which, I take it you all need a ride home tonight."

"We're gonna Uber," I explain, my words borderline slurred.

"Like hell you are. I'm only a few blocks from you. I'll drop you off on my way home."

"How do you know where I live?" I ask way too loudly.

"Because I've dropped Aaron off there."

"Oh." My cheeks flush.

"Finish your drinks and we can head out. I'm going to go get paid." He nods to the table and then spins on his heel, heading in the direction of the bar.

"You are so obvious," Henna slurs next to me.

"What?" I look away from Abel's backside to see my friend watching me with knowing eyes.

Well hell, if drunk Henna is picking up on it then there's no way sober Abel isn't.

"I see the way you look at him." She smiles, leaning to the side to lay her head on my shoulder. She turns her big eyes up to my face and bats her lashes dramatically. "Peyton's in love." She sighs loudly.

"Peyton most certainly is *not* in love. I'm a little smitten, but make no mistake, there is no *love* involved."

"So, what you're saying is you want to bang my brother," Aaron chimes in.

"I do not want to *bang* anyone. Who even says that anymore? Bang." I snort.

"Doesn't matter how I word it. Still true." He shrugs, taking a pull from his beer.

"Considering you're drunker than I am, I'm going to pretend like it's the alcohol talking."

"Blame it on whatever you want, doesn't change the facts."

"And what are the facts exactly, Aaron?" I lean forward, causing Henna to pop up off my shoulder.

"That you have a thing for my brother."

"I do not have a thing," I lie and fail miserably at doing so. Even I don't believe the words coming out of my mouth at this point.

"Who has a thing?" Abel suddenly reappears, seemingly out of thin air.

"Peyton," Aaron tells him, leaning in close to his brother.

"Peyton what?" Abel questions, his gaze going to me.

"Peyton is ready to go home," I interrupt in hopes of derailing Aaron.

"Peyton," he slurs, "has a thing for you, little brother." He shoves Abel's shoulder.

"Oh my god." I groan and shake my head. "Don't listen to him. He's so drunk he doesn't know his ass from his nose."

"Eww." Aaron crinkles his nose. "How would I not know my ass from my nose?"

"On that note." Abel laughs, hooking his brother under the arm and lifting him to his feet. "I think it's time we get you home."

"I'm not going home," Aaron objects.

"He's coming home with me." Henna leans across the table and wiggles her eyebrows at Abel.

"Oh my god, Henna. We get it." I push off my stool, swaying slightly when my feet hit the floor.

"You okay?" Abel's eyes are glued on me.

"Yeah, just stood up too fast. You get him, I'll get her." I hitch my thumb at Henna.

"Maybe I should just take turns getting all three of you." He gives me a knowing look.

"Nah, I got this." I swipe my hand through the air. "Come on, Henna Boo." I pull her up next to me. "Let's get you and lover boy home."

"Lover boy." She giggles.

"Lead the way," I tell Abel, hooking my arm around Henna's shoulder and securing her to me.

"Okay." He gives me one last look before he guides his brother from the bar, me and Henna fast on his heels.

Getting Henna into the car proves even more difficult than getting her *to* the car. She tends to get a bit lovey and as such, she keeps grabbing my face and telling me how much she loves me.

"Abel, a little help." I finally give up after my fourth attempt at guiding her into the backseat.

Abel shuts the door once he has Aaron in and crosses to the other side of the car. Stepping around Henna, he swoops her up so he's cradling her like a baby. I'm instantly jealous of my too drunk friend.

"You're hot." She giggles, petting his face. "Peyton and you are two hot tamales. You should make sweet love and create some equally beautiful babies." Her words are so slurred I can barely decipher what she said.

"What did she just say?" Abel cocks a brow at me.

"Ignore her. When she gets drunk she talks in cursive."

He looks at me for a long moment like he's trying to figure out what *I* just said, then out of nowhere he bursts into laughter.

"You're funny," Henna tells him.

"And you're getting into the backseat now." He leans down and plops her in the car next to Aaron, shutting the door before she can try to escape.

"Sorry, she's like a wild animal sometimes."

"Nothing I haven't seen before." He chuckles. "Here." He steps back and pulls open the passenger door for me.

"Thank you." I smile, trying to ignore the way my heart whooshes in my chest.

Abel shuts my door and crosses around the car, hopping into the driver's side moments later.

"I'm hungry," Henna announces loudly from the backseat. "Can we get pizza on the way home?"

"Pretty sure all the pizza places are closed," Abel tells her, starting the car.

"Boo! How about burgers?"

"I don't know of any burger places open twenty-four hours between here and your house," he tells her, slowly backing out of his parking spot before pulling out into the road.

"Let's go to Jack's!" Aaron announces it like he's just had an *ah ha* moment.

"I am not taking your ass to Jack's in your current condition."

"Why not? Claudia and Jack won't be there."

"You hope they won't," Abel argues.

"What's Jack's?" I chime in, curious as to what they're talking about.

"It's a little diner across town. Our aunt and uncle own the joint. Best burgers in the world," Aaron answers.

"Best burgers in the world, huh?" I stare at the side of Abel's face which causes him to glance in my direction.

"Oh no. Not you too." He shakes his head before his eyes slide back to the road.

"Oh come on. We're hungry." Aaron starts kneeing the back of Abel's seat.

"Fucking hell," Abel grumbles. "Fine! I'll take you to Jack's, but so help me, Aaron, you make an ass of yourself, you're the one that's going to have to apologize to Jack and Claudia the next time you see them."

"I'm not going to make an ass of myself." Aaron laughs.

"Yay burgers!" Henna celebrates.

"Any chance we can just take them home and they won't notice?" I ask Abel under my breath.

"Um, I heard that." Henna knees the back of *my* seat.

"What is with you two kneeing seats?" I turn and glare at her. "If you don't stop, we're going to kick you both out of the car and you can find your own way home," I warn, playfully serious.

"I know why she wants to kick us out of the car," Henna whisper yells to Aaron.

"So she can get all up on my brother's nuts," Aaron finishes her thought.

Heat floods my cheeks and I know I must be a hundred shades of red at this point, but I do my best to laugh it off in hopes of hiding my embarrassment.

"You two are children," I tell them, avoiding looking at Abel as I turn back toward the front. "Sorry about them," I murmur.

"Don't be. Nothing I haven't dealt with many times before. My brothers try to pretend they're all holier than thou but get a little alcohol in them and they are just as fucked up as the rest of us."

"At least you have siblings. Try being an only child with parents who are so overprotective you could barely breathe most of your life."

"I take it you didn't get to do much as a child?" he asks, keeping his gaze locked on the road.

I'm thankful that despite Henna and Aaron's outrageous attempts to mortify me further than I have already done myself, Abel moves along like nothing was said.

"You could say that. My mom was the more lenient one. But my dad, that man needed to take a serious chill pill. He got even worse after my mom passed."

"I'm sorry." It isn't until Abel apologizes that I realize what I said. I'm not one to typically share such personal things with someone I barely know. Guess that's what happens when you drink too much alcohol. You become all loose tongued.

"It's okay. It was a long time ago."

"How old were you when she passed?" he asks, ignoring Henna and Aaron's playful moaning and laughing in the backseat.

"Fifteen."

"How did she die? If you don't mind me asking."

I'm hesitant to tell him, knowing that's how his wife died, but I don't see a way to avoid answering without coming across as rude.

"Cancer." His expression shifts the moment the word leaves my mouth.

"Did she have it long?" he asks after a few beats of silence.

"Just a few months. One day she was perfectly healthy and a year later she was gone."

"Wow." He blows out a slow breath. "That had to be hard."

"It was. But I like to think she's still here with me. I swear sometimes I can even hear her laugh. Or feel her next to me when I'm baking our favorite pie in the kitchen. I don't know if she really is or not, but it helps to picture that she's here."

"I get that." He nods, eyes glued to the road.

"Aaron," Henna moans, the sound echoing through the car.

"I swear to god if any body parts come out back there, I'm cutting them off," Abel warns, flashing a smile in my direction.

I'm happy for the shift in conversation. Alcohol may make me happy, but it can turn me into a crying drunk in a matter of seconds, and no one wants to deal with that. I think I've suffered enough embarrassment for one night.

"Are they always like this?" he asks me.

"Yep." I nod. "You should try sleeping in the room next to them. Let's just say our walls are not very thick."

"I think I'd move." He laughs.

"I've been tempted as of late." I smile, dropping my head back against the headrest as my eyes stay fixed on the side of Abel's face.

Henna breaks away from Aaron's mouth long enough to comment, "You would never leave me."

"Keep telling yourself that," I joke.

"Fucking finally." Aaron sits upright as Abel slows and pulls into a parking spot next to a small, rundown diner.

"I say we let them sit by themselves," Abel suggests, a smile on his face as he puts the car in park and kills the engine.

"Let's do it," I agree, swinging open the car door before sliding out. The ground sways slightly under my feet and I have to grip the top of the door to keep myself from toppling over. Luckily Abel doesn't see.

"Come on, you two," he calls into the backseat before slamming the door shut.

"We had to help them out of the bar," I remind him, meeting his gaze over the top of the car. "Maybe bringing them here wasn't the best choice."

"They could use a little food and time to sober up. Otherwise they'll feel like hell tomorrow. Besides, this is the one place I know won't kick us out."

"Well, at least there's that," I agree, watching him cross around the car toward me right as Aaron and Henna stumble out of the same door.

"You know Claudia and Jack's rule. If you're too drunk to walk through the front door then you're too drunk to be here.

Think you can manage to get inside without falling on your face?" he asks Aaron.

"Fuck you, man. I've got this."

"Okay." Abel chuckles, extending his arm to me. "Shall we?"

"I'm not that drunk. I can walk inside on my own."

"And?" he questions, arm still extended.

I open my mouth to argue but realize that I don't want to and quickly snap it closed. Linking my arm through Abel's, I allow him to walk me to the front door. After guiding me inside, he waits at the door, holding it open for Aaron and Henna who somehow manage to walk inside without any assistance.

"You two sit here." Abel barely touches Aaron's shoulder and he falls into the booth, causing all of us to laugh.

"Where are you sitting?" Henna gives Abel a curious look as she takes the seat across from Aaron.

"Peyton and I will be in the next booth over."

I don't miss the way her eyes narrow in on my face or the knowing smile that lights up on her own.

"It's not like that. We just don't want to deal with you two." I gesture between her and Aaron.

"Sure it's not." She gives me a disbelieving look.

"You are quite possibly the worst friend ever," I tell her, wagging my finger in her direction.

"Ouch," she says as I follow Abel to the next booth over.

"I'm so sorry about her," I say, sliding into the booth.

"I'm sorry about him." He hitches his thumb backward in the direction of his brother as he takes the seat across from me.

"They really are a match made in heaven, aren't they?" I laugh, reaching for a menu tucked behind the napkin holder.

"That they are. Good thing they're not like this all the time."

"Oh lord, I don't think I could be her friend if that's how she acted all the time. Don't get me wrong, drunk Henna is fun but as you have witnessed tonight, she's also a master of embarrassing her friends."

"Ah, she wasn't that bad." He grabs himself a menu.

"Wasn't that bad? She pretty much told you I want to jump your bones in five different ways."

"Yeah, but if it's true who really cares?"

I blanch, not sure what the hell to say to that.

"Relax, Peyton." He smiles, dimple and all. "I'm just messing with you."

"Ha. Ha," I deadpan. "So funny." I flip open my menu, not able to make out a single word on it right away. I have to give my vision a second to adjust to the tiny letters before I can read it.

Guess I'm a little more intoxicated than I thought.

"So, what's good here?" I ask, keeping my gaze on the menu.

"Everything."

"You have to say that; your family owns the place," I tell him, looking up to see him watching me. "What are you getting?"

"What I always get." He shrugs. "A burger and fries."

"Perfect," I say, shutting the menu. "That's what I'll have too."

Chapter Thirteen
Abel

"This is so good." Peyton moans around a mouthful of food.

"I told you."

"Yeah, but a lot of people say stuff like that. Best place ever, yada yada." She swirls her hand in the air. "Very rarely is it actually the case."

"Well, I'm glad to hear that this was not one of those cases."

"Me too." She grins before taking another bite of her burger. She waits until she's chewed and swallowed before continuing, "So, your aunt and uncle own this place?"

"Yep. Have since I was a kid."

"That's awesome. I've always thought it would be cool to own my own business."

"Then why not do it?"

"Me?" She snorts. "I'm not cut out to be a business owner. I like being able to shut off my brain at five o'clock and not think about work again until I'm back in the office the next morning."

"If you did open your own business, hypothetically speaking of course, what would you do?"

"Hmm, I don't know. I've never really given it that much thought. I think maybe a clothing boutique, seeing as I have a slight obsession with clothes and shoes. Or maybe a bookstore."

The mention of a bookstore brings Finley to the forefront of my thoughts. I've never met someone who loves books the way she did.

"Why a bookstore?" I push past the sudden tightness in my chest.

"Because I love bookstores."

"I take it you're a big reader?"

"I wouldn't say that. I do enjoy a good murder mystery every now and again, but I wouldn't say I'm a big reader. I just really love bookstores."

"Any specific reason why?"

"My mom." She turns her eyes downward for a long moment before her gaze comes back up to mine. "She loved to read. When I was little, we used to stop by the little bookstore in town every time we'd be out running errands. She'd spend hours browsing the shelfs and would usually walk out with several new books each time we went. My dad used to joke that he needed a second job to support her reading habit." She smiles at the memory.

"I used to know someone who loved to read like that."

"Oh yeah?" She pops a fry into her mouth.

"Yeah." I clear my throat.

"Was it your wife?" She hits me with a sympathetic look, only further confirming my suspicions that Aaron must have told her. Her eyes flash to my wedding ring and then come back up to mine, her features softening.

"It was," I confirm after several moments of silence have passed between us.

"Did she like to read anything in particular?"

"She loved everything, but mostly romance. It would fascinate me, watching her read. I could tell what was happening based on her expression. She felt every character and story so deeply while she was reading it was almost like they were a part of her."

"Sounds like my mom." She gives me a sad smile. "Tell me more about her."

I don't have to ask to know who she's talking about, but for some reason I do anyway. "Who?" My voice comes out thick.

"Your wife."

"Finley," I say her name aloud to someone other than Claire for the first time in a very long time.

"Finley." She nods. "What was she like?"

"Unlike anyone I had ever known before or since." I let out a slow sigh, sitting back in the booth. "She was fearless, strong, stubborn as all hell." I pause, having to physically push past the knot in my throat. "She was beautiful, full of life, and had more courage in her little toe than most people have in their entire bodies."

"You really loved her."

"Still do." I shrug.

"And you always will. We don't stop loving people just because they are no longer here. If anything, we love them more once they're gone."

"Yeah," I agree, nodding slowly.

"I'm sorry. We don't have to talk about this." She must read something on my face that gives her the impression I'm not enjoying this conversation.

"No, it's okay. I need to learn how to talk about her," I say, surprising even myself.

Isn't this what I've been trying to accomplish for the last three years? Being able to talk about her without feeling like I'm dying. And while yes, it's not an easy conversation to have, something about having it with Peyton makes it a little easier. Maybe because she's so easy to talk to, or maybe because she knows what it feels like to lose someone the way I lost Finley.

"Will you tell me about how you met."

"Well, we actually met at a bar. I was there meeting my brothers for drinks. She was sitting at the bar drinking water. We locked eyes and the rest was kind of history. I knew right there, in that moment, that I had to know her. So, after my brothers left, I sat down next to her. It was the start of the best night of my life. Then she ghosted me the next morning and I spent the next few weeks trying to track her down like a crazy stalker."

"Wait, what do you mean she ghosted you?" She laughs.

"I mean, she snuck out sometime after I had fallen asleep. I didn't know her last name, something she had purposely kept from me I later found out. We didn't exchange numbers and I had failed to learn where she worked or lived over the course of our night together. I woke up the next day and she was gone."

"Oh my god. So then how did you two end up together?" She leans forward, placing her elbows on the table.

"I had a private investigator buddy of mine track her down."

"You didn't?" Her eyes go wide, and I can tell she's fighting off a smile.

"Oh, I did." I laugh at the memory.

"So, what happened?"

"He finally located an address where she lived with her sister, Claire."

"Claire," she repeats, seeming to piece together the dots.

"Claire is Finley's sister," I confirm. "So anyway, I showed up at their apartment and Claire answered the door. She said Finley was out of town but agreed to give her my number. A few days later she finally text me."

"Did she say where she'd been? Why she'd left?"

"No." I shake my head. "I could tell she was keeping something from me, but I was so happy to be talking to her again that I didn't really push it. It wasn't until I accompanied my mom to chemotherapy one day that it all came together."

"Wait, your mom has cancer?" Concern wrinkles her forehead.

"Had. She's been in remission for nearly three years."

She flattens her palm against her chest and lets out a slow breath, the situation obviously hitting a little too close to home.

"So Finley was at the hospital?" she prompts me to continue with my story.

"She was coming out of chemo as we were going in. Imagine my shock to see her sitting in that wheelchair. I didn't even know she was sick."

"Wait, so she was sick when you guys met?"

"She was, but I didn't know that at the time. Not that it would have changed how I felt about her. Nothing would have changed how I felt. But I understand her reasoning for not telling me." I pause, taking a long drink of water. "I found out later that she found out about her brain tumor the day we met. When she left me the next morning, she did so under the impression that she wouldn't be alive long enough for it to matter. She thought she was sparing me."

"But she did live."

"She did." I nod. "She survived the surgery and was on the mend. That's when our relationship really took flight. The few weeks that followed were the happiest of my entire life. But then we found out the cancer had spread, and everything changed. We no longer had our whole future ahead of us like we had hoped. Now we were staring at months, possibly weeks, and there wasn't a thing we could do about it."

"Did they try chemo again?"

"They said they could, but it wouldn't cure her. At best it only would've bought her a couple of months longer. She opted to live out the remainder of her time on her own terms."

"I get that." Peyton sits back, dropping her hands in her lap. "Sometimes it's better that way. Especially when you know the chemo won't work. My mom stopped treatments after they were unsuccessful. I was so mad at her at the time. I didn't understand why she was giving up. Now I realize that she wasn't giving up. She was accepting that there was nothing she could do and choosing to live for however long she had left."

"Quality over quantity. That's how Finley put it. She didn't want to spend six months so sick she could barely get out of bed if she could have three good ones where she could be herself."

"When the outcome is the same either way." Peyton shrugs. "Doesn't make it any easier for those of us who are on the outside holding onto hope, looking for a miracle."

"It certainly doesn't. You know, I don't think I truly believed that she was dying until those last few days. Even on bad days she was still just Finley. My beautiful wife who always wore a smile and could crack a joke even in the heaviest of situations. I think I had convinced myself that she would eventually get better. Only she never did."

"I was the same way. I refused to believe that my mom was going to die. Problem with that is I didn't make peace with it when I should have. I was holding out for that miracle for so long that when I finally realized it wasn't coming, I was out of time.

And then I was just angry. Angry at her. Angry at myself. Angry at the world."

"Yeah, I know a thing or two about feeling angry."

"How long were you two married?"

"Not long, though it felt like she'd been my wife forever. We actually eloped in Vegas a couple weeks after she received her terminal diagnosis."

"I'm so sorry, Abel. I can't even imagine what that must have been like for you."

"It's hard to think about but impossible not to. My best and worst memories are all wrapped up in those few months I got with her. Sometimes, when I open my eyes first thing in the morning, for a brief moment I forget that she's gone. There's no pain or loss. No heaviness in my chest. It's all just... gone."

"But then it washes over you all at once and you're forced to relive it over and over again." She finishes my thought so clearly, it's as if she can see inside my head.

"Exactly."

"Oh my god! Aaron!" Henna's loud cackle pulls our attention to the booth behind us. My gaze slides beyond Peyton right in time to see my brother's shirt go flying across the room.

"What the fuck," I mutter, running my hand down my face as I slide out of the booth.

By the time I reach their table, Aaron has his belt off and his pants unbuckled.

"What the fuck are you doing?" I look at him like he's lost his damn mind, because honestly, I think he has.

"Henna bet me a blow job that I wouldn't strip right here in this booth."

"And you thought it would be a good time to prove her wrong?" I glare at him.

"Well, yeah." He laughs.

"Did you forget that our aunt and uncle own this place?"

"There isn't anyone here." He gestures around the empty diner.

"There are two waitresses and the cook, not to mention that more customers could walk in at any moment."

"You know, for the rebellious sibling you're kind of a stick in the mud."

"And for someone who pretends to be so mature, you're acting like a two-year-old," I bite back.

"Here." Peyton appears next to me, Aaron's shirt dangling from her fingers. "I think that's our cue to leave," she tells me, her gaze bouncing between Henna and Aaron. I can't tell if she's pissed or amused at their ridiculous behavior.

"Yeah, I think so. Put your shirt back on and let's go," I tell Aaron.

"But we're still eating." He gestures to his plate that's practically wiped clean.

"Hate to break it to you, but you're all out of food." I point to the dish.

"Fuck." He groans. "I really wanted another fry." He laughs when Henna bursts into a fit of giggles across from him.

"You two." Peyton shakes her head before leaning down to grab Henna by the wrist. "Up you go." She tugs.

"You're so pretty." Henna grabs Peyton's face the moment she's upright.

"And you're still way too drunk." Peyton smiles at her friend, and for the first time I really allow myself to see how beautiful she is.

I mean, I've known it all along. But right now, I don't know, it's like I'm seeing her for the very first time and my god is she breathtaking.

"I love you." Henna leans in, so close to Peyton a mere inch separates their faces.

"I love you too, but so help me, Henna, if you try to kiss me again, I'm going to let your ass fall," she warns, wrapping an arm around her friend's shoulder.

"Wait, what do you mean if she tries to kiss you again?" Aaron perks up, sliding his shirt over his head before pushing his way out of the booth.

"Wouldn't you like to know," Peyton teases, turning her attention to me. "I left some cash on the table to take care of our checks," she tells me.

"No, I've got it covered." I shake my head. "You take her out to the car, and I'll settle up." I place my keys in her hand.

"I already left money."

"And I said I've got it covered," I repeat.

"Look at you pretending to be a gentleman." Aaron punches me in the shoulder and I'm tempted to knock him on his ass.

"Why don't you shut up and go with them, yeah?" I gesture toward the girls right as Peyton begins to turn, her arm looped around Henna's waist.

"I like you better when you drink," he tells me.

"I like you better when you don't," I fire back.

"Dick," he mutters, quickly spinning around and following the girls out of the diner moments later.

I grab Peyton's money off the booth and replace it with my own, waving at Bernie as I make my way to the door.

By the time I make it outside, Peyton has managed to get everyone in the car and is standing next to the passenger door when I approach.

"Here." I hand her the money back.

"You know, I'm capable of paying for my own meal." She stuffs the cash in the front pocket of her jeans.

"I know." I smile, crossing to the driver's side of the car.

Chapter Fourteen
Peyton

The drive back to mine and Henna's apartment is a quiet one. Every time I look at Abel it's like I can actually see the wheels turning inside that gorgeous head of his.

I didn't expect him to open up to me about his wife the way he did, but the fact that he did makes me feel special. I get the impression it's not something he talks about often. And while I'm glad he feels like he can talk to me, another part of me feels a little defeated because of it.

Any hopes I had that maybe we could explore this thing between us went out the window the moment her name left his lips. It became apparently clear to me, even in my inebriated state, that even if Abel was open to the possibility, I would be in constant fear that he would be comparing me to her the whole time, and truthfully I don't know that I'd be able to fill such big shoes.

He loves her, that much is so clear it might as well be written on his forehead. And it's not that he loved her, or still loves her. It's how he loved her. The way he spoke of her. As if the sun rose and set with her. The kind of love one doesn't easily get over.

It breaks my heart. For the both of us. Because deep down I know we could be really good together. Unfortunately, I can't see us ever getting to a point to find out.

I let out a slow breath as Abel pulls into a parking spot outside of our building. I'm ready to be home. To be away from the man who puts me so on edge I feel like I'm going to tumble over the side of a cliff at any moment. But at the same time, I'm sad. Sad to say goodbye. Sad for this night to be over. Sad to watch Abel drive away, not knowing when I'll see him again or if I even want to.

"We're here," I say aloud, turning to see Henna passed out in the backseat and Aaron not far behind her. "And she's out," I tell Abel, watching him glance in the rearview mirror.

"I'll carry her up." He unlatches his seatbelt.

"You don't have to do that. I can wake her up."

"She's pretty wasted. I can't imagine you'd have an easy time getting her upstairs. I'll grab her and you can make sure my brother doesn't fall down the stairs and break his neck."

I consider his offer for a moment, realizing he's probably right.

"Deal," I answer, pushing open the passenger side door before climbing out. "Come on, Aaron." I peel open his door and offer him my hand.

"We here already?" he asks groggily, looking around.

"Yep."

Aaron clumsily climbs from the backseat and stands upright. I offer him my arm to steady him, not that I'm much help. While I didn't get nearly as drunk as he and Henna, I still had quite a few and can still feel the effects swimming around in my head.

I close the door and turn right in time to see Abel emerge from the backseat; Henna cradled in his arms.

Shutting the door with his hip, he joins Aaron and me at the front of the car.

"Lead the way." Abel nods toward the building.

I ignore the pang of jealousy in my stomach at the sight of Abel holding my friend and quickly guide Aaron down the sidewalk toward our apartment building.

We reach our floor in no time, and while Aaron stumbled a few times on the way up, he did pretty well all things considered.

Fishing my keys out of my purse, it takes me three attempts to get the key in the lock. I click it over and push the door open, standing to the side to let Aaron and Abel pass.

"Where should I put her?" Abel asks, turning back toward me as I close the door.

"Down the hall. Last room at the end." I gesture in the vicinity of Henna's room.

Abel nods and heads off in that direction, Aaron following closely behind.

I take a moment to straighten up the living room, trying to make it look halfway presentable. It's not dirty or anything, just a little messy. Had I known Abel would be coming over I would have made a better attempt at cleaning up after myself earlier.

I grab the throw blanket bundled in a ball on the chair and fold it. I'm draping it across the back of the couch when Abel emerges from the hallway.

"You get her all settled?" I ask, turning to face him.

"She didn't even flinch when I laid her down. She's really out." He chuckles.

"Yeah, she doesn't drink like that often. I'm betting she won't again for a long while considering how awful she's going to feel when she wakes up." I slide off my shoes and cross the living room to deposit them in the coat closet next to the front door.

"Aaron either." He shakes his head.

"Those two were a hot mess tonight."

"That they were."

"Sorry you had to deal with that."

"Nah, it's not a big deal. Besides, I had fun."

"You did?" I cock a brow.

"I did." He smiles.

"Me too," I admit, shifting my weight from one foot to the other, not really sure what the hell to do.

"Well, I guess I should be going." Abel slides by me, but pauses at the door, cocking his head in my direction. "My friend, Sven is having a party at his house on Saturday. I know Aaron is going which means Henna probably is too. Would you maybe want to come?"

"You're asking me to a party?" I blurt, a bit surprised by this fact.

"I guess I am." He gives me a sly smile.

"What time?"

"Seven-ish."

"I'm having dinner at my dad's at six, but I could maybe meet you after."

"Okay, that works. I'll text you the address."

"Pretty sure you don't have my number." I smile, watching him pull his cell out of his back-pocket moments later.

"Guess I should probably get that." He flicks his finger across the screen, then looks up at me.

It takes me a good ten seconds to realize he's waiting for me to give him my number.

"Oh, uh." I ramble off the number so fast I have to stop and repeat myself a second time.

"There. Got it." He messes with his phone for another few seconds before locking it and shoving it back into his pocket.

A moment later, my phone dings from my purse that I dropped in the chair when we entered the apartment.

"I text you so you can save my number."

"Okay, cool." I feel a slight blush cross my cheeks, not sure why something as simple as him giving me his number has heat rushing to my face.

"So, I guess I'll see you Saturday?" He reaches for the door, yanking it open.

"Yeah, Saturday," I agree, stepping forward to hold the door open as he steps into the hallway.

"Goodnight, Peyton."

"Goodnight, Abel."

I wait until he starts to walk away before letting the door close.

"So, Peyton, how's work? Your dad said you'll be travelling to New York with your boss soon. That's exciting," Tina says, scooping a large helping of pot roast onto her plate.

"Yeah. It's not for another six weeks but I'm pretty excited. I've never been to New York before." I slide some potatoes onto my fork and shove them into my mouth.

"Oh, it's amazing. I visited there several times when I was younger. If you want any recommendations on places you should see while you're there, I'm your girl."

"Thank you, I'll keep that in mind."

"Anything else new going on?" My dad pulls my attention to where he's sitting at the head of the table, the same place he's sat for as long as I can remember.

"Not really." I shrug, shoving another bite into my mouth.

"How was the wedding last weekend?"

"It was really good. Way over the top which is total Sam."

"We sent her a card the other day. Wanted to give her a little something," Tina interjects.

"You didn't have to do that."

"I know, we wanted to. It's just a shame we couldn't make it to the wedding," she says, leaving out the part where they weren't invited.

While Sam and I have been friends for years, she's never taken the time to get to know my family. Which is totally fine. It's not the kind of friendship we have. Because of this I didn't expect her to invite my parents and wasn't upset when she didn't.

"Yeah, it was nice. I'm just glad it's over."

"Was Sam a difficult bride?" Tina asks.

"I wouldn't say difficult. She just demanded a lot of my time the last couple of weeks leading up to the wedding."

"Were there any attractive guys there?" She sips her tea, looking at me over the rim of the glass.

"Tina." My dad clears his throat.

"What?" She gives him a pointed look.

"It's fine." I'm used to it by now. My dad and Tina weren't dating but two weeks the first time she started in on me about finding a good man.

I think it was her way of trying to bond with me. And while I love that she cared enough to try, I wish she had chosen another topic in her efforts, because now it's kind of a thing with her. She always has to know what's going on in my love life. Though up to this point I've kept things pretty vague with her.

"Well, were there?" she presses.

"Not really," I lie, Abel's face flashing through my mind.

Having his cell phone number for the last two days has been absolute torture. I've had to talk myself out of texting him every five minutes, reminding myself that he only gave it to me because of the party.

A party he invited you to, a little voice in my head sings happily. I push it down, refusing to let myself go there right now.

"Have you been seeing anyone?" she continues.

"Nope." I shake my head. "I told you, after the last one that I've written off men for a while."

"I didn't think you were serious."

"Of course I was. I'm tired of dealing with immature men. They're either too scared or too self-absorbed to commit to a relationship. I'm focusing on myself for a while."

"Well I think that's wonderful," my dad chimes in. I think secretly he's hoping I'll stay single forever.

"Thanks, Dad." I snort, jumping when my cell dings on the table next to me.

I look down at the device and then back up to my dad, who is firmly against phones at the table.

"Sorry, it's work," I tell him, knowing good and well it isn't.

"Okay." He nods, grabbing his water glass before taking a long drink.

Snatching my cell phone off the table, my heart kicks up speed when I see the text from Abel displayed across the screen.

Abel: 1152 Conner Court Drive.

I smile, quickly typing out a response.

Me: I'll head that way in a little bit.

"Work?" Tina says and I look up to see her staring at me with a knowing look on her face.

"Yeah." I clear my throat and force the smile from my lips.

My phone pings again and I look down.

Abel: See you then.

A swell of nerves washes through me. I've tried to remind myself several times since Thursday that Abel was just inviting me to invite me. Because it's the friendly thing to do. But more than once I've let my mind get the better of me and have found myself questioning if that's really why he invited me or if it's because he wants to see me again. Of course, I've quickly squashed the thought every time it's taken root, because truthfully, I don't want to get my hopes up.

I resist the urge to text him back and instead place my phone back on the table face down.

"So, Dad, how's the vacation planning coming along?" I turn the attention to my dad before Tina has a chance to push the matter further.

He and Tina are going on a cruise in a few months. They've been planning it for a while.

"Well, we've got a few places picked out that we definitely want to see while we're there. Other than that, I think we're mostly going to wing it."

"Wing it?" I chuckle. "I didn't know you knew how to wing it."

"Give me a little credit. Back before I met your mother I was very much a fly by the seat of my pants kind of man."

"Yeah, that's not hard to picture at all," I joke, knowing my dad can't even go to the store without a detailed list of what he's getting, complete with what store and aisle he will find said items in. "So, what you're really saying is that Tina told you that you weren't going to plan every second of this trip and didn't give you a choice in the matter."

"Pretty much." He laughs at himself.

"Sometimes you just have to let go and let life take you where it wants." Tina reaches over and pats the top of my dad's hand.

"She's right you know."

"Says the girl who's exactly like me."

"There is a difference between being prepared and mapping out every step I take before I take it."

"Even still, you definitely took after me in that department."

"Considering mom never planned anything a day in her life, I guess you could say I am." I smile, remembering how spontaneous my mom used to be and how anxious it would make my dad.

I still remember my eighth birthday when my mom up and decided we were going to the zoo. My dad stressed the whole way about the route we would take, what animals we would prioritize seeing, and where we could eat along the way. Normally, he would have had the details planned weeks before we went. To this day I think she did that intentionally. I think she knew she was going to take me to the zoo the whole time and purposely didn't tell my dad so he wouldn't try to control every aspect of what she referred to as *my* day.

After she was gone his need to control anything and everything around him reached an all-time high. Thank god he met Tina when he did, otherwise he would have driven himself and me into a loony bin.

Tina has been good for him in ways I never thought he needed. They didn't meet until a few years after Mom had passed and while I knew right away that he truly cared for her, I think he was afraid I would think he was replacing Mom. Of course, I never felt that way. I've only ever wanted him to be happy. The day he told me he and Tina were getting married is probably one of the happiest I can remember post Mom. To see him so happy was something I never thought I'd see again.

While most women wouldn't want to step into another woman's shoes, Tina did so gracefully. She never got upset when my dad would talk about my mom. In fact, she encouraged it. She has somehow been able to accept that he will always love my mother. Just so long as he loves her too, then that's enough for her.

So while Tina does drive me a little bonkers from time to time, she makes my dad happy and that's all I could ever ask for.

My mind wanders to Abel.

I wonder if I could be like Tina. If I could step in and fill that void in his life and not feel like his second choice every step of the way. Honestly, I don't know how she does it, but for my dad's sake I'm glad she does. Without her I don't know where he'd be in life.

We spend the next hour in easy conversation. While I may not visit as often as I should, I always feel lighter after doing so. Something about being in this house, with two people I know who love me unconditionally and the memories of my mom and my childhood swirling around me. In some weird way it reaffirms my place in the world. While I may not matter to all, to some I mean everything. It's funny how often we find ourselves needing little reassurances like that.

After making an excuse about being tired, I leave my dad's a little earlier than I normally would have. As much as I enjoyed myself, the later it got the more anxious I became. So much so that I feel on the verge of having to pull over because I fear I might throw up.

I can't remember a time I've been so nervous to go to a party. It's just a party. A few friends gathering together to have some drinks and share some laughs. So then why does it feel like this is so much more?

Because you want it to be more.

Damn that voice in my head and how right she always seems to be.

Rolling down the window, I take a deep breath of the warm evening air and instantly feel better. I just need to get out of my head and, like Tina said, let life take me where it wants to.

Unfortunately, sometimes that's easier said than done. Especially when Abel Collins is involved.

Chapter Fifteen
Peyton

It's right after nine o'clock when I finally reach the address Abel sent me. Pulling up the long drive, my eyes widen as I reach the end that opens up to a huge house with so many windows it looks almost like a glass house.

My nervousness multiplies substantially as I pull off the side of the driveway behind a long line of cars and kill the engine.

Why did I think I could do this? Why did I think I could show up here and feel completely natural? Well, it doesn't. Nothing about this feels natural. In fact, I feel so out of place I can barely pull in a steady breath.

Grabbing my phone off the passenger seat, I pull up Henna's number and hit call.

It rings twice before her bubbly voice comes on the line, muted slightly by the loud hum of music and conversation going on around her.

"Hey. Where are you?" I ask, nervously picking at a spot on my steering wheel.

"At Sven's. Where are you?"

"I'm outside."

"You're here?" she squeals, clearly happy about this fact.

"I am."

"Then why aren't you inside?"

"Because I'm scared to walk in by myself," I admit in a moment of vulnerability.

"Peyton." She sighs and I swear I can picture her rolling her eyes at me.

"Is he here?"

"Is who here?" she asks, but then answers her own question. "Abel?"

"Yes."

"Yeah, he's here. I just saw him not too long ago with that Claire girl."

"Claire's here?"

"Yeah, she came with Abel."

"Oh." My heart crashes inside my chest. Welp, that answers *that* question. He really was only inviting me to invite me. I try to push past the way that makes me feel and focus on Henna. "Are there a lot of people inside?"

"A ton. But it doesn't feel crowded or anything because this place is *huge*." She over exaggerates the word. "Are you coming inside or what?"

"I don't know."

"What do you mean you don't know? You drove all the way here."

"I know, but now I'm thinking maybe this wasn't such a good idea."

"Why, because Claire's here?" She reads me like a pro.

"Well that and I don't really know anyone."

"First off, I'm here. You don't need to know anyone else. And second, don't worry about Claire. She's been hanging out with Nick all night. The two seem to be getting quite cozy."

"Oh yeah?" I question, not sure why this makes me feel a whole hell of a lot better.

I know that Claire is Abel's friend, his sister-in-law too, but I'd be lying if I said I wasn't a little threatened by her. She's Finley's sister, which means her and Abel no doubt share a very deep and special connection. That happens when you share a loss with someone.

"Yes, now stop being weird and get your ass in here."

"I'm not being weird."

"Yeah, okay. Says the girl sitting in her car too afraid of a boy to come inside."

"I'm not afraid of a boy."

"No, you're just afraid of what that boy makes you feel."

"What are we, teenagers?"

"You tell me. You're the one acting like one."

"Gahhh," I half yell, half laugh.

"Just get your ass in here."

"Fine, but you have to come out and walk me inside."

"You're joking, right?" She laughs.

"No, Henna, I'm not joking. Seriously, come outside."

"Oh my god. Fine. Give me a minute."

"Okay, thank you."

Pulling down the visor, I check myself in the mirror. After leaving Dad's I touched up my makeup and applied a soft pink lipstick that highlights my lips without actually really changing the color.

My hair is pinned back on the sides, hanging in loose waves down my back. It's my go to style when I want to try but not really look like I'm trying.

I close the visor just in time to see Henna making her way toward me. She's dressed in a slinky red dress, her long black hair flowing in the wind as she walks.

Seriously?

I glance down at my dark shorts and white off the shoulder top, wishing like hell I would have asked Henna what she was wearing before settling on this outfit. It's cute and all but now I'm gonna have to walk in next to Henna, looking like that.

"What the fuck?" She lifts her arms as she approaches.

"What?" I swing open the car door and climb out.

"You asked me to meet you outside. You didn't say I'd have to walk all the way down here to get your ass."

"Oh, shut it." I wave her off, shutting the car door before clicking the lock button on my key fob. Shoving my keys into my pocket, I turn and face Henna. "Um…" I gesture to her dress.

"What? You don't like it?" Her hands go to her hips.

"No, it's not that. I just didn't realize it was *that* kind of party."

"What? The kind where you can wear a cute dress?"

"Um, err, yeah," I stutter.

"Girl, you know me. Any excuse I can get to pull one of these bad boys out of the closet." She smiles. "Besides, you look super cute."

"Cute." I look down at myself. "Great. That's exactly what I was going for." I let out an audible sigh.

"Fine. You look hot!" she corrects. "Is that better?"

"No, because now you're just telling me what I want to hear." I purposely choose to be difficult. "Come on." I take off toward the house, stepping past her. "Let's get this over with."

"God, listen to you. You act like this is some formal dinner that you can't wait to get through. It's a party, Peyton. You know, the kind where people have fun." She quickens her stride to catch up to me. "You used to know how to have fun."

"I do know how to have fun."

"Not since you've gone celibate."

"I haven't gone celibate," I argue.

"Sworn off dick then. Does it really matter how you put it? You stopped putting out and now you're lame."

"You make it sound like I was such a slut."

"Please. You've never been and will never be the kind of girl that can be classified as a slut. But you have been wound a little tight since things went belly up with that last ass hat you were dating. Maybe you need to get laid."

"Oh my god, Henna, I do not need to get laid," I say a little too loudly as we climb the stairs to the front porch.

"Well that's a shame." His voice comes out of nowhere and I stop so sudden my upper body jerks forward. It takes only seconds before I spot Abel at the far side of the porch. He must have been watching us walk up and probably heard every word we said.

My insides instantly warm and I can feel a flush flood my cheeks.

"I, uh, hey." I can't seem to make my mouth work all of a sudden.

"Hey." He grins, lifting his beer to his lips before taking a pull. "I was starting to think you weren't coming."

"Sorry, it took me longer to get here than I thought it would. This place is really out there."

"Yeah." He looks around. "It's kind of out in the middle of nowhere."

"Well, I'm gonna let you two talk," Henna interrupts. "I need to find Aaron."

"He's in the game room. Pretty sure Claire and Nick are putting a beating on him and Sven at pool."

"Oh, I'm sure he's loving that." Henna laughs, throwing up a half wave as she takes off inside the house, leaving me standing on the porch all alone with Abel.

"So." He smiles, and my insides seize up.

"So." I rock back on my heels nervously.

"You look really pretty." He gestures toward me.

"Um, thanks. You too," I say. "I mean, you look really handsome."

Stupid, Peyton. Geez. Get your shit together.

"Thanks." He chuckles. "You want something to drink?"

"I probably shouldn't. I have to drive home later."

"Technically you don't." He grins, that damn dimple making me weak in the knees. "Usually at these parties everyone crashes here. Sven has about ten bedrooms and wrap arounds in the living room and basement so there's plenty of sleeping space."

"Is Henna staying?"

"I believe so, yes. Is that a deciding factor for you?"

"If she stays I might, but if she's not staying I probably won't."

"Well then, let's find out." He grabs my hand and tugs me toward the door.

The minute we step inside we're accosted by loud music and the roar of laughter and conversations taking place all around us. Abel pulls me through the house so quickly I don't have time to look around.

I can tell you that the place is incredible. High ceilings. Expensive furniture. No doubt decorated by a professional designer. Not to mention each individual room is about the size of my entire apartment, maybe bigger.

We find Henna in the back, in what I assume is the game room considering there are arcade games, a ping pong table, a pool table, along with many other little things set up throughout the space. She's standing next to the pool table laughing at Aaron who looks aggravated.

"I take it you beat him." Abel slides in next to Claire who's looking quite pleased with herself.

"Didn't know I could play pool." She smiles, her gaze sliding to me for a split second before going back to Abel. "Turns out I'm actually quite good."

"'Bout time someone put my brother in his place." Abel laughs.

"Okay, who's next?" Nick appears at Claire's other side, dropping his arm over her shoulder. The action causes her smile to spread and it becomes very obvious that she's into him and that he's into her. I relax a little.

"I think me and Peyton might like a go," Abel volunteers us.

"Um, you might want to rethink that. I'm quite possibly the worst pool player ever."

"Oh, come on. You can't be that bad. Who knows, maybe you'll surprise yourself. I know I did," Claire encourages me.

"Please." Abel pouts out his bottom lip and I instantly wonder how much he's had to drink. He seems so much more laid back than usual. There's a playfulness to him that I don't think I've ever seen before.

"Fine." I cave, knowing there's no way I can resist that face. "But don't say I didn't warn you."

"You're going down," Nick playfully boasts, crossing to the opposite side of the table where he proceeds to collect the balls and place them in the rack.

"Probably," I mutter, walking over to where Henna is consoling the sore loser that is her boyfriend.

"Hey." She smiles when I slide up next to them.

"Hey."

"Here." Abel appears at my side, sliding a pool stick into my hand. "Hey, Henna, are you and Aaron planning on staying here tonight."

"That was the plan." She nods.

"Perfect." Abel smiles at me. "I'll be right back." He hands me his pool stick and quickly walks away.

"What is he up to?" Henna cocks her head to the side.

"No idea," I answer honestly.

"I see we scared your partner before the game even began," Nick calls over to me from across the table.

"Abel doesn't scare off," Claire informs him. "He'll be back."

As if right on cue, Abel reappears with a fresh beer in one hand and a red solo cup in the other. Stepping up next to me, he holds the cup out to me.

"If I remember right, you're quite fond of long islands. Though I can't promise I'm very good at making them."

"I said I wasn't drinking." I smile, taking the drink anyway.

"No, you asked if Henna was staying and she is," he corrects. "Therefore, so are you. Now taste it and tell me how I did."

I try to fight the smile threatening to spill across my lips but it's no use. You would think I would've learned by now that my attempts are in vain when Abel is involved.

Lifting the cup to my lips, I take a tentative sip.

"Well?" He waits for my reaction.

"Not bad," I admit. "A little heavy handed on the liquor but it's pretty good."

"I'll keep that in mind for next time." He winks, turning his attention to the pool table when Nick announces that they're ready.

We spend the next hour alternating playing pool with Claire, Nick, Sven, Henna, Aaron, and a couple others. Despite my best efforts, we lose every single game. By the time we finally call it quits, I've downed two of Abel's long islands and am feeling quite good. Not drunk but buzzed enough that I've relaxed a little and let my guard down.

"Hey." Claire slides up next to me when Abel leaves to make me another drink.

"Hey." I smile.

"Can we talk for a minute?" she asks, gesturing outside.

"Yeah, of course." I nod, following her to the back door before stepping onto the deck with her. While it was warm earlier, the air has a chill to it now, and I rub my hands up and down my arms in an effort to warm myself. "What's up?" I ask when Claire walks to the banister and looks out over the expansive backyard, having yet to say a single word.

"I just wanted to talk to you about Abel," she says, eyes trained forward.

"Okay," I draw out, waiting for her to continue.

"He likes you." She lets out a soft breath. "I can tell by the way he looks at you. I wasn't sure I'd ever see him look at another girl that way."

"Claire," I start, but she cuts me off before I can even think about what I want to say. Hell, I haven't even processed her first statement before she continues to say more.

"I know he puts on a brave face, but inside he's barely holding it together. I just need to know that you're not only having fun. But that you like him too. Because the last thing he can take right now is opening his heart to someone only to have it stomped on. I don't think he'd survive it."

"I would never," I start.

"Do you like him?" She cuts me off again.

"I really do," I admit.

"Good." She smiles, her gaze coming to mine. "Just don't hurt him. I may not look like much, but I will throw down for that man, no questions asked."

"Understood." I smile back despite the seriousness of her words. I can't help it. It's sweet how much she cares about him.

"Good," she repeats. "I love Abel. My sister loved him. I just want to make sure he's in good hands."

"Oh, we're still getting to know each other. And he's made no advances toward me. I get the impression he just wants to be friends."

"Oh honey." She shakes her head. "A man doesn't act the way Abel acts around you if he just wants to be friends. Truth be told, I don't even know if he knows it yet. But he will. And when he does, I need to know you won't hurt him."

"I would never," I answer truthfully.

"I can see why he likes you, ya know?" She grins.

Before she can elaborate, Abel walks outside, his gaze jumping between the two of us.

"Hey," he says to us both.

"Hi." I smile, taking the drink he extends to me.

"Everything okay out here?" he asks.

"Everything is great," Claire answers. "Peyton and I were just getting a little fresh air."

"Okay." He nods, deciding to accept this as an answer even though I can tell he knows there's more to it.

"I'm gonna run inside and find Nick. He said we're gonna try our hands at beer pong next." She laughs. "I've never played, but who knows. Maybe I'll be good at that too." She bumps her shoulder into Abel as she passes him. "I'll catch up with you later," she calls out, seconds before she disappears inside.

Chapter Sixteen
Abel

"You doing okay?" I lean against the deck railing, my body angled toward Peyton.

"I am." She takes a drink before looking up at me with a smile that makes my insides feel funny.

"Good." I take a drink of my beer in hopes of dulling the feeling. It's not a bad feeling. Maybe a little scary, but not bad. "So, what were you and Claire really talking about?"

"Nothing." She shrugs. "We were talking about Nick. I think she likes him."

"Yeah, you got that impression too?" I chuckle.

"I think it's pretty obvious any way you spin it."

"Out of everyone here, Nick is the last person I would have expected Claire to connect with."

"Why's that?"

"I don't know. She's just so…nice. And caring. And she has her shit together. Nick? Not so much."

"I don't know. He seems okay to me."

"He's a good guy," I admit. "Just not someone I would have picked for Claire."

"Well, lucky for her, you don't get a say." Peyton taps me on the chest with her pointer finger. I catch her hand mid motion and wrap my fingers around it, pressing both of our hands against my chest.

I don't know why, but I find it impossible to let go. I keep waiting for that familiar feeling to return—the weight, the heaviness, the guilt—but to my surprise it's nowhere to be found.

"You're beautiful." I voice my thoughts aloud.

"How much have you had to drink?" she jokes, shifting her weight from one foot to the other like she doesn't know how to stand still.

"Five beers. But don't worry, I know what I'm saying. This isn't the beer talking." I reach out with my free hand and tuck a chunk of hair behind her shoulder, feeling her shudder under my touch. "You *are* beautiful."

"Abel." Her voice shakes as my hand slides from her hair to her neck.

"Yeah?" I stroke my thumb across her jaw, my eyes glued to that spot.

I don't know how it happens. One minute I'm watching my thumb move across her skin, the next I'm leaning in, the urge to be closer to her too strong to resist.

"Abel." Her voice sounds small and I pause a mere inch from her lips. "If you kiss me, I'm not sure I'll ever recover."

"I'm not sure I will either," I whisper, closing the small gap between us. The instant my lips brush hers a wave of electricity passes over my body.

It's like grabbing ahold of an electric fence. The shock flows through me, and even though every part of me is screaming let go, I can't. Because beyond the pain there is something so much more. Something unexpected. Something I didn't even realize I needed until this very moment.

Her.

Chapter Seventeen
Peyton

His lips are like fire, branding my skin in the most delicious way possible. His touch is everywhere; my hair, my face, my chest, the backs of my thighs as he hoists me up against the closed bedroom door.

It's so overwhelming.

I squirm under his touch. A part of me wants to pull away, the other part never wants him to stop.

I don't know how this happened. One minute we were on the deck. The next he's kissing me in a way I don't think I've ever been kissed before. Like he's a starving man and my lips are the only thing that will satisfy his hunger.

When he suggested we go upstairs to somewhere more private I thought maybe we'd talk. Maybe he'd tell me that kissing me was a mistake. What I did not expect was for him to pin me against the door and kiss me even harder, even deeper, with even more need.

And now I'm lost to him. The frenzy of his hands. The power of his lips. The way he groans deep in his throat, making me ache for a man in a way I've never ached before.

I want him so badly it's painful. No, strike that. I *need* him. Like my lungs need air. It's like he is the only thing tethering me to Earth and the moment he lets go I will float away.

"Abel." I pant against his mouth when he lowers me to my feet, his fingers opening my shorts with ease.

"I want you," he pants, kissing me as he slides my shorts down my thighs. "I need you." He hitches his thumbs into my panties and tugs them down. "I have to have you." He swipes his tongue across my lower lip, causing me to let out an audible moan.

And then his hand slips between my legs and I melt into a puddle of mush under his touch. How can I not? How could I possibly resist a man that has this much power over me.

The connection we share – the chemistry – it's unlike anything I have ever felt before and am fairly certain will ever feel again.

"Tell me you want me," he pleads, his lips against my mouth.

"I want you." I let out a soft cry when he plunges two fingers inside of me.

As if this is the undoing of us both, he slides his hands down to the hem of my shirt and lifts, depositing it somewhere on the floor, before, with one hand, he quickly removes my bra. I'm exposed, vulnerable, and damn if it isn't the best feeling in the world.

Snaking his arms around my waist, he lifts me and turns, taking the few steps across the room to the bed, before setting me on top of the thick comforter the moment he reaches it.

His eyes roam my body. A hunger behind them that would make even the strongest woman putty in his hands.

He slides off his shirt and I can't stop my gaze from roaming his broad chest. I pause on the tattoo scribbled right above his heart. *Finley.* A dull ache forms in my chest but I push it away. I can't let his pain become mine.

I force my gaze to shift to his defined abs, dipping lower when he undoes the buckle of his pants.

It's enough to redirect my attention.

Reaching into his back pocket, he pulls out his wallet and removes a condom from one of the slots. I hold my breath as he removes his jeans and boxers in one quick movement. He places the condom wrapper in his mouth and rips it open with his teeth before rolling it onto his impressive length.

He places his hands on the bed and slowly crawls up my body. By the time he settles on top of me, I'm shaking like a tree in the middle of a windstorm. My branches fly every which way and my leaves are torn from their home and flutter to the ground beneath me.

"Peyton." He stills on top of me, his erection heavy against my thigh. "Are you sure this is what you want?" Where he's been confident, he now seems unsure and this has me scrambling to reassure him.

"I'm sure." I nod. "I'm very sure. I want this. I want you." I pull his face down to mine and kiss him gently.

"I can't promise you anything," he murmurs against my lips. "As much as I want to, I can't right now."

"I'm not asking for anything." I spread my legs, causing his body to settle between them. "I just want this. You. Right now." I lift my hips, letting out a soft whimper when he presses his length against my core. "Please," I moan, so desperate I'd probably get down on my knees and beg for it at this point.

Abel kisses me, slow and deep, silencing me. His movements are slow and calculated. The soft stroke of his hand down my side. The light nudge of his hip against my inner thigh as he spreads me wider. The gentle way his fingers touch me as he lines himself at my entrance.

I hold my breath, waiting for the moment of impact. Waiting for the moment that I know will change everything. And when that moment comes, it's like everything in me comes alive all at once. Like my body is recognizing this is who it's been searching for.

Tears blur my vision, all of my senses overwhelmed as Abel begins to slowly move inside of me. I'm lost to the feeling. To him. Floating away on a cloud I never, ever want to come down from.

It's not long before soft and sweet morphs into hard and carnal, Abel taking something from me that he so desperately needs. That I'm more than willing to give to him.

I lift my hips, meeting him thrust for thrust as we move together in perfect synchronization. Each one taking us higher and higher. Bringing us closer and closer, until both of us are dangling off the cliff, fighting like hell to hang on.

My fingers slip and I go tumbling down, free falling into the abyss as my body explodes around Abel, taking him down with me.

It takes several beats before we're able to catch our breath. Abel's body covers mine like a heavy blanket, his heart hammering so hard and fast I can feel it against my chest.

In a euphoric bliss, I move my fingers lazily up and down his back, but it's not long before my mind starts to run away from me, and I can tell by the way he withdraws into himself that he's doing the very same thing.

"I'm sorry." He lets out a heavy breath and rolls off of me.

"Sorry?" I question, propping up on my elbows to watch him slide out of bed.

"I don't know what I was thinking." He shakes his head as if to remove a thick fog that's closing in around him as he begins to get dressed.

"Abel." I sit up and push off the bed, making quick work of collecting my clothes. "There's no reason to be sorry. I'm not," I tell him, stepping in front of him with my clothes balled up against my chest.

"I don't want to lead you on. I promised myself that I wouldn't."

"How are you leading me on?" I grab his chin and force him to look at me. "We didn't do anything wrong. We're both consenting adults who did something we wanted." I'm shocked by how confident and sure I sound. Normally, I'd be running for the door the moment he crawled out of bed. But not this time. Not with Abel. I want him, and damn if I'm going to be ashamed of that.

"I know. But the problem is, I like you. Like really like you. And honestly, Peyton, it scares me a little."

"I feel the same way, and it scares me too."

"I'm not capable of giving you what you want."

"Why are you so sure you know what I want? Maybe this is what I want. Maybe I just want to have sex with a man I'm very attracted to. Is that so wrong?"

He seems to think on this for a moment, his expression softening slightly.

"I'm making it weird, aren't I?"

"Truthfully, a little."

"Fuck, I'm sorry. I just don't know how to do this anymore."

"How to do what?"

"This." He gestures between us. "I haven't had anything more than random one-night stands since…"

"Since Finley died." As I finish his sentence for him, my heart cracks straight down the middle. Only it's not breaking for me, it's breaking for him. I can see it; the uncertainty, the fear, the indecision. It's etched into every feature of his face.

He nods slowly.

"I don't know how to do this with someone I know. Someone I actually really like."

"We don't have to make this something. We don't ever have to do this again if you don't want to."

"That's the problem. I do want to."

"Why is that a problem?"

"Because feelings always get in the way when sex is involved."

"So, we won't let them." As if it's that easy.

Already my feelings have multiplied by a trillion and that's after only one time. I can't imagine how I will feel a week from now, or even a month. He's under my skin, but there's no way in hell I'm going to tell him that. Because I don't want this to end. Not when it's only just beginning. There's something here. Something buried deep beneath the pain and guilt he holds onto like a vice. Something that tells me Abel and I could be good together. More than just good, if the sex is any indication. Hell, we could be epic. And that's what I want. The epic kind of love. And while I know I'll never replace Finley, and I would never want to, I'm hoping maybe there's enough room in his heart for the both of us.

So instead, I plaster on an easy smile and do the only thing I can. I pretend. I pretend like I'm capable of a casual relationship in hopes that it grows into more.

Maybe that makes me stupid and weak, that I would bend on what I want to make a man happy. But isn't that what a relationship is? Bending when we need to and standing firm when necessary. I see the battle he's waging inside himself, so this is the time that I bend.

"You really think you're capable of just sex?" he asks, still not convinced.

"Why don't we try it and find out. Because I don't know about you, but I want more." I drop my clothes and reach up, locking my hands around the back of his neck. "I want so, so much more." I press up on my tip toes and trail my tongue lightly across his bottom lip.

"Fuck me." He groans and I feel him starting to harden against me.

"Is that my answer?" I pull back, a knowing smile on my face.

"What do you think?" he asks, seconds before I find myself pinned between Abel and the bed. A place I've decided I never want to leave.

"There you are." Henna spots me right as I hit the bottom step leading into the great room.

"Hey." I try to act completely normal even though I'm freaking out a little on the inside.

"Where have you been?" She eyes me curiously.

"I was outside for a while and then I went upstairs to the bathroom. Those Long Islands didn't agree with my stomach." I run my hand along my belly.

"Is that why you look so out of sorts? Were you up there getting sick?"

"I'm better now," I say without actually answering her question.

"You sure?"

"Yep. I feel great."

"Okay, well we're all going down to the hot tub. I wanted to see if you want to join us."

"I don't have a suit."

"You don't need one. Sven has an entire closet of swimsuits."

"Of course he does." I laugh.

"So, what do you say?"

"Um, can I get back to you on that? I want to find Abel real fast and see what he's up to."

"Yeah, okay. Just don't wait too long or there won't be any spots left."

"Yeah. Yeah." I shoo her away, waiting until she's disappeared from view before giving Abel, who was hiding around the corner at the top of the stairs, the all clear.

He peeks his head out and hits me with a wide smile before he comes bounding down the stairs.

"I think I'm going to like this sneaking around thing," he murmurs as he passes me.

I don't know how we ended up deciding to keep this 'casual' relationship between us. After a little talking, we both agreed it would be easier for now. Easier for whom I'm not yet certain. A part of me thinks he's ashamed of me. Maybe not me *specifically*, but of being with me. Like people will think less of him because his wife died.

Eventually he's going to see that all anyone wants is for him to move on and find happiness again. Am I hoping that he'll find that with me? Of course I am. But again, something I will keep to myself… for now.

"So, do you want to go to the hot tub?" I ask, following Abel down the hallway into the massive kitchen. He heads over to the back counter where there are several liquor bottles lining the top.

"Nah, I'm not a fan of hot tubs."

"Me either," I admit. "Besides, even if I did get in, I wouldn't last more than five minutes. I overheat so easily."

"Then it's settled." He knocks his hip with mine as I watch him make me another drink.

"So, what do you want to do?" I ask, looking at the side of his handsome face.

"I can think of a few things." He smiles, turning to hand me my finished drink.

"Again?" I wiggle my eyebrows playfully at him.

"Good god, woman. You're insatiable." He chuckles, popping the top off a bottle of beer before sucking half the contents back in one long pull.

"Me? You're the one that started it the third time." I wave my finger at him, laughter vibrating through my voice.

"Well, maybe if you weren't so damn addicting." He leans in.

"Oh, so it's my fault." I slide my nose against his.

"Damn straight." He smiles, pulling back when a random guy comes strolling into the kitchen.

"Come on. Sven has an incredible movie room downstairs. What do you say we grab some blankets and go hide out down there? He has just about every movie you can think of."

"I'd like that." I nod, turning to follow him out of the kitchen.

I don't know how we got here. How we went from awkwardly flirting, to having sex, to uncertainty over if we could continue to have sex, to having more sex, to existing like normal people. One thing that's become crystal clear over the course of this night is that Abel Collins is one hell of a roller coaster ride and so far, I've only gone down the first hill.

I don't know what will come of this. Maybe it'll blow up in my face. Maybe it'll turn out to be the best damn thing I've ever done. Either way I'm strapped in and the ride's already moving. There's no getting off now.

Chapter Eighteen
Abel

"Hey there." Aunt Claudia slides into the booth across from me. "How's the shake?" She gestures to the frozen drink in front of me.

"It's good." I smile, twisting the glass in between my hands.

"Everything okay?"

"If I tell you something, do you think you could keep it just between us?" I ask.

"How many times have you asked me that and how many times have I told you no?" She gives me a knowing look.

"Never." I chuckle.

"Exactly. So, lay it on me, kid." She's referred to me that way since I was a literal kid. I have a feeling she's not going to stop anytime soon.

"I met someone," I say, letting the words I've been holding in so desperately flow freely from my lips.

"You met someone?" she repeats, waiting for me to continue.

"Peyton." I smile at her name, still not sure how it makes me feel that I can't even say her name without smiling.

After the other night I can't think straight. She's on my mind constantly, except she's not the only one there. I swear I've never felt so conflicted about something in my entire life. And while we haven't actually spoken since Sven's party, I have a feeling she's probably thinking about me just as much.

"You look happy," Claudia observes, pulling me back to the present.

"I am. Well, for the most part."

"For the most part?" she questions.

"Well, the thing is, we're trying this whole casual thing, and to keep things as uncomplicated as possible, we've decided to keep it between us. At least for now."

"And so you're telling me why?"

"Because I need some advice and you're the only one I could think of that won't judge me and will give it to me straight."

"Well at least I'm good for something." She gives me a toothy grin.

"You're good for more than that. But I really do need your advice."

"Okay." She waits for me to continue.

"The thing is, I really like this girl."

"Okay, so what's the problem?"

"That *is* the problem." I scratch the scruff on my chin. "On one hand, I feel happier than I have in a very long time. On the other I feel guilty."

"Because of Finley?"

"That, and because I feel like I'm leading her on."

"Did she agree to the casual relationship?"

"Yes."

"Then why do you feel like you're leading her on?"

"Because she wants more. I know she does. And I want to give her more. It's the first time since Finley died that I can actually see myself being with someone else. But I'm afraid I won't ever get to the point where I *can* give her more. I'm afraid I'm broken and nothing she can do will fix me."

"Abel, you're not broken. And she doesn't need to fix you. You lost someone you love very much. Learning where you fit into life after that person is gone is probably one of the hardest things to do. But Abel, you can do it. You just have to let yourself."

"I feel like I shouldn't let myself."

I've spent countless hours going over and over this in my head. Why I should. Why I shouldn't. Why I feel the way I feel.

Why I feel guilty for not feeling more guilty than I do. It's exhausting. And while this whole thing with Peyton just started two days ago, already I feel like I'm fighting a battle I can't possibly win.

"You can't think that way. Finley would want you to be happy, to move on. You know that. The only person holding you back is you."

"But I don't know how."

"Well, you can start by taking that off." She gestures to my left hand where my wedding band sits on my ring finger.

I shake my head, the thought making me almost queasy. "I can't," I croak.

"Yes, you can. And you need to. Finley's gone, Abel. Nothing and no one will bring her back. You have to find a way to let her go. You can start with that ring."

I twirl the band around my finger but can't find it in me to remove it.

"Do you like this girl?" Claudia asks, pulling my gaze back to her.

"I do."

"If you want a future you have to learn to let go of the past."

"I worry that if I let this go too far I'll realize I can't love her the way I love Finley."

"You're never going to love anyone the way you do Finley and you shouldn't want to. What you two shared was special, rare, and can't ever be replaced. But that doesn't mean you can't love someone just as much. That love will just be different and that's okay. It doesn't make it mean any less."

"I want to let her go and yet I don't know if I can. I miss her so much. Every single day, every moment that passes, I think of her. Of what our lives would be like if she were still alive. Of all the things we could have done together."

"But you're chasing a ghost. Finley isn't coming back, no matter how much you wish it so. You owe it to yourself to see where this new relationship might go. You said you agreed to something casual, so keep it casual and let it develop naturally. If it's there, then you'll know and if it's not, then you move on."

"You make it sound so simple."

"There's nothing simple when it comes to matters of the heart, but some things are easier than others and this is one of them. All you have to do is open yourself up to the possibility. When you're ready, you'll know."

"I'm pretty sure I don't know much these days." I snort.

"I'm sure it feels that way sometimes, but Abel, you are stronger than you think you are. And you will get past this. Maybe in six months, maybe in five years, but one day, one day you're going to wake up and the pain will be gone. Not the memory of what you lost or how it felt, but that gut-wrenching pain. The kind that makes it hard to get out of bed in the morning. That pain will eventually fade, and when it does, you'll find your place again. That much I can promise you."

"When did you become so smart?"

"*Become*? Pretty sure I was just born this way." She laughs, patting the back of my hand. "I've gotta get back to work. Poor Olivia over there looks like she's about to blow a gasket." She gestures to the young girl running around the dining room like she's got mini rockets attached to her feet. "You'll be okay?"

"I will," I reassure her.

"If you need to talk more, you know where to find me. I'm always here for you, no matter what."

"I know, thank you, Aunt Claudia." I watch her slide out of the booth, her lips hitting the side of my head moments later.

"I love you, Abel. I promise, you'll get through this."

"Love you too." I smile, watching her take off toward the kitchen.

My phone ringing abruptly pulls me from sleep. I groggily search for the device on my nightstand, swiping my finger across the screen and pressing it to my face without even looking at who is calling.

"Hello," I grumble into the phone.

"Abel, it's Chuck." My eyes pop open and I'm suddenly wide awake.

"Chuck. What is it? Did you find her?"

"I did. She popped up on my radar yesterday when she was booked in Rock Hill, South Carolina."

"*Yesterday*? And you're just now calling me?" I don't try to hide the irritation in my voice.

"I had to be sure we had the right Cherie Holt before I contacted you."

"So, does this mean you're sure it's her?" I ask, careful not to be too hopeful.

"It's her, man. I cross referenced her information with what I have on Finley. This is her mom."

My heart thuds so loudly against my ribs I can hear the sound in my ears. We finally found her. After three long years we've finally found Finley's mom.

When I first had my P.I. friend, Chuck, look into her, he wasn't hopeful that we'd find her. She jumped addresses so often and never held a job, and if she did, she was paid under the table. So tracking her down led to dead end after dead end. So, we stopped looking and Chuck put a flag on her name so that if she was picked up by police or brought to court on any legal charges he would be notified. Looks like our waiting game has finally run its course and Chuck's patience has paid off.

"Fuck, man. I don't know how to thank you."

"You thanked me by paying me, remember? I'll text you the address of the station where she's being held. They got her on drug charges, but I don't know how long they'll hold her. If you're going to see her, now's the time to do so. If you wait too long you might miss your window."

"Send me the info. I'll leave today," I tell him, thanking him again before quickly ending the call.

I pull up Claire's number and hit call, and it rings twice before she picks up.

"Good morning." I hear the smile in her voice.

"Claire, we found her. Finley's mom. Chuck found her."

"What?" She sounds as shocked as I feel. Neither of us ever really thought this day would come.

Finley had chosen not to tell her mom she was dying. That was a choice she had the right to make. But after she was gone, I felt like I had to let her know. She was a piece of shit mom who cared more about drugs than her own daughter, but at the end of

145

the day she was still her mom. I can't help but feel like a small part of her still cares and deserves to know that her daughter is gone.

Claire agreed with me and together we started the process of trying to track her down. I don't know what I hope to accomplish by going to see her, but I know I have to.

"She was arrested on possession in Rock Hill, South Carolina. Chuck says he doesn't know how long they'll hold her, so we need to go now."

"Now, as in today?"

"Now as in *now*. Can you get off work?"

"I'll call in sick if I have to. There's no way I'm letting you do this alone." She doesn't hesitate. "Why don't you start packing and I'll get online and see what flights I can find. I'll call you back as soon as I have something."

"Sounds good." I end the call, throwing the covers back before quickly climbing out of bed.

Peyton: Are you free tonight? Henna is staying at Aaron's house. Thought maybe we could order pizza and watch a movie…among other things.

I read Peyton's message as I sit in the airport terminal with Claire waiting on our flight to be called. She was able to get us plane tickets for four o'clock in the afternoon. In just a few short hours we will be in South Carolina. I'll be in Finley's hometown for the first time ever. A part of me hopes it will make me feel closer to her, though I know it probably won't. Finley hated South Carolina and ran away from it the first chance she got. She ran away from her drug addict mother and the horrible environment she was raised in. And here I am, running toward it in an effort to somehow reconnect with her.

I stare at the message for a solid two minutes before deciding to text her back.

Me: Sorry, wish I could. Had to leave town unexpectedly. I'll text you when I'm back in Chicago.

Her response comes almost immediately.

Peyton: Oh, okay. No problem. I hope everything is okay.

Me: Everything's fine. I just had something come up that I have to take care of.

Peyton: Do you know when you'll be home?

Me: Not sure yet. Could be a day. Could be a few. I won't know until I get there.

The dots bounce across my screen for several moments and then disappear, like she was typing something but changed her mind. They reappear again after a few seconds before her next message fills the screen.

Peyton: Be safe. Text me when you're home.

Abel: Will do.

I lock my phone and let out a hard breath, shoving the device into my bag.

"Everything okay?" Claire nudges my shoulder with hers.

"Yeah, everything's fine."

"Was that Peyton?" she asks knowingly.

"Yeah."

"I like her." She smiles.

"Yeah, me too." I shrug like it's nothing.

"She seems like someone that would keep you on your toes. You need someone like her in your life."

"Why, when I have you?" I divert, not wanting to get into this with Claire right now.

I need to figure out what the hell it is we're really doing and how I feel about it before I share it with Claire. Talking to my aunt is one thing. I'm not ready to have to answer a ton of questions I'm sure Claire will have when I'm not sure I have any answers to give.

"Ha. Ha. Aren't we the funny one today?" She crinkles her nose at me.

"I'm always the funny one," I counter.

"You wish." She rolls her eyes.

"I'm trying really hard not to be offended right now," I tell her on a laugh.

"But it's working as a distraction, isn't it?"

"So that's what you're doing? Trying to distract me?" I give her a disbelieving look.

"Maybe." She shrugs. "Or maybe I'm trying to let you down easy because really, Abel, you aren't that funny."

"You're lucky I love you, Claire Roberts."

"You're lucky I love you, Abel Collins," she fires back.

Before I can think of a witty comeback, our flight number is called and everything I've been trying so hard not to think about comes boiling back to the surface.

The questions that have sounded over and over in my head since I received Chuck's call this morning.

Am I doing the right thing?

What if I get there and she's gone?

What if she's even worse than when Finley left?

What if she's better and Finley missed it?

That last one I seriously doubt considering she was arrested on drug possession. But there's one question that sounds louder than all the others. The one that's been eating at me all day.

Would Finley be okay with this?

She made her wishes known before she died. She had no desire to see or contact her mom, even in her final days. I just don't know if it's that she really didn't want her mom to know or if it's that she didn't want her mom to give her one last chance to disappoint her.

Either way, there's no going back now. I've committed to seeing this through and that's exactly what I plan to do.

"You ready?" I look up to see Claire is already standing, her carryon bag slung over her shoulder.

"As ready as I'll ever be." I push out of the chair, grabbing my bag off the floor before following her to the loading gate.

We arrive in Rock Hill just after seven in the evening. It's muggy and much warmer than I expected it to be. The drive to the police station has been a quiet one. I think Claire, like myself, is nervous about what we're going to find once we arrive.

When the Uber slows outside of the police station, I'm not sure if I want to get out or to tell him to drive me back to the airport. Claire doesn't give me the chance to choose because the moment the car stops she's climbing out.

"Well, this is it." She steps up next to me as soon as I exit the car.

"This is it."

"It's now or never." She loops her arm through mine and together we make our way into the police station.

We have to jump through a few hoops in order to get to see Cherie. One of which involves Claire lying and saying she's her daughter and I'm her son-in-law. I didn't feel good about it, but it wasn't all a lie. Technically, I really am her son–in–law, although it feels weird to think that when I've never met the woman.

We're taken to a nearby room and have to wait nearly thirty minutes before a knock sounds against the door. My stomach twists into tight knots as it swings open and an officer steps inside, followed by a woman I'd never guess as Finley's mom if I didn't know otherwise.

She looks nothing like her daughter. Where Finley was dark hair and perfect skin, her mother is gray, wrinkled, and severely strung out looking. She looks at Claire first and then her eyes move to mine. When she meets my gaze, it takes everything in me not to lose the contents of my stomach. Her stare is vacant, detached, like she wouldn't know who we were even if she actually knew us.

I know instantly that coming here was a mistake.

"You have ten minutes," the officer informs us once Cherie is seated at the far end of the table, caddy corner from both Claire and I who are sitting on opposite sides.

The door slams closed, leaving an eerie silence in its wake.

"Do I know you?" Cherie finally speaks, her voice strained and hoarse.

"Cherie, I'm Claire Roberts. I'm your daughter, Finley's sister," Claire starts, approaching her cautiously.

"Finley." A flash of recognition crosses her face before the blank stare returns.

"Yes, Finley," Claire continues. "This is her husband, Abel." She gestures to me and the woman's eyes slide in my direction again.

"My Finley isn't married." She narrows her gaze at me.

"She did get married." Claire draws her attention back to her.

"Where is she? Where's my daughter?" Her voice goes up and she starts looking around the room like someone is going to jump out of the walls and attack her.

"That's why we're here, Cherie. We've been looking for you for a very long time. We wanted to tell you sooner, but we didn't know how to find you."

"Tell me what?" she barks, growing irritated. "What do you want? Why are you here?"

"If you'd let me, I'm trying to explain." Claire's patience is the thing of legends. I can't even open my mouth because if I do, I might lose my shit. "Finley, your daughter, she passed away three years ago from cancer."

This seems to get the woman's attention and for the first time since sitting down she shows some sort of real emotion.

"What do you mean she passed away?"

"She died."

"She's not dead." She shakes her head. "What kind of game are you trying to play? Who sent you?"

"No one sent us. And I'm not playing a game. It's true. She came to live with me in Chicago. She met Abel and fell in love. Then she got sick."

"You're lying. Where is my daughter?"

"I've already told you. She's gone."

"She's not gone." Cherie smacks the table, the sound echoing off the walls around us. "Why are you lying to me? What do you want?"

"We don't want anything!" I explode, not able to hold it in for a moment longer. "Your daughter, the one you didn't give a shit about. The one you chose drugs over, time after time after time. *That daughter.*" I make sure I have her full attention before continuing, "She defied all odds. She escaped you and this fucking life." I gesture around the room. "And she was happier than she had ever been. And do you want to know why you didn't know she died?" I lean in close but make no attempt to lower my voice. "Because she fucking hated you and she didn't want you to know," I seethe, anger pouring out of me like hot lava.

"Abel." Claire lifts up in her seat, placing her hand against my chest. "That's enough."

"No, you know what, I knew better than to come here but I thought maybe, *just maybe*, you'd actually give two shits that your *only* daughter died. But look at you." I sneer at her. "You don't care about anything except when you're going to get out of here and get your next fix."

"Abel." Claire tries again but I'm not being silenced.

"You really are a piece of shit," I spit.

"Abel." Claire stands all the way, her voice harsher than I've ever heard it before. "I said, that's enough." She glares at me and it suddenly dawns on me that I've never seen Claire mad before. And damn is she pissed. I'm not sure if it's at me or Cherie or the situation. Probably a combination of all three.

I take a deep breath and try to reel myself in for Claire's sake.

"I may be all of those things," Cherie begins, causing Claire to reclaim her seat. "I was a horrible mother. Awful. The absolute worst, but I love my daughter." Tears well behind her eyes and for the first time I think maybe she's hearing us. "I deserved the chance to say goodbye."

"Well, your daughter didn't think you did," I respond, much calmer.

"Maybe she was right." She shrugs, tears breaking free and streaking down her sunken cheeks.

"We just thought you should know," Claire says. "We don't want anything from you. We aren't here for any reason other than to share this information with you. And now that we have, I think it's time we go." Claire pushes to a stand. "Abel." She jerks her head toward the door.

"Will you tell her I'm sorry?" Her broken voice halts me as I reach the door. "When you visit her grave, tell her I'm so sorry."

"You can tell her yourself," I say, knowing she never will. Raising my fist, I knock hard on the door. It swings open moments later revealing two officers standing on the other side. "We're done here," I tell them, storming out of the room.

I can't get out of the station fast enough. I'm so pissed I can't see straight, yet it's exactly as I expected so I don't know why I'm so mad. I knew this was likely how we would find her. I didn't come here for any reason other than to tell a mother her daughter had died. That's it. So why do I feel like I'm the one that received the bad news?

"Abel." Claire catches up to me outside where I'm pacing the sidewalk, not sure what to do with all this anger.

"She fucking told us, Claire. She told us what kind of person she was, and we came anyway. I thought I'd feel better. I thought this was the right thing to do. But seeing her." I gesture toward the station. "Seeing firsthand what Finley grew up with, it makes me fucking sick." I tug at the ends of my hair.

"Finley was dealt a shit hand. There's no denying that. But she didn't let her childhood or how she was raised define her and neither should you."

"I'm not. I swear to God I'm not. I just… Fuck… That woman." I throw my hands in the air.

"She's the worst of the worst. But Abel, we knew that coming in."

"I don't think I realized it would be this bad." I stop pacing when Claire steps in front of me.

"I did." She gives me a sad smile. "And I tried to tell you. But you were so hellbent on doing this for Fin that you wouldn't hear otherwise. I knew it wouldn't make you feel better."

"So, what? This is your *I told you so* speech?"

"This is my, *we came here and did what we said we were going to do and now it's time to close this chapter* speech."

"Well it's a shitty speech," I tell her, her gaze slicing to mine seconds before we both start laughing.

"And to think I said you weren't funny." She bends over, holding her stomach as laughter rumbles through her.

I don't think our laughing has anything to do with me being funny or not, but everything to do with our current situation. When you find yourself at the end of your rope sometimes the only thing to do is laugh.

And so we do. We laugh until tears fill our eyes. We laugh until our stomach's cramp. We laugh until neither of us can physically laugh anymore.

And then we do the only thing we can. We make peace with the situation, knowing we did everything we set out to do. Whether it turned out the way we wanted or not, our job was done.

You can't control what life throws your way; you can only control how you react to it. Finley said that to me after she found out she was dying. I never understood how she could be so strong, even then, even when facing the end of her life, she still found some way to make it okay.

"What do you say we find an old burger joint and eat ourselves into a coma?" Claire smiles at me.

"I think that's the best idea you've had all day."

Chapter Nineteen
Peyton

Abel: Are you home?

My heart rate picks up speed at the sight of Abel's name on my phone. It's been five days since Sven's party – since the most incredible night of my life – and this is the first time I have heard from him other than the brief text conversation we had on Monday when he said he was going out of town.

Outside of that it's been radio silence. I'd be lying if I said it didn't bother me more than it should.

Me: Yes.

I type out my response with shaky fingers.

Abel: Are you alone?

Me: Yes.

I wait for him to say more. One-minute passes, then two. I start to grow impatient. But just as I begin to type out another text a knock sounds at my front door.

Tossing my phone onto the coffee table, I cross the living room. Given the messages we just exchanged I can only guess it's Abel and this makes me equally excited and nervous.

I look down and assess my current situation. Pink tank, gray jersey shorts, my hair in a messy knot. Not good.

Shit.

I consider darting to the bathroom to throw on a little lip gloss and take my hair down but I know I don't have time.

"Who is it?" I call through the door.

It's times like these that I really miss having a peep hole. Why we don't have one is beyond me. I thought that was something that was standard but apparently, it's not.

"It's me." Abel's deep voice vibrates from the other side of the door causing goosebumps to erupt across my skin.

Unlatching the deadbolt, I pull the door open, but before I have time to say anything, let alone react, Abel's lips are on mine and he's backing me into the living room.

He kisses me hard, his hands roaming feverishly, clawing at my clothes as he kicks the door closed.

"Bedroom," he growls against my mouth.

"This way." I manage to break away from his assault long enough to grab his hand and pull him down the hall toward my bedroom.

The moment we're tucked inside, he's on me again. His mouth on my neck, his hands up my shirt, his erection digging into my stomach.

"I need you," he murmurs against my mouth, stepping back long enough to remove my tank in one quick motion.

"Then I'm yours." My hands slide down his torso to the buckle of his jeans, popping them open with ease.

"So, are you going to tell me what's going on or am I going to have to pry it out of you?" I ask, my head laying on Abel's chest as I trace lazy circles on his stomach with the tip of my finger.

"What do you mean?" His hand slides through my hair, playing with the ends.

"I knew the instant you walked in the door that something was wrong."

And I did too. I could sense it in the urgency of his kiss and the intensity of his touch. He needed an escape and I am where he chose to find it.

"It's been a long few days. Let's just leave it at that."

"Does it have something to do with why you had to leave town?" I ask.

"Peyton," he sighs, his hand falling away from my hair.

"You can talk to me, ya know? I think you'll find I'm a pretty good listener."

"I thought we agreed what this was." He shifts beneath me, forcing me to sit up.

"What? Because we're having sex, we can't be friends too?" I question, trying to keep the hurt from my voice.

"I didn't say that." He props up against the headboard and I swivel to face him, pulling the sheet up around my chest.

"You kind of did. Just not in so many words." I smile to try to lighten the heavy mood that's suddenly settled over the room.

I don't know why he does this. It's like before and during sex he can't get enough of me but as soon as it's over he retreats into that head of his and completely shuts me out.

"It's just... complicated."

"And you think I can't handle complicated?" I cock my head to the side. "Abel, talk to me." I lay my hand on his thigh, stroking it gently with my thumb.

"We went to see Finley's mom." He lets out on a rushed breath.

"*We?*"

"Me and Claire."

"Oh, okay." Even though I know his relationship with Claire is purely platonic, I can't ignore the jealous twist in my gut just the same.

"We've been looking for her for three years, ever since Finley passed."

"Wait, you didn't know where she was?"

"Finley's mom is a drug addict. Has been for years. It's why Finley moved here. To get away from her and be with her sister. When she got sick, she didn't want her mom to know. I never really understood why. I mean I did, but I didn't. She was still her mom, you know?"

"So, she didn't know..."

"That her daughter had died? No." He shakes his head. "I hired a P.I. to track her down, but because she didn't have a real residence and never obtained legitimate employment it was like she didn't exist. No credit cards, no bank accounts, nothing."

"So how did you find her?"

"She got arrested on drug possession. That's why I had to leave so abruptly. I didn't know how long they would hold her, so I knew my window was limited." He scratches his jaw where his facial hair has grown from a mild scruff to a short beard. I have to admit; it looks incredible on him.

"Did you see her?" I ask when he doesn't continue.

"We did."

"And?"

"And she was exactly who Finley said she was. I don't know why I had hoped she'd be different. Why I convinced myself that telling her about Finley would somehow make me feel better. In the end it only made me feel worse. It made what she had been through as a child more real. If that makes sense."

"It makes complete sense. Sometimes you can't fully understand a situation until you come face to face with it yourself."

"Exactly." He blows out a breath. "After we told her I wanted to get out of there." He looks up, his expression hesitant. "I wanted you."

"Why do you say that like it's a bad thing?" I try to pretend like his words don't affect me, but they do. More than I would ever admit to him.

"It's not a bad thing. But it terrifies me. The entire flight home you were all I could think about. When I saw you standing in that doorway, I don't know what came over me. I just needed you." He gives me an apologetic smile. "I haven't *needed* someone in a very long time. It's hard for me."

"I get that. You lost someone you love, Abel. But eventually you're going to have to learn to start letting people back in."

"I'm working on it." He shrugs.

"Okay, enough with the heavy." I pat his leg before sliding out of bed.

"Where are you going?"

"*We* are going to get out of this apartment."

"And do what?" He watches me slip on my shorts, his gaze honing in on my bare chest. I can't stop the smile that curves up the corners of my mouth.

"Something. Anything. I don't care." I latch my bra before snagging my tank off the floor.

"What if I just want to stay here with you?" he asks, making my heart flip inside my chest.

"I mean, I would love that. But Henna will be home soon, and I'm guessing you don't want to be here when she gets here."

"Yeah, that's probably not the greatest idea," he agrees, finally moving off the bed.

I get why he doesn't want anyone to know about us right now. This whole thing is still so new and it's hard to keep things casual if everyone and their mother knows. Casual means uncomplicated and people tend to complicate things.

That doesn't mean I'm not still holding out hope that this will become something more. I'd have to be crazy not to be. Abel is the entire package. He's good looking, funny, extremely talented, among many other things. He's everything I've been waiting for and so much more. With the exception of what he's been through, that does tend to make this situation a little trickier. But I'm willing to put in the work because Abel is worth it. He's so, so worth it.

"How did you find this place?" Abel gestures around the dimly lit, basement style restaurant.

"Henna. She has a knack for finding places that most people have never heard of."

"She must, because I was pretty certain I had eaten at just about every restaurant in Chicago and I didn't even know this place existed."

"Don't say that, because then I'll have to make it my mission to see how many times I can prove you wrong." I smile, lifting my wine glass to my lips.

"I don't know, that might be fun," he counters with a shrug.

"Okay, then." I lean forward. "You're on."

"So what, you're going to take me to the most obscure places in the city to see if I've been there?" He chuckles.

"Pretty much." I laugh, taking another drink of wine.

"Okay, but we need to heighten the stakes." He leans back, crossing his arms over his broad chest.

"What do you have in mind?" I ask, liking the sound of where this is going.

"For every place you take me that I've already been to you owe me a dare."

"A dare?" I question with a smile.

"I can dare you to do anything and you have to do it."

"Hmm." I consider this offer. "Okay, I'll agree to that under one condition."

"Which is?"

"That if you haven't been there *you* owe me a dare."

"Trying to even the playing field I see." He laughs.

"What fun would it be if I didn't? And seeing as you've never been here before, I think that means you owe me a dare."

"The game hasn't started yet," he objects.

"Oh yes it has. You made the rules; I'm just playing along."

"You know, I had you pegged all wrong."

"And why do you say that?" I cock a brow.

"Here I thought you were this sweet, innocent person. I'm starting to realize you have a bit of a dark side," he teases.

"Oh, you haven't seen anything yet." I bite down on my bottom lip to contain my smile. "Are you ready for your first dare?"

"Now?" He looks around. "Our food isn't even here yet."

"It doesn't need to be."

"I'm going to regret this, aren't I?" He laughs.

"I don't know." I shrug playfully. "Maybe."

"Shit," he grumbles with laughter in his voice. "Alright, hit me."

"See that piano over there." I point to the corner. "I dare you to go over there and play a song."

"You want me to walk over and start randomly playing a song?" He gives me a funny look. "Am I even allowed to do that?"

"I don't know." I giggle.

"I don't play piano."

"Liar."

"How do you know I'm lying?"

"Because you're a musician."

"Just because I'm a musician doesn't mean I can play any instrument."

"Can you play piano?" I ask him flat out.

"Yes."

I can't stop the laughter that bubbles out of me.

"Then why are we even having this conversation?"

"How did you know I can play piano?" He narrows his gaze at me.

I shrug. "Some secrets I will never tell."

"Shut up." He chuckles, shaking his head.

"I'm just kidding. The night Aaron, Henna, and I came to see you play, Aaron mentioned that when you were younger you used to love going to music stores. That you would walk in and play every instrument they would let you touch, and that the piano was one of them. I just assumed from there."

"That asshole talks too much," he mutters under his breath with a smile on his face.

"So, time to pay up," I announce, my gaze going from him to the piano and then back to him.

"Fine." He takes a long drink from his glass and stands. "This one's for you," he tells me, giving me a mischievous smile before setting off across the room.

Moments later, I watch him settle behind the piano, his fingers silently skirting along the keys. No one pays any attention to him until the first note rings out, and then I swear, every eye in the room is on him.

I don't recognize the song at first. The beat is familiar, but I can't pinpoint where I've heard it before. That is until he starts singing.

As soon as the first line leaves his lips, it hits me and it's all I can do not to buckle over in laughter.

Abel Collins, in the middle of a crowded restaurant with countless people watching, is belting out a slower, piano version of "I Wanna Sex You Up" by Color Me Badd.

I don't know if I'm more amused or surprised by his selection of song. Amused because, come on, he's singing Color

Me Badd. Surprised, because truthfully, I didn't know he had it in him.

He seems so serious most of the time, like he's almost afraid to have fun. I remember being the same way after my mom died. I felt guilty any time I smiled or laughed; like I didn't have the right to feel okay anymore. It kills me that he carries that weight.

But over time those feelings faded for me. I'm sure they will eventually for him too. It's like one day it was there and then, without even realizing it, it was gone. Like time magically healed the broken part of me that felt like I was doing something wrong for simply living my life.

Abel's eyes dart across the room and find mine, a slow smile pulling at his mouth as he sings over one particularly sexual part of the song. I cover my mouth with my hand to muffle my laughter, shaking my head at him.

His smile widens and he sings louder, his incredible voice making a song I never particularly cared for, one that I feel the overwhelming urge to download this minute.

He's completely unphased by the laughter and whistles coming from the other patrons and keeps playing until the very end.

When he finishes, everyone in the restaurant erupts into applause. Abel stands from the piano and takes a half bow, smiling like I'm not sure I've ever seen him smile before.

His gaze comes back to mine and he laughs. Pushing away from the piano, he crosses the room back to where our table is located against the far wall.

Bypassing his seat, he stops directly next to mine and crouches down so that his face is level with mine.

"Happy?" he asks, so close I can feel his breath on my face.

"Tremendously," I admit, letting out a surprised gasp when he dips and presses his lips to mine. It's not just a peck either. It's a full blown, his tongue down my throat kind of kiss with everyone in the restaurant here to bear witness.

When he pulls back, I'm flustered and heat is spreading across my cheeks like wildfire.

"Has anyone told you you're adorable when you blush?" He gives me a knowing smirk, then stands upright, taking his seat across from me seconds later.

"Um." I look around the room, seeing several sets of eyes dart away the moment I do.

"Um, what?" He leans back in his chair after picking his wine glass off the table.

"I thought we were keeping this hush hush?" I question, not trying to mask my confusion over his sudden outpouring of PDA.

"We don't know anyone here and they don't know us." He shrugs. "Why, do you have a problem with me kissing you in public?" He smiles over the rim of his glass, clearly sensing that I do not.

"Not at all. I'm just a little confused. You're kind of all over the place," I tell him honestly.

"I know I am," he admits, his smile faltering. "But it's you."

"*Me?*"

"You make me feel…" He blows out a breath. "I don't know how to explain it that would make any sense."

"Try."

"Deep down I don't think I'm ready. I'm not ready for a real relationship and everything that goes with it. Sometimes I wonder if I ever will be. But when I look at you, when I'm with you, things just feel… different."

"Different good or different bad?"

"Different good." He smiles. "Really good." He takes a drink. "I'm not saying I want to alter what we agreed to. I think keeping things casual is the best thing right now. But I like how I feel when I'm with you."

"I like how I feel when I'm with you too," I admit.

"Come home with me after this." His request catches me off guard.

"To your place?" I question.

"Why not?" He shrugs. "At least there we don't have to worry about someone coming home."

"Okay." I don't even have to think about it.

"Okay." He grins. "Then it's settled."

"I guess so." I blush again, not sure why the hell I even am.

I swear, Abel makes me feel like a giddy teenager all over again. All the butterflies and emotions flood me like high rising water, taking me under its swift current.

Chapter Twenty
Abel

Tonight has been exactly what I needed. Peyton is the perfect distraction. Beautiful. Funny. Easy to talk to. She makes me feel better in a way I can't explain.

She deserves better than me, this I know with complete certainty. But I'm selfish and I want all of her, even though I'm not willing to give her the same.

"Okay, where were we?" Peyton reappears from the kitchen with two waters in her hand.

"You were about to tell me your two truths and a lie," I remind her.

"Um, no I wasn't." She laughs, plopping down on the couch next to me before sliding a water into my hand. "I went last. It's your turn."

"Are you sure? I feel like I just went," I tease, tipping the bottle to my lips.

"I'm positive. But nice try." She laughs.

"Okay, let's see." I tap my chin dramatically. "I hate to fly. My favorite vegetable is corn. And the color orange makes me cringe."

"Hmmm. That's a tough one." She thinks on it for a moment. "The truths are, corn and the color orange?" she guesses.

"Nope." I grin.

"Really?"

"Really." I lift the beer bottle to my lips and take a drink.

"You have to at least tell me what I *did* get right."

"The color orange *does* make me cringe."

"Okay, so then you hate to fly."

"Yep," I confirm.

"But you've flown several times, have you not?"

"That doesn't mean I like it."

"Fair enough." She nods. "So, corn is not your favorite vegetable?"

"Nope."

"Then what is?"

"Asparagus." I chuckle when she curls her nose.

"Asparagus? That has to be one of the worst vegetables there is."

"Your opinion. I happen to really like it."

"Gross." She shakes her head.

"Your turn." I laugh, settling deeper into the couch.

"Okay." She pauses. "My favorite color is pink. I used to be a cheerleader in high school. And I hate rap music."

"Easy," I tell her. "Your lie is that your favorite color is pink."

"Incorrect. My favorite color *is* pink."

"Well, shit. Okay. You weren't a cheerleader in high school."

"Wrong again."

"You hate rap music?" I cock my head, finding this little piece of information surprising.

"Despise it." She nods.

"Really? I find it hard to believe you hate *all* rap music."

"I'm not saying there hasn't been a song or two over the years that I've enjoyed, but rap music as a whole isn't my thing. All the bass gives me a headache."

"So then you *were* a cheerleader in high school?" I give her a sly grin. "Let's talk more about that."

"Let's not. I'm embarrassed even thinking about it." She covers her face with her hand.

"Don't be embarrassed. The thought of you jumping around in a tiny little skirt is really doing it for me."

"Is that so?" She giggles.

"In fact, I think you should show me what you got."

"What?" She snorts, shaking her head no.

"I'm serious. Show me."

"There is no way I'm cheering in front of you."

"I dare you," I challenge.

"Nope."

"I triple dog dare you."

"What are we, twelve?" She laughs.

"Oh come on. One cheer." I pout out my bottom lip.

"Lord." She lets out a loud, dramatic sigh, pushing herself up off the couch. Setting her water on the coffee table, she crosses to the other side where there's an open space between the table and the television. "Don't laugh." She narrows her gaze at me.

I make an X motion across my heart.

"I can't believe I'm doing this," she mutters to herself as she gets into position. "Give me a V. Dot the I. Curl the C. TORY. Turn around, touch the ground, bring it up, and break it down," she chants, rolling her arms and clapping. "Let's go, Warriors. Come on, let's go, Warriors." She waves her hands in the air at the end of the cheer. "Go Warriors!" she yells, kicking her leg.

I clap, the smile on my face no doubt giving away how amused I am by this.

"Yep, I can totally see it now," I tell her.

"Shut it." She sticks her tongue out at me, her hands going to her hips.

"Can you do all those flips and jumps too?" I ask.

"Some."

"Show me."

"I am not flipping and jumping in the middle of your living room." She looks at me like I'm crazy.

"Fine, let's go outside."

"Seriously? It's like ten o'clock at night."

"And?"

"And, it's dark outside so you won't be able to see me."

"Pretty sure there are these things called streetlamps. I'm sure I could see you just fine. I just think you're scared."

"I'm not scared." She crosses her arms over her chest.

"You sure?" I challenge, purposely pushing her buttons.

"You know what, fine." She stomps over to the door and slides on her flip flops. "But if I fall and break an ankle because you have me tumbling in the dark it'll be on you." She rips open the front door and quickly exits the apartment before I've managed to get up off the couch.

"Hey, wait for me," I call, jogging outside after her without bothering to put any shoes on.

She kicks off her sandals on the sidewalk, then crosses to a flat patch of grass in front of my building.

"I can't believe I'm doing this." She looks forward, blowing out a hard breath.

I'm just about to tell her she doesn't have to, that I was only screwing with her. But before I have the chance, she takes off running, doing some cartwheel type thing before flipping backward, her hands barely touching the ground.

"Holy hell. What was that called?" I ask, pretty impressed.

"Round off into a back handspring." She smiles. "I took gymnastics for twelve years."

"It shows." I grin. "What else can you do?"

"I used to be able to do a lot, but I'm pretty out of practice."

"You don't look out of practice to me."

"Trust me, I am. You'll know when I can barely walk tomorrow." She laughs. "Why don't you give it a try?"

"You want me to try to do that?" I snort.

"Why not?" Her smile widens.

"Because I'd break my neck is why not," I tell her like it should be obvious.

"I bet you could do a cartwheel."

"I bet you I cannot."

"Come on. Try."

"Not a chance."

"You mean to tell me that I came out here and did a back handspring, barefoot, in the dark, for you, and you won't even attempt something as simple as a cartwheel."

"Yep, that's what I'm telling you." I laugh when she gives me the cutest fucking mean mug I've ever seen. "Tell you what, how about we take this party back upstairs and I'll do my best to make sure you're not sore tomorrow."

"And how do you plan to do that?"

"By giving you a massage." I hold my hand out to her.

"A massage, huh?" She raises an eyebrow in question but still takes my hand.

"I'm actually pretty good at it. Or so I've been told."

"I think I'll be the judge of that," she tells me, pausing to slip on her flip flops before following me back inside.

Chapter Twenty-one
Peyton

It's still dark outside. I don't know how late it is, but I know it's pretty late. Abel dozed off a little while ago, but for whatever reason I haven't been able to make myself get up and leave.

Finally deciding I can't wait any longer or I might fall asleep, I get up and make my way into the kitchen to get a drink of water. And even though I know I should gather my things and head home before it gets too late, I find myself roaming Abel's apartment instead.

There's not a lot in the way of personal items. He has a wraparound couch, a coffee table, a television mounted on the wall. All the things a normal apartment would have, yet there are no pictures, no figurines, or little mementos from his life. Nothing. Nothing except a small silver vase that sits on the mantel above the fireplace.

It catches my eye, even in the dimness of the room, and I find myself drawn to where it sits. It isn't until I'm standing directly in front of it that I see the letters etched along the bottom.

Finley

I read the name twice before it dawns on me what this is… Finley's ashes.

From the bits and pieces I've picked up along the way I knew that Finley was cremated. What I did not know was that Abel still had her ashes, or that they were sitting in the room I've occupied with Abel most of the night.

It doesn't bother me. I mean, why would it? But it does give me this weird feeling. Like there's not enough room in this apartment for the both of us. I know that probably sounds bad. I guess you'd have to be in my shoes to understand the feeling. I've known all along that Abel's heart belongs to another. I guess I'm just now realizing what that means for me.

How can there possibly be a future for us? How could I ever stack up to this perfect girl? The one he loved so dearly, who died way too young.

It's nights like tonight where it's easy to pretend. It's easy to forget about the ghost that stands between us. The one, after three years, Abel still hasn't been able to let go of.

She must have been some girl. To earn the love of a man like Abel and have it given to her so whole heartedly, even years after her death.

I wonder if a man will ever love me like that. A love that defies everything, even death.

"What are you doing?" I jump at the sound of Abel's voice. Turning to face him, he's leaning against the opening of the hallway, watching me.

"Sorry," I fumble. "I was just getting ready to head out and I saw this."

"I haven't been able to let them go yet," he says, his eyes going to the urn. "Half of them are buried with her headstone. This half." He gestures to the mantle as he crosses the room toward me. "This half…" He stops next to me, his eyes on the urn. "She told me that when I was ready…" He trails off as his gaze slides to mine. "I keep waiting to be ready, but the thought of taking her and letting her go feels more impossible than anything I've ever done. Aside from watching her die."

"They say time heals all wounds. I don't know if I believe that's true," I say, looking to where Finley's urn sits in front of us. "Some wounds heal quickly. Some take a little longer. And then some, the really deep ones, I don't think they ever truly heal. It's more like they form a permanent scab. It's enough so that we don't bleed out, but it never heals more than that."

"I keep waiting for the day. The day I wake up and know it's time. I'm starting to wonder if that day will ever come."

"I get that feeling. Losing a mom is different than losing a spouse, but I think both are monumental losses." My eyes go to his chest where Finley's name is tattooed in beautiful cursive.

"I got it a few weeks before she died," he says, clearly seeing where my mind has gone. "I thought somehow it would help me keep her alive, even after she was gone."

"I did the same thing." I hold up my left foot, and without explaining the meaning behind it, I gesture to the feather tattoo that runs along the top.

"Thank you for being here." His statement has my head turning upward to find his eyes locked on me. "You make it easier somehow. Easier to think. Easier to breathe."

The tight knot that's been lingering in my chest skyrockets into my throat and I find myself unable to form a single word.

"I know I'm all over the place. And I know I'm probably giving off some really confusing signals. But the truth is I really like you, Peyton. I'm just trying to figure out how to carry those feelings with all the others that are jumbled up in my head." He blows out a breath, angling his body so that he's facing me head on. "Just be patient with me, okay?"

"I like this." I gesture between the two of us. "I hope you know I don't expect anything from you. I just really enjoy being with you."

"I enjoy being with you too," he says, reaching out to trail his hand lightly down my arm.

"There's no pressure here, I hope you know that," I reassure him, even though in my heart all I really want is for him to be mine. Really *mine*. But I also know that trying to force it will only push him away. So, I'm trying to play it his way, in hopes that it goes my way in the end.

"I do. And I can't tell you how much that means to me. You've brought light back into my life. After spending three years stumbling around in the dark, I need some time to adjust."

"I understand." I reach up, cupping the side of his face. "I should probably go." I let my fingers slide through his ever-growing beard before falling away completely.

It would be so easy to lose myself in him. So easy to let my guard down and act on my heart. But I can't be that careless.

"It's pretty late," I say, taking a full step back. "And I have to work in the morning," I continue, remembering that one very important thing. "Crap, my car is at my apartment."

"It's okay. I'll drive you home."

"Abel, you're tired. I can order an Uber."

"At this time of night?" He shakes his head. "Not a chance. I'll take you."

"Okay," I concede, knowing by the look on his face there's no way he's going to let me leave otherwise.

"Let me just grab a shirt." He looks down at his bare chest and my gaze follows his, my eyes locking in on Finley's name above his heart seconds before he turns and walks away.

Chapter Twenty-two
Peyton

Abel: So I was thinking…

I smile at my phone that's lying face up on my desk. Picking it up, I slide my finger across the screen to unlock it right as another message comes through.

Abel: How would you feel about sushi tonight?

Me: Are you done with our game already? Three dares and you're ready to throw in the towel?

I laugh to myself, remembering last weekend when I took Abel to Perry House, a small little eatery on the outskirts of the city. Per the rules of our game, every place we go that he's never been, he owes me a dare. So far, I'm three for three and it hasn't even been two weeks. While the other two dares were fun, last week it took a turn into something else. I blame the wine or Abel or maybe it was a combination of them both. Whatever it was, when *I dare you to take me to the bathroom…* came out of my mouth, I was equally shocked and excited by the fact that he didn't hesitate for a second.

I guess it's safe to say I've checked *have sex in a public bathroom* off my list. Not that it actually existed on my must do list, as it was never something I considered doing. But that didn't make it any less amazing, and the excitement over the possibility of getting caught only added to the intensity of it all.

Abel: Throw in the towel? After last time? Not a chance.

I cover my mouth with my hand to stifle a laugh.

Abel: I just thought if I picked the type of restaurant the odds would be better stacked in my favor. You've had three dares. I think it's about time I got one.

Me: And what, do tell, are you planning on making me do if you win?

Abel: Oh no, I'm not telling you that.

I try to shake away the ridiculous smile lighting up my whole face but it's useless. That damn thing isn't going anywhere. Not when Abel is involved.

Me: Guess I'll have to find a sushi restaurant you've never been to.

Abel: Good luck with that.

Me: We shall see.

Abel: So tonight? Meet at my house at seven?

Me: It's a date. I'll see you then.

"Someone looks happy." I look up, jumping slightly at the sight of my boss, John, lingering in my office doorway.

"Oh hey." I lock my phone and lay it face down on my desk. "Henna being Henna," I blurt out the first excuse I can think of.

"What did she do this time?" He smiles, sliding into the office.

"You don't even want to know." I force a laugh that I think sounds somewhat natural.

"Now, why does that only make me want to know more?" He chuckles, stopping directly in front of my desk.

"So, what's up?" I completely dodge the topic, folding my hands in front of myself.

"I wanted to touch base with you about our upcoming trip to New York. I know it's still a couple weeks out, but I want to make sure everything has been communicated to you about your flight and hotel information."

"Yes, Bev sent everything over the other day. I didn't know we were flying first class."

"Anytime I can, I do. Trust me, you'll never want to fly coach again after this trip."

"Great." I smile. "Because that's all I can afford. Not that I fly much."

"I don't know. Depending on how this trip goes I might look at taking you with me to more of these things in the future."

"Really?" My face lights up with excitement.

"Really." He nods. "Did you have any questions about the itinerary?"

"I don't think so, though I've only skimmed it. I was going to go through it more thoroughly later."

"Be sure that you do."

"Was that all you needed?" I ask when he continues to linger. "Or are you avoiding someone?" I arch a brow. It's not uncommon for John to sneak into my office every now and again to avoid having to deal with Janice.

She's a hell of a tech whiz, and basically keeps this place running all by herself, but she tends to be quite needy. John's too polite to tell her to go away so instead he finds places to hide out.

"She's been on my ass today about upgrading the servers. I keep telling her I'm waiting until the next roll out but she's determined to get her way now."

"Just be firm with her. Tell her no."

He gives me a knowing look. "When have you ever known Janice to take no for an answer."

"Remind me again, who owns this company?" I ask, leaning back in my chair.

"Yeah, yeah." He turns, peering through the glass walls of my office into the hallway. "I think the coast is clear. I'm going to try to run out and grab some lunch while I can." He spins on his heel and heads for the door. "Thanks for letting me hide out," he calls over his shoulder, pausing at the door to look both ways.

"Anytime." I giggle, watching him take off speed walking down the hallway moments later.

"Ugh. I feel like shit." Henna drops her purse on the chair before kicking off her shoes. "Today has been the worst."

"Rough day I take it."

"Just one of those days where nothing seems to go right."

"I know those days."

"I say we order pizza, crack open one of those bottles of wine on top of the fridge, and binge watch Outlander. I'm still like six episodes behind."

"Wish I could but I have plans tonight," I tell her, drawing her attention to my pale, yellow sundress that I partnered with floral white sandals.

"Plans with who?" She narrows her gaze at me.

"Just a friend from work."

"A friend from work? Which friend?"

"You don't know him."

"Oh, so it's a *him*." A slow smile turns up the corners of her mouth.

"It's not like that." I lock my iPad and lean forward, setting it on the coffee table in front of me.

"You say that and yet that cute little outfit you have on says otherwise."

"It's just a sundress."

"Just a sundress." She snorts. "Your other friends might buy that line but you forget who you're talking to."

"Honestly, Henna, it's just dinner with a work *friend*." I put an emphasis on the word friend. "Speaking of which, I should probably get going." I stand, smoothing the front of my dress.

Even though I'm not scheduled to meet Abel for another half an hour, my anxiousness over seeing him coupled with Henna's twenty questions has got me ready to get out of here.

"So where are you and this friend of yours going?" Henna's eyes follow me as I head into the dining room to grab my purse off the table.

"Tachiais."

"Tachiais?" she questions. "You don't even like sushi."

"I like sushi," I disagree. "It's just not my favorite thing in the world."

"Uh huh." She studies me for a long moment. "Well, you have fun with your *friend*," she calls after me as I head toward the door.

"I will. Don't wait up." I give her a little wave as I quickly exit the apartment.

"So," I gesture around the restaurant. "Tell me the truth. You've never been here, right?" I ask.

I spent half the day researching every Sushi restaurant in the city, trying to find the perfect one that I was certain Abel hadn't been to.

He doesn't answer, instead he slowly shakes his head, a wide smile forming on his mouth.

"Shit. You have?" I bite down on my lower lip.

"A couple of times, actually."

"No way." I shake my head in disbelief.

"Yes way. But." He leans back, his smile still firmly in place. "To be fair, there isn't a Sushi restaurant I *haven't* eaten at in Chicago."

"That's not possible. There are tons," I tell him, having not actually known just how many there was until today.

"I'm aware."

"So then what? This was some kind of set up?" I narrow my gaze at him.

"I wouldn't say set up." He chuckles.

"How is it that you've eaten at every Sushi restaurant in the city when I didn't even know most of them existed until today?"

"Sushi is my mom's favorite. And because I'm the youngest, and was the last to leave the house, and because my father despises Sushi, I was the one that got roped into going with her every time she got a hankering for it. We hardly ever went to the same place twice. Needless to say, it didn't take us that long to mark them all off the list."

"So then why lure me here under false pretenses?"

"I didn't. I suggested Sushi, you agreed."

"Yeah, because you conveniently left off the part where your mom is some kind of Sushi queen."

"I think someone is a little salty that she lost," he teases from across the table.

"I'm salty because the game was rigged," I fire back.

"So," he leans forward, rapping his fingers lightly on the table. "Do you wanna know what your dare is?"

"Well, tell me already," I interject when he doesn't continue.

"Nah." He grins. "I think I'll make you sweat for a while."

"You're an evil, evil man." I slowly shake my head, not able to fight the smile that slides across my lips.

"Okay, we've eaten dinner. Had drinks. And are now standing in front of your apartment building. Don't tell me you've decided to waste a perfectly good dare." I cross around the front of the car to join Abel on the sidewalk.

"Not a chance." He takes my hand when I reach him. "I've just been saving it."

"Well the offer expires at midnight, so you better get on with it already."

"So impatient." He chuckles, tightening his fingers around mine as he pulls me toward the entrance of his building.

"I mean it, Mr. Collins. Midnight."

"What happens at midnight? Do you leave me with only a glass slipper?" He stops at the door, glancing down at me for the briefest moment before pulling it open and guiding me inside.

"That depends, you got a pair of glass slippers laying around?" I quip.

"Fresh out, unfortunately."

"Shame." I giggle when he knocks his hip into mine.

"Okay." Abel stops in front of his apartment door. "I'm ready to tell you my dare now." He fishes his keys out of the front pocket of his dark jeans, his ocean blue eyes locking with mine. "I dare you to stay the night with me."

"What?" I question, assuming there's more to it.

"I dare you to stay the night with me," he repeats, the hesitance on his face endearing.

"That's what you want to use your dare on?" I gawk at him like he's lost his damn mind. He could have dared me to do anything and this is what he chooses?

"You never stay." He shrugs.

"I never knew you wanted me to," I tell him truthfully, my heart kicking up speed in my chest.

"Neither did I." He reaches out, his fingers lightly grazing underneath my chin as he guides my face upward.

"But you do now?" My breath hitches as he slowly leans forward.

"I do." His lips brush gently against mine. "Stay with me," he repeats his request, sucking my bottom lip into his mouth.

I swear my body just about takes flight from the swarm of butterflies flapping wildly inside my stomach.

"Okay," I agree without a second of hesitation.

Why would I hesitate? The man I'm falling for hard and fast asked me to stay the night with him. I know it may not seem like much to some, but to me it says the world. Because it means that whatever this is between us is evolving. It's growing into something that's beyond just hooking up. I see it when he looks at me, feel it when he touches me, hear it when he speaks to me. This is more for him, just like it's more for me.

It isn't until Abel pulls back and his hand slides along my cheek that I realize something…

My gaze follows his hand as he lowers it, my heart drumming so hard in my ears I can't hear myself think.

He's not wearing his ring.

I blink, looking to his other hand, thinking maybe I'm turned around.

Nope, no ring.

My stomach twists and my mind spins in every direction. *He's not wearing his ring.*

I had gotten so used to seeing it that I stopped paying attention to it, which is probably why we went the entire evening and I didn't notice.

But I've grown accustomed to the cold bite of the metal when he touches me. Which is why as soon as his hand slid across my face I knew.

He's not wearing his ring.

I try not to get too carried away. Maybe him taking it off has nothing to do with me. *Or maybe it has everything to do with you,* a little voice in my head interjects.

I want to silence that voice, push her down to the deepest pits and never hear her again. But it's already too late. The thought is already there. The hope. It's gone from a simmer to a complete boil and now I'm afraid there's no stopping it from bubbling over.

Abel turns, having no clue about my sudden internalization over the fact that he's not wearing his wedding ring, and inserts his key into the door, pushing it open moments later.

Chapter Twenty-three
Abel

My eyes dart open and instantly land on the waves of blonde hair spread out across the pillow next to me. I can't resist the urge to reach out and run my fingertips through it. Peyton doesn't stir when I do.

I didn't plan last night. When the evening started, I had a much more creative use of my dare in mind. But then I saw her from my balcony. She was climbing out of her car, the wind whipping through her hair and causing her dress to flutter in the breeze.

She looked so beautiful that I nearly forgot how to breathe. Like a perfect angel sent down to Earth just for me. And that's exactly how she looked with the sun glittering off her blonde waves. An angel.

I look at my hand as it slides through Peyton's hair. It's been two days since I took off my ring, yet every time I look down I expect to see it there. It's strange but was something I needed to do. Claudia was right, it was time.

When I slid the band from my finger it felt like someone had stuck a knife in my side and was turning it over and over again. The pain was enough to put me on the verge of vomiting.

But then something strange happened. A sort of calm washed over me. It was like this heavy weight had lifted. I felt lighter than I had in years and I knew, in that moment, that Finley was with me. That she was there, telling me it was okay. That I was doing the right thing.

I roll onto my back and look up at the ceiling where the bright morning sun peering through the blinds casts stripes of light across it.

Peering back toward Peyton, I let out a slow breath. I keep waiting for the panic to claw at my chest and my stomach to coil the way it always did when I'd wake up next to some random girl after a night of drinking, but I don't feel an ounce of that. That has to mean something, right?

In fact, if anything I feel happy. It's been so long since I've felt the sensation I had almost forgotten the feeling.

And yet there's still that voice – the one telling me that I can't possibly give her what she needs.

That's what scares me the most. How could I ever be enough when I have so little of myself left to give? Peyton doesn't deserve someone who can only give her half a heart. She deserves someone that can give her his everything.

I want to be that man. I want to be that man for her. But deep down I know I can't be. I already gave myself to another, and when she died she took me to the grave with her.

Deciding there's no way I can possibly go back to sleep; I gently toss back the covers and roll out of bed. Grabbing my shirt from the floor, I slip it over my head, then tiptoe out of the bedroom in an attempt not to disturb Peyton.

Pulling the door closed softly behind me, I pad out to the kitchen and start a pot of coffee. Before Finley, I never drank the stuff. I couldn't stand it. But after living with her and Claire, I just got in the habit of making a pot every morning. When I moved to California, the first morning I woke up there I immediately went to the coffee pot and started brewing a pot. It took me a good two minutes to realize that I was making coffee for no one. Because I was alone and I would always be alone.

The thought of never brewing a pot of coffee again was so unsettling that I poured a cup and made myself drink it. I did it again the next day and the next, until one day when I sat down and put the steaming cup of coffee to my lips, it didn't taste quite so bad. Somewhere along the line I had gotten used to it.

I've been a coffee drinker ever since.

It takes a few minutes for the pot to run through. I pass the time by tidying up the kitchen and putting away the dishes I left on the counter to dry the night before.

I've just grabbed a coffee cup from the cabinet when Peyton appears in the doorway of the kitchen wearing the sundress she had worn the night before.

"Hey." She smiles, running a hand through her hair.

"Hey." I smile back. "Coffee?" I grab a second mug before waiting for her response.

"Yeah, coffee sounds great." She moves to the far counter and hoists herself up onto it, her legs dangling off the edge beneath her.

"Did you sleep okay?" I glance in her direction as I fill our mugs.

"Really good, you?"

"I slept pretty good as well," I admit. "Sorry if I woke you." I gesture back toward the bedroom.

"Oh, no, you didn't. I'm usually a pretty early riser. Especially when I'm in a strange place."

"Did you just refer to my home as a *strange* place?" I quirk a brow in her direction.

"You know what I mean." She crinkles her nose playfully.

"How do you take your coffee?" I ask, turning with both mugs in my hands.

"Just black is fine." She reaches out, taking the cup from me the moment I reach her.

"Gross." I grin as I lift the warm cup to my lips.

"Gross?" She giggles. "Are you or are you not drinking your coffee black?"

"I am," I tell her after I've swallowed, the liquid warming a path all the way to my stomach.

"Then how am I gross exactly?"

"Because it *is* gross." I laugh at the confused expression on her face. "I don't drink it because I like it."

"Then why do you drink it?"

"I don't know. Because it's part of my habit now. I mean, why do you drink it?"

"Because I like it." She gives me a funny look, then tips the cup to her lips, taking a tentative sip.

"You mean to tell me you actually like the taste of coffee?"

"I do." She sets the mug on the counter beside her.

"I could maybe understand if you loaded it down with cream and sugar or something but just plain, black coffee?"

"Just plain black coffee." She picks up the cup and takes another drink, smacking her lips together at the end. "Mmm." She hums, setting the mug back down.

"Gross." I chuckle, taking another drink of my coffee. While I may have gotten used to the flavor, that doesn't mean I actually think it tastes good.

"Again, says the man drinking his coffee the exact same way," she quips, her gaze going toward the other room when her ringtone starts playing through the apartment. "Crap," she grumbles, sliding off the counter to go in search of her phone.

I slip around the corner right in time to watch her snag it off the coffee table and hold the device to her ear.

"What the hell? I'm fine," she says, then pauses to listen before continuing, "I had too many glasses of wine last night and crashed on my friend's couch."

There's a long pause where I assume she's listening to the person on the other end of the phone.

"I'm sorry I didn't call. I didn't know I had to." Another wave of silence.

"Okay. Okay." She sighs, pinching the bridge of her nose between her thumb and forefinger. "Yeah, I'll be home in a few." Pause. "Okay, bye." She ends the call and drops the device back onto the table.

"Everything okay?" I ask, pulling her attention to where I'm leaning against the wall, watching her.

"Yeah. I forgot to text Henna last night to let her know I wasn't coming home." She lets out an audible sigh. "Apparently, this is something she never does that she expects me to do."

"Sorry I got you in trouble," I tease, winking.

"You better be. Now I'm going to have to face the inquisitor when I get home."

"The inquisitor?" I chuckle.

"Yeah. There's no way she bought a line of what I just told her. Which means she'll make it her mission today to figure out where I really was and who I really was with."

"So then tell her."

The instant the statement leaves my lips her eyes widen, but then she seems to become aware of her reaction and quickly tries to mask it.

"I thought we were keeping this between us?" she speaks slowly.

"Yeah, we are, but there's no reason for you to lie to your best friend over it. It's not fair of me to ask you to."

"So I'm just supposed to tell her the truth?" She seems unsure, like maybe this is some kind of trick.

"If you trust that she can keep it to herself, then yes, tell her the truth."

"And what exactly is it that I'm telling her? That her boyfriend's brother and I have decided to have casual, uncomplicated, amazing sex and we don't want anyone to know about it?"

"Amazing, huh?" My lips quirk up as I push off the wall and cross the room toward her. "How amazing?" I set my coffee cup on the table next to her phone before stepping up directly in front of her.

"Mind-blowingly amazing." She smiles sheepishly, the slightest pink hue creeping up her cheeks. "I have to go." She stops me right as my lips reach hers.

"You don't have to leave right this minute," I tell her, sliding my arms around her to secure her body to mine.

"I told Henna I'd be home in a few minutes," she weakly objects when my lips slide against hers.

"A few minutes is pretty broad. Did you mean ten minutes or thirty? Or maybe sixty?" I trail kisses from the corner of her mouth down to the crook of her neck. She leans her head back, giving me easier access.

"Abel," she half moans, half pleads.

"What?" I murmur against her skin. "You want me to stop?"

She hesitates for a moment before grabbing my head in her hands and pulling my face back up to hers.

"Never." She kisses me, deep and demanding, just as hungry for me as I am for her.

I can't explain it, but there's something about her. Something that makes me want her in a way I haven't wanted a woman in a very long time. I crave her. She's like my new addiction and I want to keep pushing the boundaries to see how high I can get before I plummet over the edge.

Chapter Twenty-four
Peyton

"I knew it!" Henna slaps her hand down on the kitchen table where she's sitting across from me. "I knew you were lying yesterday. A work friend." She snorts. "I told Aaron something was going on with you two and he said I was crazy."

"You can't tell Aaron." I interrupt her rant. "You can't tell anyone."

"What? Why the hell not? This is the juiciest news I've gotten in a while."

"I'm serious, Henna. We're keeping things casual. Because of that we don't want a lot of people knowing."

"You don't or he doesn't."

"Well, he doesn't," I admit, knowing I've wanted to shout it from the rooftops ever since the night of Sven's party. "I think it's so it'll be easier to cut ties when whatever this is has run its course."

"Are you listening to yourself?" Henna leans back in her chair, a strange look on her face.

"What?"

"Since when do you, Peyton, have things such as casual sexual affairs? And since when do you let the man determine what kind of relationship you have?"

"I've had casual flings before."

"No, you haven't."

"What about Carter?"

"You dated him." She shakes her head.

"After we had a casual fling."

"Not the same thing and you know it," she argues. "It may start casual, but it never stays that way for long. You're incapable of being with a man and not forming feelings."

"So your argument isn't that I can't have a casual affair, but that I can't have one without falling for the guy?" I question.

"Exactly."

"Not everything is so black and white. Circumstances change when the people involved in them do."

"So you're telling me that you're having amazing sex with one of the hottest guys in existence and you don't have any feelings."

"Not a single one," I lie.

"Oh my god." She smiles, giving me a look that says she's got it all figured out.

"What?"

"You're in love with him," she accuses.

"Don't be ridiculous. We've only been seeing each other, if that's what you can even call it, for a couple of weeks."

"And? I knew I loved Aaron after the night of Sam's bachelorette party. One night. That's all it took."

"You didn't tell me that."

"Yeah, and you didn't tell me you were screwing his hot brother, either. So we're even."

"Have you told him how you feel?" I ask.

"Have you told Abel how you feel?" she counters.

"No, because truthfully I don't know how I feel. And it wouldn't matter even if I did. He doesn't want a relationship."

"So what? You just accept that as his final answer and move along?"

"It is what it is, Henna. I can't change that." I push away from the table and walk toward the living room, needing to move for a moment.

"You're scared." She follows me to the couch and takes the opposite end from me when I sit down.

"It's casual sex, Henna. What do I have to be scared of?"

"The fact that you're in fucking love with him for one."

"I've already told you, I'm not in love with him."

"No, you gave me some BS excuse as to why you can't be. Not that you aren't."

"Well I'm not."

"I call bullshit."

"Seriously, Henna, this is why I didn't tell you. You always make things so much bigger than they are."

"I'm going to pretend that you didn't just say that to me." She narrows her gaze.

"I'm sorry. I'm just tired and I don't want to do this with you."

"Do what? Have a conversation with your best friend about a guy you're very clearly into?"

"That's exactly what I *don't* want to do." I run my hands down my face. "Because if I do, if I let myself for even one moment entertain the idea that I could feel more, than I'm completely screwed."

"Why are you screwed?"

"Because he's still in love with his wife," I tell her like it should be that obvious.

"He will always love his wife. But Peyton, that doesn't mean he can't love you too."

"Maybe someone should tell him that," I grumble, not sure where this is coming from. When I left Abel's, I was on top of the world, now I feel irritable and frustrated.

"I hate to break it to you, girl, but whether you admit your feelings out loud or not, they're still going to be there. Whatever you're afraid of, it's already too late."

"Shit." I plop my head backward onto the top of the couch cushion. "I tried to resist him, you know?" I straighten back up. "I knew it was a guaranteed broken heart, yet even then, I couldn't do it. I couldn't."

"Sometimes we meet people who make us lose sight of all reason. Trust me, I know that better than anyone." She laughs.

"What should I do? If I tell him that I'm falling for him." I throw her a menacing look to keep her from saying what I know she's about to – that she was right. "If I tell him, it'll scare him off for sure."

"I agree, that might be a lot right out of the gate. My advice, give it some more time, really lay on that Peyton charm, and before he knows it, he's going to love you too. If he doesn't already."

"He doesn't," I say, very certain of this fact.

But he took off his wedding ring.

There she is again, that stupid voice spreading her false hope through my heart like wildfire.

"Are you sure about that?" Henna questions.

"Yeah, I'm pretty sure." I give her a knowing look.

And he told you to tell Henna.

"I mean, sometimes," I hesitate. "Sometimes he looks at me and I feel like there's no way he can't feel it too. When we're together it's unlike anything I've ever felt before. It can't be just me, can it?"

"Based on what I've witnessed between the two of you, I would say no, it isn't just you. Even Aaron has made comments about the way Abel looks at you. If Aaron is noticing then you know it must be pretty obvious."

"Claire said something to me at Sven's. She said she could tell Abel cares about me."

"See." Henna leans forward and smacks my leg. "If she's telling you then it must be true."

"I just don't wanna get my hopes up, ya know?"

"Honey, I hate to tell you that's not going to prevent you from getting hurt. You opened yourself up to that the moment you let him in." She gives me a sympathetic smile. "But life is unpredictable. Sometimes when we're so sure something is going to go one way it does a complete one-eighty and darts in the other direction. This could be the best thing that ever happened to you. And unless you're willing to ride it out, you may never even know it."

"So you're saying I should dive in."

"Sink or swim, baby. That's my motto." She winks.

"Such wisdom," I deadpan. Seconds later we both burst into laughter.

I didn't realize how badly I'd needed this. How badly I'd needed to tell someone, to talk to someone. To air out my concerns and face what I'm too scared to face on my own.

While I don't always agree with Henna's logic, I have to say that this time she might be right. The only way to know how this will end is to have the want and courage to see it through.

I can't imagine walking away from Abel now, especially not after last night. Falling asleep in his arms will go down in history as one of the best nights of my life.

So, I really don't have a choice to make. I love him. *There*. I'm admitting it. I love him. And that's all I can do. Love him and hope that one day he loves me back.

"What are you doing two weeks from today?" Abel asks, rubbing his hand up and down my shin as we sit facing each other, legs stretched out on the couch between us.

"Two weeks from today." I try to figure the date in my head. "Two weeks from today I'll actually be in New York."

"You're going to New York?" His hand stops moving. "Who are you going with?"

"My boss and another co-worker."

"And how well do you know these people?"

"Pretty well, why?"

"Just asking."

"Just asking?"

"I just want to make sure you're safe."

"I can promise you that I will be. I'll be in good company."

"That's all I need to hear." He resumes rubbing my leg, this time in a slow, circular motion.

"Speaking of New York, I could really use a ride to the airport Friday morning."

"What time do you leave?"

"Four." I drag my bottom lip through my teeth.

"In the morning?"

"Yeah." I laugh at his reaction.

"I'll have to check and see if I have a gig the night before. I'll let you know."

"Okay. If you can't, Henna already said she could. I would just," I pause. "I'd much rather ride to the airport with you."

"You would, huh?" He grins, amused by how flustered I get for no reason.

There is a reason. It's *him*.

"Most definitely."

"Would you ever move out of Chicago?" he asks, seemingly out of the blue. "Talking about New York made me think of it."

"I don't know. I guess it would depend on the circumstances. Why?"

192

"Just curious." He lifts his shoulder in a half shrug. "Sometimes I think about moving, starting over somewhere new."

I ignore how the thought of him leaving makes me feel.

"Where would you go? Back to California?"

"Nah, I'm not much of a West Coast kind of guy. Don't get me wrong, it's beautiful there, but I don't know. It just never really felt like home."

"I get that."

"Where would you go? If you could pick anywhere in the world to live, where would it be?"

"In the world or in the country because those would be two very different answers."

"Let's start with if you could live anywhere in *this* country, where would you live."

"Hmmm." I hum aloud. "That's a tough one. I guess if I had to pick it would be Maine."

"Maine?" He seems surprised by my response.

"I've never been but I've always been obsessed with the idea. But I'd wanna live on the coast. I want to be able to see a lighthouse from my backyard and be able to hear the waves of the ocean at night."

"Just a quiet little costal town in Maine." He leans his head back onto the armrest.

"Exactly."

"I like that."

"What about you? Where would you go?"

"I don't know. Probably south. I've always loved the Florida Keys. Maybe I would find me a little beach cottage. I could spend my days on the beach and my nights playing music at the local bars."

"Do you think it's something you'll ever do?"

"I don't know. Maybe."

"Maybe?" I playfully smack his leg.

"Unlikely," he tries again.

"That's a little better," I agree with a smile.

Abel laughs, the full sound bouncing off the walls around us. I swear he laughs at me more than anyone else. Either I've done a really good job at convincing him that I'm funny. Or, and the more likely of the two, he's laughing at me – as in *at* me.

"Why are you laughing at me?" I pout out my bottom lip in dramatic fashion.

"Because you're fucking adorable." He sits up, pulling my feet into his lap. "Tell me about this." He runs his finger across the feather tattoo on my foot.

"My tattoo?"

"Yeah."

"After my mom got really bad, and we knew she wouldn't be with us much longer, I started spending every free moment I had with her. I would sit next to her bed and read to her, talk to her, just be with her. I wanted to hold onto every single second that I could for as long as I had." I pause. "One evening, I was sitting next to her, going on and on about whatever stupid thing was happening in my teenage life at the time. And Mom was just looking at me. But then something in her expression changed, and I don't know, there was just this look on her face that stopped me mid-sentence."

"What happened?" he asks when I don't immediately continue.

"She told me that she had a dream the night before. That she saw herself as a bird, flying high and free, watching over all those that she loved. She said she didn't think it was just any dream, but a telling of what was to come. She was going to come back as a bird and she promised that when she did, she would leave feathers for me to find, so that when I needed her the most, *they* would remind me that I'm not alone. That she's here with me." I have to fight back the well of emotion that lodges in my throat. "Nine days later, as they lowered my mother's casket into the ground, a feather floated down from the sky and landed directly next to this foot." I wiggle my toes.

"Your mom."

"Who knows. Could be. Or it could have just been a crazy coincidence, but I like to believe it was her. Which is why on my eighteenth birthday I went and got this tattoo. Whenever I'm feeling sad or I'm just missing my mom, I look down at my foot and it makes me feel a little better. Like she's here."

"I get that." He runs his fingers along his chest where Finley's name is hidden beneath the material of his shirt.

"Why don't you tell me about some of your tattoos?" I gesture to the arm that's sleeved from wrist to shoulder.

"These?" He holds up his arm, giving it a quick onceover. "None of them are even half as meaningful as what you just shared with me."

"Except one." My eyes go to his chest.

"Except one," he agrees. "I think I'll eventually get more. I guess I've just been waiting for something to inspire me. What about you? Do you want more tattoos?"

"Nope." I shake my head. "That one hurt like a bitch." I point to my foot. "I have no desire to feel that kind of pain ever again."

"Not a fan of the needle, huh?" He chuckles.

"I know some people say it's therapeutic, but it didn't feel that way to me. It just felt painful."

"They're always painful. Sometimes that's the point."

"Well it must be over my head because I don't get it."

"That's fair. It's not for everyone."

"Clearly." I gesture to myself. "Anyway, so yeah, that's the story on the tattoo." I sit up and glance at the clock on the wall behind me. "Ugh." I groan, turning back toward Abel.

"What the heck was that about?" He chuckles.

"You have to leave for your gig in an hour." I pout out my bottom lip and make the most pitiful face I can come up with.

"An hour." He narrows his gaze at me and my skin instantly prickles. "I can think of a lot we can do in an hour."

"Can you now?"

"Most definitely." He shifts up onto his knees. Wrapping his hands around the backs of my legs, he pulls me down the couch in one swift tug and settles in on top of me. "You are under my skin, Peyton Rivers," he murmurs, dropping his mouth to mine.

"You're under mine." I whisper back.

Chapter Twenty-five
Peyton

The two weeks with Abel are effortless. We don't talk about feelings or the future or anything of any real substance. But we'd laughed. We'd made love. And we'd spent the last few days really getting to know each other. And the more I learn, the harder I fall.

It's impossible not to love a man who's impossibly perfect for you in every single way imaginable.

But as much as I've loved every minute with Abel, I'm grateful for my upcoming business trip to New York. I need a minute to remove myself completely. A moment where I can think, without the cloud of Abel consuming me.

I'm drowning in him.

Plain and simple.

I think it will be good for me to take a step back.

"You about ready?" Henna pops her head into my bedroom as I'm zipping my suitcase.

"Yep." I pull the case to the floor and roll it toward her.

"Nothing like last minute packing." Henna snorts. "What happened to my planner?" she teases.

"She's been a bit preoccupied," I say, knowing that may be a bit of an understatement.

"I'll say." She smiles as I slide past her out into the hallway.

"Thank you again for driving me." I stop at the front door and slide on my flats. "I really didn't want to leave my car at the airport."

"And miss getting up at four a.m. Never," she drones out sarcastically.

"Drink some coffee and perk up, buttercup. I need you alert and awake. I'd like to make it to New York in one piece."

"Yeah, yeah. I'm awake," she says, both of us jumping when a knock sounds on the door.

"Who in the…" Henna trails off, stomping toward the door.

Again, this is where a peephole would come in handy. But Henna doesn't care, she tears the door open without a moment's hesitation.

"Well, well, well," I hear her say as I turn, my eyes honing in on the man standing in the doorway.

"Abel?" I say, my voice coming out as shocked as I feel.

"Hey." He rocks back on his heels. "I thought maybe I'd see if you still wanted me to take you to the airport."

"I thought you had to work last night?" That's the reason he gave me when he said he couldn't take me. Why we had our physical goodbye before his gig.

"I did. But when I went home afterward I couldn't sleep. And since I couldn't sleep and you need a ride, I thought why not." He shrugs.

"So you're taking her to the airport?" Henna steps back, allowing Abel to enter the apartment.

"If that's okay." He looks at me and I immediately nod.

It's okay. More than okay, actually.

"If it means I can go back to bed, I'm all for it," Henna interjects.

"You can go back to bed," he tells her.

"Praise the gods." She lifts her arms up and sways them in the air.

"Gee, thanks." I shake my head at her.

"No offense. I love you and all. But this is way to freaking early for me to be awake." She takes a step toward me. "You'll call me as soon as you land in New York."

"I will."

"Have a fun trip and be safe." She gives me a tight hug.

"I will."

"Thanks, Abel. You have no idea how much I love you right now." She steps back, her gaze going to the man behind me.

"I do what I can." He chuckles.

"Well, we should really get going. I have to be at the airport in less than thirty minutes." I turn toward Abel.

"Here." He leans down and grabs the handle of my suitcase. "I'll take this down and meet you at the car."

"Okay, thank you. I'll just be a second," I say, watching him pull open the front door and disappear outside moments later.

"Eeeek." Henna makes a squealing noise the instant the door snaps closed.

"What?" I hit her with a questioning look.

"Are you really that blind or are you purposely trying to avoid all the signs?"

"What signs?"

"Girl, that man is head over heels."

"No he isn't," I disagree.

"He shows up at your house at four o'clock in the morning to drive you to the airport even though you already had a ride."

"Yeah, because he's a nice guy, and because he couldn't sleep."

"Sure he couldn't." She rolls her eyes. "Or maybe he's going to miss you and wanted to see you for a few minutes before you leave."

"Not likely."

"You're so stubborn. You can't even admit to something when it's staring you right in the face."

"On that note." I sling my purse over my shoulder. "I'm leaving."

"Okay." She smiles and throws me a little wave. "Love you," she calls after me as I reach the door.

"Love you too," I call back, throwing her one last look before exiting the apartment.

When I reach Abel's car, he's already inside. Slipping into the passenger seat, I lay my purse on the floorboard before snapping my seatbelt in place.

"Thank you again for this," I tell him, knotting my hands nervously in my lap. Why I'm nervous is beyond me. Maybe it's the flight. I've never been a huge flyer. Or maybe it's because I wasn't mentally prepared to see Abel this morning and the soaring feeling in my chest is harder to control than normal.

"It's my pleasure," he tells me, starting the car before backing out of his parking space.

The drive to the airport is quiet. Abel hums along to the music that's playing softly from the speakers, while I stare out the window and watch the sleeping city of Chicago pass by.

I've always loved being up and out while the rest of the world sleeps. It makes me feel a little less small.

"So you're flying back on Monday, right?" Abel breaks the silence as he pulls into the airport.

"Yes. I think my flight gets in around noon."

"Do you want me to pick you up?" he asks.

"If you want to." I try to sound indifferent.

"I do."

"Okay. I can text you the exact time once I get to the hotel and have a chance to look at my return flight details."

"Sounds good."

"You know, you don't have to walk me in," I say as he drives past the drop off area into the parking lot.

"I know. I want to."

"Okay." I have to fight the ridiculous smile that's threatening to split my face apart. He finds a spot relatively close and throws the car in park before killing the engine. By the time I get out of the car, Abel already has my suitcase out of the trunk and is waiting for me.

Grabbing the suitcase handle with one hand, he reaches out with the other, sliding his fingers around mine before leading me toward the airport.

As we approach the doors, a wave of anxiety washes over me and I instantly want to ask him to take me back home.

"You seem nervous," he observes, guiding me inside.

"I *am* nervous."

"You'll be fine," he reassures me, squeezing my hand.

"I'm a nervous flyer. I'll be okay once I'm in the air."

"Peyton." My attention is drawn behind me when I hear my name being called. I turn just in time to see John speed walking toward me. "Hey." He smiles when he reaches me. "You made it." His eyes slide to Abel and I don't miss the way his brow furrows.

"I did." I pull his gaze back to me.

Abel shifts next to me.

"Abel, this is my boss, John. John, this is Abel…"

"Her boyfriend," Abel interrupts me, releasing my suitcase to extend his hand to John.

I watch the interaction with wide eyes, still trying to decide if I actually heard him right. Did he just introduce himself as my boyfriend?

"Nice to meet you, Abel." John shakes Abel's hand, his gaze once again falling to me. "I didn't realize Peyton was seeing anyone."

"It's still new," I explain. Not that I really owe him an explanation. But Abel's little announcement has me feeling a bit off kilter.

"I see." John nods. "Well, it was nice to meet you, Abel." He looks between the two of us, his eyes eventually settling on me. "We should probably get going," he tells me.

"Yeah, okay." I shift, turning toward Abel. "Thanks again for the ride."

"I'll pick you up on Monday," he tells me, grabbing my forearm before tugging me toward him. His arms wrap around me, securing me in a tight cocoon that I never want to leave.

I inhale his scent, knowing how much I'm going to miss it while I'm gone. How much I'm going to miss him. And while I know I will only be out of town for four days, four days without Abel feels like an eternity.

Abel pulls back slightly and tips my chin up, laying a light kiss to my mouth right in front of my boss.

"Call me when you land." He kisses me again.

"I will," I promise, feeling all sorts of flustered when he releases me and takes a full step back.

"You ready?" John steps up next to me.

"Ready." I reach for my suitcase, throwing Abel a smile and a small wave as I turn and follow John toward security.

201

"So, a new boyfriend, huh?" John gives me a sideways glance as we sit next to each other at the hotel bar, enjoying an evening cocktail.

We arrived in New York early this morning and spent a good portion of the day exploring. Diego, John's partner of sorts, has been here several times and proved to be a rather handy tour guide to have around. And while I enjoyed my first day in the Big Apple, I haven't been able to shake Abel from my thoughts.

Him showing up at my house unannounced to take me to the airport. The way he introduced himself as my boyfriend. How he kissed me in the middle of the airport lobby without a care in the world who saw. It got the wheels turning and ever since then I haven't been able to get them to stop.

"Yeah." I smile, the thought of Abel as my *boyfriend* making it impossible not to.

For all I know, he just said that for show. We haven't actually discussed what we are beyond that first night when we agreed to keep things casual. And even though I know I should ask Abel about it, I'm not ready to come off of this high I'm feeling just yet.

"When did that happen?" John asks, taking a sip of his scotch and water.

"Like four weeks ago."

"Four weeks and you haven't told me?" He draws back playfully, his palm flattened against his chest.

"We've been keeping it low key." I shrug.

"Well, it didn't seem that way this morning when he practically pissed all over your leg."

"What?" I bark out a laugh.

"I'm just saying, I know when a man is marking his territory and he was marking you good."

"He was not."

"Oh yes, he most definitely was."

"Why would he feel the need to do that with my boss, though?" I wonder aloud.

"Because I'm a man," he states the obvious.

"But you're my boss."

"And, you think they're aren't bosses out there that hook up with their employees?" He gives me a look that says I should know better.

"But you're not that kind of boss," I point out.

"No, but he doesn't know that now, does he? Besides," he takes a long drink, setting the glass back on the bar in front of him. "I'd be lying if I said I wasn't tempted."

"Tempted?" I question, my eyes making a quick pass around the room in search of Diego. He stepped out to make a phone call and has been gone for quite some time. While I adore John as a boss, I'm starting to feel this conversation might be going somewhere I don't want it to and I could really use a buffer.

"You're beautiful, Peyton. You know you are."

"John." I raise my hand to stop him.

"I'm not hitting on you," he promises. "As much as I wish I *could* be that kind of boss, I'm just not. I didn't get to where I am by mixing business and pleasure."

Thank goodness for that. I release the breath I was holding.

"But I will say this. He's one lucky guy. I just hope he realizes it."

"Me too," I mutter under my breath as I lift the wine glass to my lips and empty the remainder of the contents into my mouth.

"There you are," John says, his eyes moving to somewhere behind me. I turn to see Diego reclaim the seat to my left.

"Sorry, Natasha was having trouble getting Em down so I had to read her a story."

"Aww, that's so sweet." I smile at him. "How old is she now, three?"

"Yep. As beautiful as her mama and as crazy as her pops." He chuckles.

"Sounds like you could use another drink." John signals the bartender for another round.

"None for me. I think I'm going to call it a night. Waking up at three this morning has me dragging." I slide out of my stool, grabbing my purse from the bar. "What's the game plan for tomorrow? I know we have a luncheon."

"Yeah, meet me in the lobby at eleven."

"Okay." I nod to him and then to Diego. "You two have fun," I tell them. "And don't drink too much."

Chapter Twenty-six
Peyton

Abel: Is it Monday yet?

I smile at the text message Abel sent a couple of hours ago. He's playing tonight so he must have sent it between sets.

Honestly, I feel the same way. While I've enjoyed my time in New York, the city really is something to be seen, and I've met some amazing people over the course of the last three days, I'm so ready to be home I can barely stand it.

Me: Almost.

I type out a quick response, then drop my cell phone onto the bed as I get ready to jump in the shower. We have to be at the airport tomorrow by eight in the morning, so I want to have as much done as possible tonight so that the morning goes off without a hitch.

When my phone signals an incoming message I'm a little surprised. I didn't expect Abel to text me back right away.

Only when I grab my phone it's not Abel's name I see, but Sam's.

Sam: You're dating Abel!?!

My stomach lurches and before I can think of one single thing to say, another message comes through.

Sam: Aaron just told Andrew. I can't believe you didn't tell me.

My fingers hover over the key pad for a long moment before I finally start to type a response.

Me: We aren't dating. We're just hanging out. And I haven't told you because it's not anything serious.

I watch the dots bounce across the screen as she types her reply.

Sam: That's not what Aaron said.

Me: What exactly did Aaron say?

Sam: That you two spend practically every night together.

While that's a bit of an overstatement, considering Abel plays three or four nights a week, it's not completely untrue. We do pretty much spend all of our free time together.

Me: We don't. But even if we did, that's none of Aaron's business.

I pull up a separate message and immediately text Henna.

Me: You told Aaron?

I switch back to my conversation with Sam right as another message comes through.

Sam: I'm just saying, I can't believe I didn't hear it from you.

Me: I'm sorry I didn't say anything. You were on your honeymoon when it all began and I haven't really seen you since you've been back.

I give an excuse I hope will be enough to pacify her.

Meanwhile, Henna messages me back and I switch out of Sam's message into Henna's.

Henna: He swore he wouldn't say anything.

Me: Well, apparently he told Andrew and now Sam is blowing me up wanting to know why I haven't told her.

Henna: Shit. I'm so sorry. I'm calling him right now.

I switch back to Sam's message.

Me: We should plan dinner next week and I'll fill you in.

Sam: Fine, but I'm still mad at you.

I shake my head, firing off another response.

Me: Yeah. Yeah. Love you.

Sam: Love you too.

I drop my phone, running my hands through my hair. Freaking Henna. I knew she couldn't keep her mouth shut. Especially when she's dating the brother of the man I'm currently hooking up with.

My mind wanders to Abel and a nervous knot forms in the pit of my stomach. Does he know that Aaron knows? That now Sam and Andrew know too?

206

I consider sending him a message but decide against it. If he doesn't know yet, I certainly don't want to be the one to tell him.

Then again, I can't really see him caring that much. At least I hope he won't. After all, he did introduce himself as my boyfriend to my boss of all people.

In a way I think maybe John was right. Maybe him doing that was a show of claim so that John wouldn't try anything with me on our trip. Not that he would have, anyway. He's proven to me over and over again that he's not that kind of guy.

But if Abel felt compelled to do that than obviously he cares enough to not want me hooking up with other guys. It's not something we ever discussed. I guess I just never saw a need for it. I just assumed...

Another thought hits me with force, nearly knocking me off balance. What if he's hooking up with other girls? What if he has been this whole time?

"Stop being stupid, Peyton," I say aloud as I gather my toiletries. When would he even have time to hook up with someone else if he wanted to? Every night he's either with me or he's working. So unless he's hopping around doing daytime bootie calls, I can't see this being a thing.

My phone pings again right as I enter the bathroom. Dropping my shampoo and body wash on the vanity, I head back toward the bed to grab it.

A rush of warmth spreads through me at the message staring back at me.

Abel: I miss you.

I clutch the phone to my chest, letting the happiness I feel spread over me like a warm blanket on a cold night.

He misses me...

I let out the most girly squeal. The kind you reserve for when you're alone and there's no one around to judge you. The sound echoes off the walls back to me and it only makes me smile wider.

I can't help it. That's what Abel does to me. He takes me from uneasy and questioning everything, to so insanely happy I can barely contain myself, all in the matter of one sentence.

I miss you.

It's such a small thing, missing someone. But to me it feels enormous. It feels like the clouds have parted and the skies are opening up, showing me a clear path to the man I now know I am undeniably in love with.

Me: I miss you too.

I have to resist the urge to type out an additional message professing my love for him right here and now.

It feels too soon, feeling about him the way I do. And yet it feels like I've loved him my entire life, if that makes any sense.

I've always been a "think with my head and not my heart" kind of girl. I weigh the options. Not just with how I feel, but with the logistics of making an actual relationship work long term with said person.

But with Abel it's different. With Abel I care more about just being with him. Maybe that's how it should be. Maybe that's why I haven't had much success in the relationship department.

All I know is that every single thing I've taught myself over the years – the dos and don'ts when it comes to men – all of it went out the window the instant Abel kissed me.

I knew he'd ruin me and I kissed him back anyway. I knew he'd consume me and yet I'm the one who begged him not to stop. And I know he'll break me, and yet here I am, running full force into the storm to feel the wind on my face.

Maybe that makes me crazy, or maybe it means that for the first time maybe ever, I'm actually living.

I spot Abel the instant I round the corner. He sees me at the same time, our eyes locking. A slow smile crawls across his face and within seconds I'm gliding toward him, pulling my suitcase behind me.

"There she is." He pulls me to him the moment I reach him, laying an unexpected kiss to my mouth for everyone in the airport to witness. "Fuck I missed you," he murmurs against my lips, and a weird flutter runs through my chest.

"Hi." I smile at him when he releases his hold on me and reaches for my suitcase.

"Hi." He grins and I swear he's the most gorgeous thing I've ever laid eyes on.

"Hi," I say again, almost shyly.

"How was your flight?"

"It was good. First class is no joke." I take the hand he extends to me, tangling my fingers with his as he guides us out of the airport, his other hand tugging my suitcase behind us.

I feel like a giddy teenager having her hand held for the first time. Obviously that's not the case. Abel alone has held my hand countless times, and yet its effect on me never wavers.

It's also not lost on me that he's seems more at ease showing his affection to me in public. I went from feeling like a dirty little secret to feeling like a princess he wants to parade around on his arm.

We make small talk as we leave the airport. I tell Abel the highlights of my weekend. About Diego taking us around the city, about the incredible conference, about all the people I met. I talk so much that by the time we reach my apartment building he's barely had time to say two words. Yet he seemed perfectly content listening to me ramble on and on.

"Thank you for the ride." I unlatch my seatbelt as he pulls into a parking spot. "Do you maybe wanna come up?" I gesture to the building in front of us.

"I'd love to." He kills the car engine and quickly climbs out.

I bite my bottom lip in an effort to hold in my smile. I feel like I'm always smiling when I'm with him, but I can't help it. Abel makes me so insanely happy.

He grabs my suitcase from the trunk before following me up the sidewalk toward my building. I feel him close, like he's walking just far enough from me not to step on my heels.

I keep my gaze forward and focus on fishing my keys out of my purse without falling up the steps that lead to the front entrance.

It doesn't take us long to reach my apartment and the moment the door snaps closed behind us, we both turn toward each other.

He smiles. I smile.

The next thing I know, we're a tangled mess of lips and hands, tearing at each other's clothing like we can't get undressed fast enough.

It isn't until we're down to nothing but our underwear that he thinks to pause and look around.

"You're sure Henna isn't here, right?"

"Pretty sure." I giggle. "Henna. Henna, are you here?" I yell through the apartment. No answer. "I'm guessing that's a no," I tell him, pulling his mouth back to mine.

Hoisting me up, our lips don't part as he carries me down the hall, into my bedroom. Depositing me on the bed, he rids me of my remaining clothes before slowly stepping out of his boxers.

My body sings with anticipation.

"You have no idea how much I thought about this while you were away." He crawls up my body, trailing kisses across my stomach before working his way higher.

"Mmm." I hum at the feeling of his lips as they slide across my collarbone as he settles between my thighs.

"It's all I could think about. The way you taste." He flicks his tongue along the base of my neck. "The way you smell." He inhales deeply. "The way you feel around me." He slides inside of me without warning, causing me to cry out in both surprise and pleasure. "Fuck." He groans, burying himself deep.

This isn't the first time we haven't used protection, but it's the first time he's done so without triple checking with me first. I guess now it's kind of a moot point. I've been on birth control since I was eighteen. I'm pretty confident there won't be any surprise pregnancies in my future.

"Abel." I drag my nails gently up his back.

"It would be so easy." He slowly begins to move, his body sliding against mine. "To lose myself in you." He kisses my cheek. "To let myself fall." His lips move to mine. "It would be so easy." His words whisper against my mouth.

It sounds like he's saying he could fall in love with me. My heart constricts in my chest and my lungs suddenly feel unable to properly pass air.

"Then do it," I say, not even knowing exactly what I'm telling him to do. I don't get a chance to find out either, because

Abel silences me with an earth shattering kiss that rockets through me like fireworks going off under my skin.

His hands are everywhere, his lips, his touch. It's everywhere. Like he's branding me with an iron, claiming every single inch of me as his own.

And I let him. I let him claim me, over and over again. Because when it comes to Abel Collins, I want to be claimed. I want him to know that every piece and part of me is his. Especially my heart.

"Honey, I'm home," Henna sings through the house and I shoot upright, my eyes going to where Abel is sleeping in my bed next to me.

After we had physically exhausted ourselves we must have dozed off.

I shake Abel's shoulder.

"Hey, wake up," I whisper yell. "Abel." I shake him harder.

He groans, his eyes sliding open.

"Henna's home."

"And?" He rolls to his side, snaking his arm around my middle to pull me back down with him.

"And? She doesn't knock. She could walk in here at any moment."

"Well then I guess it's a good thing there's a blanket." He pulls the comforter up over us.

"You don't care if she walks in and finds us in bed together?" I turn to my side to face him.

"No." He lifts his hand to brush a strand of hair away from my face. "She already knows. Besides, it's a little late to try and sneak out now." He grins.

"I feel like a teenager waiting for my mom to walk in and find me in bed with a boy."

"Well, if we're going to get caught, perhaps we should be doing something worth catching." He lifts his eyebrows suggestively.

"Shut up." I push playfully at his chest, rolling to my back.

"Knock, knock," Henna's voice floats from the hallway seconds before my bedroom door swings open. "Are you in bed?" She laughs, stopping dead in her tracks when her eyes slide to the man next to me. "Well hell, you could have at least warned me that y'all were in here indecent and shit."

"Sorry." Abel chuckles, acting completely at ease. I don't know when it happened, but at some point things changed. I think it was so gradual that I didn't even notice until it was staring me right in the face.

"If you two are going to be done anytime soon, Aaron and I bought pizza." She gestures in the vicinity of the kitchen.

"I could go for some pizza." Abel props up on his elbow so that he's hovering above me. "You hungry?" He looks down at me.

"Starving." I smile up at him.

"Okay, we're in," he tells Henna.

"Perfect." She claps her hands together. "I'll tell Aaron to grab a couple extra plates." With that, she spins around and promptly exits the room, pulling the door closed behind her.

"You just made her day." I press up and kiss his jaw before rolling out of bed.

"I did?"

When I look at him he's already out of bed and has his boxers halfway up his legs. Meanwhile, I'm still searching for my panties.

"You might regret that later," I inform him, finally locating my underwear and bra.

"Why's that?" He slides his shirt on over his head. Thank god I grabbed our clothes from the front hall when I went for drinks before round two.

"Because you've just subjected yourself to an evening with the inquisitor." I give him a knowing look. "Not to mention your brother is out there," I address the one thing he's conveniently failed to comment on.

"So." He shrugs, tugging up his jeans.

"So, I thought we were keeping this low key." Even though *I* know that Aaron knows, it doesn't mean Abel does.

"We were."

"What do you mean *were*?" I question, having to physically fight off the excitement that starts bubbling in my stomach.

"I think we're past secretly hooking up, don't you?" He cocks his head to the side.

"Yeah, I do, but I didn't know that's what you wanted."

"Neither did I," he repeats the same thing he said to me after asking me to stay the night with him that first time.

"But you do now?"

"I do." He nods, his grin turning into a full-blown smile, dimples and all.

"So, are we officially dating then? Is that what this is?" I struggle to accept vague responses. I *need* him to put some kind of label on it so I know how to categorize it in my head.

"I guess we are." He crosses the room toward me.

"And you don't care who knows?"

"Pretty sure everyone already knows, anyway. Let's just say Henna is a bit loose lipped." He tugs me into his chest and tips my chin upward.

"You know about that?" I cringe.

"Pretty hard not to when you show up to dinner at your parents and everyone there is talking about it."

"Oh god. I'm so sorry."

"Don't be." He chuckles. "I actually didn't mind it. It felt good to talk about something that makes me happy for a change. It's been a long time since I've had anything good in my life to talk about."

"Abel." His name comes off my lips in a soft whisper.

"I told you the other day, Peyton, you're under my skin." He leans forward and kisses me softly. "Now come on, let's go eat. I'm so hungry." He drops another kiss to my mouth before grabbing my hand and leading me out of the bedroom.

"This is so good." I groan around the bite of pizza in my mouth. I hadn't realized how hungry I was until Henna plopped down an open pizza box on the table in front of me and I practically salivated.

"This is really good," Abel agrees. "I've never had this pizza before."

"You haven't." I give him a knowing look.

"Oh no, this does not qualify," he tells me, knowing exactly where I'm going with this.

"And why not?"

"Okay, someone explain to me what's going on right now," Henna interrupts, her gaze bouncing between Abel and me.

"Peyton and I have a little game we like to play whenever we go out to eat," Abel starts.

"Okay," Henna draws out. "Which is?"

"I try to find a restaurant he's never been to and if I succeed, he has to fulfill one dare of my choosing," I jump in to answer.

"And if I have been there," Abel takes back over, "Then Peyton has to fulfill one dare of *my* choosing."

"Oh, I like this game." Henna bounces in her seat.

"So, I think, because we're eating together, and he's never had this pizza place before, that I should win a dare," I say.

"And I say because she didn't pick the restaurant, the winning argument is null and void," Abel argues.

"Hmm." Henna taps her chin. "Realistically it could go either way. But, I think I'm with Peyton on this one."

"You're only with Peyton because you want Abel to have to do a dare," Aaron jumps to Abel's defense.

"Thank you." Abel nods to his brother.

"Looks like we're at an impasse." Henna leans back in her seat. "Shame. It would have been fun to witness whatever crazy thing you'd make him do."

"Fun for you maybe," Abel interjects.

I know it's something so insignificant, sitting around a table sharing a meal with my best friend, her boyfriend, and the man I'm now officially dating. It's something that happens every day, yet to me it feels monumental on a level I can't even begin to process.

Because this is the first time this has happened when there are no secrets between us. Where everything is out in the open and we can exist like a normal couple. I didn't realize just how much I needed that until now.

We spend the next two hours lounging around my apartment, laughing and talking. I've seen Abel around his brothers before but never in such a laid-back fashion. The two, I'm finding, are a lot alike in a lot of ways, yet so different from each other at the same time. It's nice to see another side of Abel.

It's just after ten when Henna announces she's going to bed. Aaron has to work early in the morning, so he decides to head out, and while I expect Abel to use Aaron's exit as an excuse to leave himself, he doesn't even budge when Aaron says his goodbyes and Henna walks him out.

Instead he pulls me closer, dropping his arm over my shoulder as he secures me to his side.

"Are you tired?" Abel traces his fingers lightly up my arm, causing my skin to prickle.

"Not really," I admit. "That nap earlier kind of ruined me."

"Yeah, me too. I guess we could always give Henna a taste of her own medicine, seeing how we're both wide awake and all."

"A taste of her own medicine?" I laugh, turning my gaze up to his face.

"You know, thin walls," he whispers even though we're completely alone.

"I like the way your mind works." I giggle when he abruptly pops up off the couch, pulling me up with him.

"We've got a lot of payback to make up for. Might as well start now." He winks before leaning down and effortlessly tossing me over his shoulder.

"Abel," I squeal, laughing when he swats my backside. "I can walk, you know."

"Yeah, but this is so much more fun."

Chapter Twenty-seven
Abel

"So, you're officially dating?" Claire smiles, knocking her shoulder into mine as we make our way down the sidewalk. Claire's new little yapper dog is bouncing happily next to her.

"I guess we are," I admit, feeling hopeful in a way I never imagined I would again.

I used to think there was no way I could love someone like that again. That there was no one on this earth that would ever compare to Finley.

But the more time I spend with Peyton, the more I realize that it doesn't have to be so cut and dry. It's not about loving them the same because they aren't the same. And it's not about Peyton replacing Finley, because no one will ever have the power to do that. It's about her claiming a part of my heart that I didn't even know existed anymore.

Over the last few weeks, she has slowly opened my eyes to all the things I was too lost in my grief to see. Possibility. Hope. A real chance to be happy again. These are all things I wrote off after Finley died.

"You seem really happy," Claire continues.

"I am," I admit. "For the first time in a long time."

"I'm glad. After everything, you deserve it."

"So where is this dog park we're going to again?" I ask when we stop and wait to cross the street.

"Just around the corner." She gestures ahead of us.

"I still can't believe you got a fucking dog." I shake my head, looking down at the little white ball of fur. "I gotta admit though, she's pretty cute."

"She is, isn't she." She smiles down at her. "Nick found her for me."

"Nick did, huh?" I question. "You two still hanging out I take it."

"Hanging out. Let's go with that." She gives me a look that says I don't want to know more.

"If he does anything to hurt you, you better tell me."

"Why? So you can go all brother on me and beat him up."

"That's exactly why."

"You're sweet, but I can take care of myself." She takes off walking and I quickly catch up to her.

"I know you can. You're one of the strongest people I know."

"Thank you for saying that." She lays her head against my bicep for a brief moment.

"Well I mean it. You really are."

"I like to think Fin passed me some of her strength when she died. Otherwise I don't think I would have survived losing her."

"But you did."

"And so did you," she counters, reaching over to squeeze my hand.

"Yeah, I guess I did. I didn't come out unscathed, but somehow by the grace of god I'm still in one piece. I think Finley had something to do with it."

"Oh you know she did. Sometimes I think she's standing behind an invisible curtain, pulling all the strings."

"I feel that way too sometimes. Like something random will happen and I'll think to myself, *okay, Fin, I'm listening*."

"That's exactly it." Claire slows as the dog park comes into view. "Look, Sadie Bell, there it is." She talks to her dog like it's a baby.

I can't help but bark out a laugh.

"Are you laughing at me right now?" Her squinted gaze slides to my face.

"Never." I feign innocence.

"Come on, baby, let's go play. Mean Uncle Abel can stand on the other side of the fence and watch," she speaks directly to the dog.

"What, am I in time out now?" I throw my hands up when Claire starts to walk away.

She gets all of ten feet before she turns back around. The way the sun hits her skin, lighting her whole face, I swear she's never looked more like Finley. But instead of hurting like I expect it to, like it used to, it actually brings a smile to my face. Because I want to remember her. Always.

"Are you coming or what?" She taps her foot impatiently.

"I thought I wasn't invited." I smirk.

"Oh shut it and come on." She laughs, waiting until I've joined them before continuing on.

"So, do you love her?" She reverts back to our previous conversation as she leans down and releases Sadie from her leash.

"I think so." I lean back against the fence that surrounds the park.

"You think so?"

"I love her," I admit to Claire at the same moment I'm admitting it to myself.

I've known it's been there, in the background…slowly simmering. I just don't think I realized it until the moment Claire asked me. Or maybe I did and I wasn't ready to emotionally deal with what that meant at the time.

"Do you love Nick?" I quickly add, hoping to steer the conversation back to her. She's been pretty hush, hush about the whole Nick thing and I'd be lying if I said I wasn't at least a little curious.

"I wouldn't say I love him, but I really, really like him."

"Think there might be a future there?"

"Guess we'll just have to wait and see." She shrugs. "What about you and Peyton? Think there's a future there?"

"Guess we'll have to wait and see."

"Darn it. Sadie's over there stealing that dog's toy." She takes off in her direction. "This conversation isn't over," she calls over her shoulder.

"Never thought it was," I mutter after she's long out of earshot.

I've just said goodbye to Claire and am making my way toward my car when my phone starts ringing. Dragging it out of my pocket, I'm a little confused when I see Henna's name flashing across the screen.

"Henna?" I question, lifting the phone to my ear.

"It's Peyton," she blurts, not bothering with pleasantries.

"What's Peyton?" I ask, a nervous knot forming in the pit of my stomach.

"She's been in an accident. We're at the hospital."

"What do you mean she's been in an accident? What kind of accident?" I can't keep the emotion from my voice.

"She was hit by a car walking across the street." The instant I process her words I feel the ground sway beneath my feet.

No, no, no... Not again.

"How bad?" I force myself to say, though I don't know how I manage considering it feels like there is a thousand pound weight pressing against my chest.

"I... I don't know."

"What do you mean you don't know?"

"I mean, I don't know. I haven't seen her since they loaded her into the ambulance."

"Fuck." I rip open my car door and quickly climb inside. Moments later, I'm squealing out of the parking lot. "How bad was she the last time you saw her?"

"She was unconscious and her arm was mangled pretty bad."

I pinch the bridge of my nose trying to keep my shit together.

"I'll be there in ten minutes," I tell her, ending the call without waiting for her response.

My mind races as I weave through the late afternoon traffic.

What if she dies?

It's the question I can't seem to shake.

Could I survive losing another person I love?

And that question in itself holds a million other questions.

Will I ever get the chance to tell her that I'm in love with her?

Will I ever get to see her smile again or hear her voice?

Am I cursed?

I've loved exactly two women in my life.

Finley, my first love. The girl who taught me so much in the short time she was in my life. The one who changed me in ways she'll never know. The one who will forever own a piece of my heart.

Peyton. It's new but it's powerful in a way I never saw coming. She's taught me how to laugh again, how to enjoy the little moments. In a lot of ways she's brought me back to life.

I love them both in very different ways and for very different reasons. But the fact still remains that I love them.

It's exactly eleven minutes later that I walk into the ER of the hospital. It doesn't take me long to spot Henna, sitting in the corner of the waiting room with Aaron who has his arm wrapped around her shoulder, consoling her.

My legs feel like they are dragging large boulders behind them as I make my way toward Henna and my brother.

As if sensing my presence, Henna looks up, tears forming in her eyes the instant she catches sight of me.

"Abel." She pushes out of her chair, wrapping her arms around my middle.

"How is she?" I ask, hugging her back.

"The doctor just came out. They're taking her into surgery."

"Surgery?" I release Henna and take a full step back.

"Tell him the rest," Aaron prompts, seeming to snap Henna out of her fog.

"She's going to be okay," she breathes.

"But I thought you said…" I gawk at her, unable to understand why those weren't the first words she said to me the moment I walked in the door.

"Her arm is shattered." Aaron stands, sliding his hand into Henna's. "They have to go in and try to stabilize it by placing rods and pins."

"But she's going to be okay?" I'm almost afraid to be hopeful.

"She's going to be okay," Henna confirms.

"I don't understand. What happened?" I ask.

"We went to lunch and we were on our way back to Peyton's office. It all happened so fast. We were waiting at a cross walk. The light turned and Peyton stepped out into the street. I was right behind her, but far enough away that when the car swung around the corner it missed me." Her chin quivers. "One minute she was rolling up on the hood of the car, the next she was on the ground and I couldn't get her to open her eyes." She covers her mouth with her hand to muffle her sob.

"She's going to be okay," Aaron soothes.

"I know. I know." Henna takes a deep breath to steady herself. "It was just so scary. And every time I close my eyes I see her laying there. It's like it's on an endless loop and I can't shut it off."

"Did the doctor say if she suffered any other injuries?" I ask.

"A concussion. A couple broken ribs. Some scrapes and bruises."

"And the person who hit her?"

"Not sure." Henna shrugs. "She was being questioned by the police when the ambulance showed up."

"Probably some stupid woman texting and driving, not paying attention," Aaron huffs.

"Peyton's dad said he's going to call the station in a little bit and see if he can find out more information."

"Is he here? Peyton's father?" I ask, looking around the otherwise empty waiting area.

"Yeah. That's how we found out what was going on. They wouldn't tell me anything until he showed up. He just stepped out to call Peyton's stepmom and update her. I guess she's on her way too." Her gaze darts to something behind me. "There he is."

I turn to see an older man with sandy colored hair making his way toward us. It isn't until he reaches us that I get a really good look at him. He's about my height, but a bit broader than me. He has Peyton's eyes, or rather she has his. It's the first thing I notice when his gaze comes to mine.

"Abel, this is Chuck, Peyton's dad. Chuck, this is Peyton's err... friend, Abel." She stumbles over what to call me.

"Sir." I reach out and take his hand which he immediately shakes.

"It's nice to meet you, Abel."

"You as well." I release his hand.

"My daughter seems quite taken with you," he tells me, giving me a once over. I'm a little surprised by his statement. I hadn't realized she had told her family about me. Then again, the subject hasn't really come up, other than her asking me a couple days ago if I was interested in meeting them. When I said yes, this isn't really what I had in mind.

"Well, I'm quite taken with her too, sir," I admit.

He nods, an air of understanding passing between us before he turns his attention back to Henna.

"She's in surgery now. The doctor said it will be a few hours. If you guys want to leave, I'd be happy to call you as soon as she's in recovery."

"We can stay and keep you company. I want to be here when she wakes up."

"Tina is on her way. Besides, she'll be out of surgery for a while before they let anyone back to see her. You've had a rough day. Go home. Take a shower. Get something to eat. I promise I'll call you as soon as I know anything."

"Okay," Henna reluctantly agrees, turning to gather her belongings from the chair. "Abel?" She turns toward me.

"I'm staying," I tell her bluntly.

"Maybe you should come with us," Aaron suggests.

"No, I'm staying," I tell him, turning to claim the seat to my right.

"Okay." My brother nods, following Henna out of the waiting room moments later.

I spend the next four hours in the waiting room of the emergency room. While Chuck and Tina have been able to distract me with some small pockets of conversation, I still haven't been able to shut my mind off. It's like it's been playing the worst case scenario over and over in my head for hours. The more time that passes, the more anxious I become. To the point that I feel seconds away from crawling out of my own skin.

I keep waiting for the doctor to walk out and say she didn't make it. People die in surgery. It happens every day. Even when you think there's nothing to worry about. I've seen the worst case scenario play out right in front of me. I've lived it. And I don't want to ever live it again.

By the time the doctor finally does make an appearance, I'm so convinced I know what he'll say I can barely stand to listen.

I keep waiting for the other shoe to drop. The inevitable *but* that always follows. Only it never comes.

According to him, Peyton's surgery went flawlessly, and while she will have a long road of recovery ahead of her, he sees no reason why she won't make a full one.

The better the news, the heavier my chest feels. The weight crushing down on me by the second, making it harder and harder to breathe.

I don't know why, or what drives my actions, but one minute I'm standing next to Peyton's parents and the next I'm in my car, speeding away like my life depends on it.

Chapter Twenty-eight
Peyton

"Hey." Henna pops her head in the door, a small bouquet of flowers in her hand.

"Hey." I cringe as I shift upright in bed.

"How are you feeling?" She hesitantly enters the room, setting the flowers on the small bedside table next to me.

"Well," I look down at my arm, "I've been better." I laugh, not really sure what else I can do at this point.

"Peyton, I'm so sorry," she starts but I immediately cut her off.

"Stop it. You didn't see that car and neither did I. Don't try to find a way to blame yourself for this. Don't go all Henna on me."

A small smile graces her pretty face.

"Go all Henna on you," she mocks, seeming to relax. "I saw your dad and Tina as they were leaving." She gestures toward the door.

"Yeah, I had to practically kick them out to get them to leave for a little bit. I swear my dad still looks at me like a helpless child."

"Because you're still his child. And," she quickly adds, "you're all he has left."

"He has Tina."

"Yeah, but that's not the same and you know it." She plops down on the edge of the bed and angles herself toward me.

"I know."

"So, have you heard from Abel?" she asks, her change of subject more painful than the physical pain I'm in.

I've been here since yesterday and he hasn't come to see me. He hasn't called. Hell, he hasn't even answered the text I broke down and sent him earlier.

I don't get it. I know from my dad that he was here the whole time. That he stayed through my entire surgery. But then once he found out that everything was okay, he took off and not one person has heard from him since. Other than Aaron, who could only confirm that he's fine and would give me no other information. I'm not sure if it's because there was no information left to give or if it was because he didn't want to give it.

"Nope."

"What's his deal, I wonder?"

"Honestly, I'd like to know the same thing. I mean, why did he even come here in the first place if I mean that little to him?" I let my fear get the better of me and find that it's easier to resort to anger.

And boy am I angry. Furious, even. I thought we had more. I thought *I* meant more.

"You don't mean that little. You should have seen him when he got here yesterday. He was wrecked with worry."

"So then what happened? Why leave and not even have the courtesy to return a phone call?"

"Something must have freaked him out. Do you think your dad would have said anything to him?"

"Chuck Rivers? That man doesn't have it in him. He would never do that to me. He knows I'm crazy about Abel."

"I didn't realize you had told them. Yesterday I wasn't sure how to introduce Abel."

"They've known for a few days. It's my dad, so I left out most details but he knows I'm happy, and that's all he cares about." I pause. "Or at least I was happy."

"Hey." Henna places her hand on my shin and squeezes gently. "Whatever this is, whatever is going on with him, I'm sure he'll come around and when he does, he'll have a perfectly reasonable and forgivable explanation."

"I don't have time in my life for people who can't make time for me."

"That's just the hurt talking."

"I don't care what's talking. I mean it, Henna. It's bad enough that I feel like his second choice. The girl he's accepting because he can't have the one he really wants."

"Stop that." Henna cuts me off before I can finish my thought. "Just stop. You are no one's second choice, Peyton."

"No?" I question sarcastically.

"Absolutely not. That man is crazy about you. It doesn't matter who came before you. It's the now that matters, and girl, to him you matter a hell of a lot more than I think you realize."

"Then why isn't he here?" I repeat forcefully.

"I can't answer that. But, you know Abel. You know that if he's not here there has to be a reason."

"Oh, there's a reason alright. I'm just not sure it's a reason I'm gonna like."

"My god, did that car knock a few screws out of place?" Henna tilts her head and studies me. "Where is my optimistic, perky best friend?"

"She got hit by a car," I deadpan, causing a quick smile to pass over Henna's face.

She manages to wipe it clean for all of two seconds before it spreads wide, laughter bubbling in her throat.

At first I think she's lost it, but then for some unknown reason, I start laughing too. And it hurts...bad. I clutch my ribs and shake my head, deciding I need to try not to do that again anytime soon.

"Have you talked to Abel?" I ask Aaron who helps ease me onto the couch.

It's been three days since my accident and while I'm so glad to be home, there's an air of uncertainty hovering over me that I can't seem to shake. But I know exactly what, or should I say, who, is causing it.

"No, sorry." He frowns, standing upright as soon as I'm positioned comfortably.

"Not your fault." I shrug, dropping my head back onto the cushion so I can look up at the ceiling, afraid that if I look at Aaron for another moment I might start crying.

It's been an emotional couple of days. As if being hit by a car wasn't bad enough, Abel's sudden unexplained disappearance is making an already bad situation so much worse.

"He's just...just be patient with him, okay? He's going through something right now."

"I wouldn't care if the sky was falling." I lift my head up and meet Aaron's gaze. "If it were him sitting here," I gesture to myself, "nothing would keep me from being by his side. Nothing."

"I get that. And I get why you're pissed. But you and Abel are two very different people. You can't expect him to always react the way you would."

"I don't expect him to react the way I would. I expect him to react the way any normal person would when a person they care about gets damn near mangled by a car. Guess that tells me where I stand."

I've looked the other way with Abel, accepted things that I would normally never tolerate. Put myself in situations I've purposely avoided my entire life. I did it because *he* was different and because *I* was different with him.

But there has to be a line, doesn't there? Something that you can't cross without sacrificing who you are and what *you* want.

And I think this might be that for me. I can tolerate a lot of things, but him not being here for me when I need him the most? That I can't accept.

"Peyton."

"If you're going to sit here and defend him when he doesn't have the decency to text me back, don't."

"Aaron," Henna interrupts, popping out of the kitchen. "Don't." She shakes her head, stopping him from saying more. "Will you come help me? I can't get the pickle jar open."

"You can't get the pickle jar open?" He turns, giving her a disbelieving look.

"What? Don't look at me like that. I seriously can't get it open."

"And what would you have done if I wasn't here?" He smiles, heading toward her.

"We wouldn't have pickles with our sandwiches," she quips.

I mouth a thank you as Aaron disappears into the kitchen. She replies with a soft smile and a nod before following after him.

Chapter Twenty-nine
Abel

I peel myself off the couch, the pounding on my door becoming increasingly louder as I cross the living room.

"Abel. Open up. It's me," Claire's voice calls through the thick wood.

I unlatch the dead bolt and pull the door open, barely looking at her before I turn and head back into the living room.

"What the hell?" She shuts the door and follows after me. "I've been calling you for two days." She waits until I reclaim my seat on the couch before continuing, "You can't do that to me. You can't just disappear."

"I'm right here, aren't I?" I hold my arms out.

"You know I worry about you."

"You don't need to worry about me, Claire. I'm a big boy. I can take care of myself." I wipe a hand over my face.

"Yeah, I can see that." She gestures to the empty beer bottles lining the coffee table. "What's going on?" Her gaze comes to mine and her expression instantly softens. "Did something happen with Peyton?"

"Well, if you qualify her getting hit by a car a couple of days ago as something happening, then yes, I guess you could say something happened."

"Peyton was hit by a car?" She gasps. "Is she okay?"

"She got a little banged up. Messed her arm up pretty good, but yeah, she's okay."

"I can't believe you didn't call me. I want to know exactly what happened, but there's something I've got to ask you first."

She pauses. "Why are you here drinking yourself into a stupor and not there with her?"

"Truthfully, I don't know." I decide to be honest.

"What do you mean you don't know?" she asks, sliding down on the couch next to me.

"When Henna called to tell me that Peyton was in an accident, I couldn't get to her fast enough. Once I was at the hospital, there was no way I was leaving. But then the doctor came out and said she was out of surgery and would be fine and I swear all I heard was that she wasn't. That she wasn't okay. That she was gone. I knew that's not what he was saying, but it felt like it was. Like this crushing weight just appeared on my shoulders and I could barely stand to wield it. I felt like I was back there all over again..."

"Abel." Claire's soft voice pulls my gaze to hers.

"I thought maybe I just needed a moment, but the weight only got heavier, and now I don't know what to do. I want to be with her. I want to be with her so badly it hurts. But I can't move under this weight."

"You're scared."

"But why am I scared? She's okay. She's home, probably wondering why I've completely abandoned her. She's okay, so why am I scared?"

"Because Finley was okay. And then she wasn't." She wraps her hand around the back of mine and squeezes. "You went numb after she was gone. You closed yourself off to meeting new people or forming any type of real relationship with anyone because you didn't want anyone to get too close. Because if they got close, and you lost them..." She trails off. "But *she* got in. Someway, somehow, she managed to slip through the cracks in your armor that no one else could seem to penetrate. She got in, Abel, but that doesn't automatically mean you're going to lose her."

"I don't think I would survive it. I don't think I'll survive losing another person I love."

"And yet you love so many in spite of that." She gives me a soft smile. "Your friends. Your brothers. Your parents. Me. You can't be afraid to love her too. You can't base how you live your life on what could happen. You have to just live it. Count each day as a blessing and never take for granted a single moment you have with the people you love."

"But what if I'm not ready to love her like that?"

"I hate to break it to you, Abel, but you already do."

"What if I'm just not ready to let her go?" I admit, my voice cracking over the words. "Let Finley go. Peyton deserves more than a part of me."

"Then give her more. Letting Finley go isn't about forgetting her. It's not about pretending she didn't exist. It's about living for her. She's right here. Can't you feel her? She's a part of you and she's a part of me. She lives through us. She lives through *you*. You owe it to her and to yourself, to do the most with the time you've been given. Time that Finley never got."

"I feel like it all happened so fast that I haven't had time to really process it all."

"That's how love works. It hits you right between the eyes before you ever see it coming."

"I don't know if I've told you this recently, or ever before for that matter, but I truly do not know what I would do without you in my life."

"Yeah. I know." She smiles. "I guess I *am* pretty great." By her tone I can tell she's teasing me.

"I mean it, Claire. You kept me going when even getting out of bed felt impossible. And you never gave up on me. When everyone said I should be moving on, you understood that I wasn't ready. You've never pushed me unless I needed to be pushed. I just want you to know how much you mean to me."

"You mean a lot to me too." She bumps her shoulder into mine.

"When I knocked on your door for the first time almost four years ago, I never imagined this is where we would end up." I relax back into the couch.

"Despite the loss that brought us together, I'm grateful to have you in my life."

"Man, we're really getting sappy here." I try to lighten the moment.

"Hey, you started it."

I think about that for a moment and realize she's right. "I'll give you that."

"So," she lets a few beats of silence pass between us. "What are you going to do? About Peyton?"

"I want to be with her." I believe each word as it leaves my mouth because it's true. I *do* want to be with her. "But in order to give her everything she deserves, I have to let go. I have to say goodbye. I have to set her free." My eyes drift to the urn resting on the fireplace mantel.

"It's time, Abel. You know it is." Her gaze drifts to where mine is now locked. "I can go with you if you want."

"No." I shake my head, my focus going back to Claire. "I need to do this on my own."

Chapter Thirty
Peyton

"There she is!" John strolls into my office with a wide smile on his face. "How are you feeling?"

"I'm good." I adjust in my chair. "My ribs are still pretty sore, but I feel good."

Now if I could just get rid of this pain in my chest...

It's been two weeks since my accident. Two weeks without Abel. Two weeks of sitting around my apartment driving myself crazy.

He text me. Once. Five days after my accident. It read: *I have a few things to take care of. I'm sorry. Please don't give up on me.*

At first I felt hopeful, but as the days have continued to pass with nothing from Abel, that hope quickly dwindled, and completely vanished when I found out from Aaron that Abel had gone to California. He didn't know why or for how long, only that he was gone. And even though I feel like I should be angrier, more than anything I feel sad. And I miss him. So much.

I'm hoping being back at work will offer a welcome distraction because lord knows I need one. My heartache is only heightened by having to endure the Aaron and Henna show every single day. It's not bad enough that I'm miserable, but then they have to go flaunt their happiness right in my face.

I know it's not intentional, but that doesn't lessen the blow. Especially when Aaron smiles a certain way, when he looks the most like Abel. Every time his dimple makes an appearance, I feel like someone has stabbed me in the chest with a knife. Because it reminds me of Abel...

"That's good. Everyone here was so worried. We're really glad to have you back." John pulls me back to the conversation.

"I'm glad to be back."

"I'm especially glad. Janice had to step in and help pick up some of your work load. I bet you can imagine the hell I've been through the last two weeks in your absence." He gives me a knowing look. "So, do us all a favor and don't go getting yourself hit by anymore cars, yeah?"

"That's the plan." I force a light laugh but it sounds foreign coming out of my mouth.

"I've got a meeting I've got to get to but if you need anything. Don't hesitate to give me a holler."

"Will do," I tell him, offering him a half wave with my uninjured hand.

I spend my morning getting caught up on emails and my afternoon in meetings, trying to play catch up with everything I've missed.

The day goes by in a blur and before I know it, I'm in my car headed home. Only I don't want to go home. In fact, it's the last place I want to be. So instead I drive.

No real destination. Just me and the road. I roll the windows down and let the warm evening air float inside, humming along to Florence and The Machine playing lightly on the radio.

I try to push out all thoughts of Abel and focus on my surroundings. On the feeling of my heart beating against my ribs. On the sound of my breath as it leaves my lungs. On the wind brushing against my face as it seeps in through the window. But he's everywhere. And try as I may, I can't shake him.

Deciding to pull over, I slide into the first empty parking spot I find and kill the engine. When I look in front of me, I'm surprised to see Jack's Diner on the corner.

I instantly go back to the night Abel brought us here. I think it was that night that I really realized he was something special. Not that I hadn't known it all along, but I feel like in a lot of ways that night was a turning point for us.

Before I realize what I'm doing, I climb from the car and head toward the diner. It takes me less than a minute to reach the front door, and I hesitate for a millisecond before pushing my way inside.

The diner looks different in the light of day. Maybe because it's filled with people now, or maybe because the sunlight illuminates the imperfections that are easier to hide at night. Like the crack running along the seam of the checkered tile floor. Or the way most of the booths are torn and tattered, or how the wall paper is peeling in the far corner behind the counter.

Or maybe this is exactly the way it looked, and I was just too high on alcohol and Abel to pay that much attention.

Reading the sign at the entrance that says please seat yourself, I quickly find an empty booth next to the door and slide into it.

I've been sitting no longer than a minute when an older woman approaches my table. It isn't until she starts talking that I realize that I've seen her before. At Sam and Aaron's wedding.

"You're Abel's aunt?" I blurt as she's in the middle of asking me if I'm ready to order.

Her eyebrows knit together and then something passes over her features and her demeanor completely changes.

"Peyton." She smiles.

"You remember me from the wedding?" I assume.

"Abel's told me a lot about you."

"He has?" I'm sure my shock shows on my face as well as in my tone.

"It's nice to finally officially meet you. I'm Claudia."

"Peyton." I gesture to myself. "But you already knew that." A nervous laugh escapes my throat.

"I was sorry to hear about your accident. I'm glad to see you're doing better."

"I am," I choke out, my mind reeling.

He's talked to her since my accident?

He's talked to her about me???

"Such a scary thing. Did they get the person that hit you?"

"They did. She was distracted on her phone. At least that's what she told the police. Her court hearing is next week."

"Well I hope she gets jail time. She deserves it, if you ask me. Young people these days, always glued to their phones all the time. No offense," she quickly adds as if assessing my age in her head.

"None taken." I smile.

"Anyway, I'm just glad to see you're okay. My nephew really cares about you, and between you and me, I didn't know if I'd ever see that day come again."

"Well I really care about him," I tell her, leaving out the fact that I haven't spoken to him since before the accident.

"I can see that." She gives me a look I'm not sure I fully understand, then quickly directs back to business mode. "Now, what can I get for you, hon?"

"Well, Abel had me try a burger the last time we were here. I've been craving one ever since."

"I'll have to pass the message along to my husband that you're a fan. He's very proud of that recipe."

"Well he should be. One of the best burgers I've ever had. And I mean that sincerely."

"So, then a burger?"

"A burger," I agree. "And while you're at it, could you throw in some fries and a chocolate milk shake?" I ask, deciding this day is already a wash. Might as well eat my feelings. What else am I going to do with them?

"You got it, hon." She slides the notepad back into the front of her apron without writing a word on it and turns, heading back toward the kitchen.

Chapter Thirty-one
Abel

The ocean waves lap at my feet as the sun begins to set over the horizon.

It's exactly as I remember it, down to the very last detail. The smell of the sea. The sound of the water as it crashes against the shore. The feeling of the sand beneath my toes.

If I close my eyes I can almost picture it. I can see Finley, her green eyes bright as her dark hair blows in the breeze.

My heart aches and I clutch the urn closer to my chest.

"I'm not ready," I whisper into the wind, letting it carry my words away.

"Yes, you are," I hear Finley whisper back.

"I don't think I can do this without you."

"I'm with you, always." Her soft voice vibrates through me as if she were actually standing next to me, speaking the words.

Emotion lodges in my throat.

"I love you so much. Every single second, of every single day. I'll never stop."

"You love her too."

"It feels different this time," I mutter to myself.

"It should. No love is the same. Just because you love her doesn't mean you love me any less."

I know it's what she would say if she could. Because that was Finley. Beautiful. Selfless. Brave.

"No, it doesn't," I admit. "I didn't think it could happen. I didn't think there was any way I could look at someone and not see you. Not compare her to you. Not wish she was you. But then I met Peyton and I don't know. I guess I can't explain it. In some weird way I just knew. I knew she was the one. Even when I fought my feelings. Even when I pushed her away. Deep down I always knew."

I know I probably look like a crazy person, standing ankle deep in the ocean, seemingly talking to myself. But honestly, I don't care. This moment isn't about what I look like to anyone who might happen upon me. It's about Finley. It's about Peyton. It's about me. And this is something I have to do.

Twisting the top off the urn, I step further into the water.

"I will love you forever, Finley Collins. Until my dying breath. You are as much a part of me as I am myself. And as much as it kills me to let you go, I promised you I would. So, here we are, on our beach. The one where you agreed to be my wife. I didn't know if I'd have the strength to do this without you, but I'm not here alone, because you're here. I can feel you, even though I can't see you. And I know this is what you want."

Tears fall freely down my cheeks as I slowly turn the urn upside down, allowing Finley's ashes to scatter on top of the water.

"Be free, my love. Until we meet again."

I watch as the tide carries her out to sea, as she slowly disappears into nothing. And for a moment I feel like I'm losing her all over again. Pain rips through my chest, gnawing at my heart. It's excruciating. Like a blade being twisted over and over again.

I walk further into the water until it's at my knees. Then my chest. Until eventually I'm completely submerged under its weight. And I let it take me, willing it to swallow me whole and take me with her. But just as the darkness starts to take me under, Peyton's face flashes through my mind.

I resurface with a sputter.

Looking around, I realize I'm a lot further from shore than I'd thought. Using the momentum of the waves, I'm able to swim back with ease.

When I reach the beach, I collapse onto the sand. Dropping my face into my hands, I do something I have never truly let myself do. I grieve. I grieve the loss of my wife. I grieve the loss of the life we could have had together. And for the first time since she died, I let myself feel every ounce of that pain. I don't push it away or try to shove it into a dark corner. I let it consume every ounce of me until all I feel is that pain.

And that's where I sit. On the beach. Watching the waves roll in. Feeling the crushing heaviness of my loss sitting down on top of me.

But then something shifts. I don't know how to explain it other than it feels like someone is physically removing the weight from my shoulders. And that's when I look down...

Lying next to me is something that sends my mind and body reeling.

A feather.

It's not colorful like the one that's inked on Peyton's foot, but the meaning behind it is just as powerful.

I pick it up, swirling the quill between my thumb and index finger as I remember what Peyton had said about her mom leaving feathers to let her know she's still here. Maybe Finley is trying to tell me the same thing.

I take a deep inhale and let it out slowly, a calm settling the storm inside of me.

"I'm free and now you are too."

"I love you," I whisper to the wind.

"I love you too," it whispers back.

Chapter Thirty-two
Peyton

"Come on, Henna, we're gonna be late," I holler through the apartment, growing more irritated by the second.

It was her idea to meet Sam and a couple of the other girls for drinks and now here we are, ten minutes before we're supposed to be there and she's still in the bathroom messing with her hair.

"I'm almost done," she calls from the open door. "Two more minutes."

"Two? You said that ten minutes ago," I remind her.

"Just hold your horses," she snips back, right as there is a knock on the door.

Crossing the living room, I pull the door open, expecting to see Aaron on the other side. Only it's not Aaron...

"Abel," I stutter, stunned to see him standing in my doorway. It's been three weeks since I've laid eyes on his handsome face and the sight of him damn near takes my breath away. "What, what are you doing here?"

His gaze drops to my arm that's held against my torso by a sling. "Are you okay?" he asks, his voice soft.

I follow his line of sight, looking down at my arm before my eyes make their way back to his face.

"I'm okay," I confirm, shuffling nervously from one foot to the other. "Why are you here, Abel?"

"I'm here for you."

"Why?"

"What do you mean why?" He seems almost confused by my question.

"Why are you here *now*?"

He pulls in a deep breath and lets it out slowly, like he's mentally preparing himself for what comes next.

"I know I owe you an explanation."

"No, actually you don't," I cut him off. Now that the shock of seeing him again is wearing off, all the anger that's been boiling right below the surface starts spilling over.

"Peyton, I…"

"Please don't," I interrupt him before he can say more. "Let's not make this bigger than it has to be. You told me from the beginning that you couldn't give me what I need. I should have listened."

"No, you shouldn't have. Can I come in? Please. Give me five minutes to explain."

"I can't. I'm going out with Henna and the girls," I say, turning toward the sound of Henna entering the room.

"Actually, you're not." Henna looks past me and nods to Abel, whom she doesn't seem the least bit surprised to see.

"Excuse me?" I narrow my gaze at her.

"We were never meeting the girls," she tells me. "I just needed you to be ready when Abel got here."

"Ready for what?" I look between the two of them.

"For our date," Abel answers.

"I'm not going on a date with you." I look at him like he's officially lost it. And hell, maybe he has.

"Yes, you are." Henna steps into my space and leans in close. "Just hear him out." She wraps her arms around my neck and gives me a quick squeeze. "I'm going to Aaron's. Don't wait up." She swivels around and slides past Abel into the hallway.

I stand rooted to the spot for a solid minute, not sure what the hell to say or do. I feel at odds with myself. My head is saying one thing, but my heart is on a completely different page.

"You disappeared."

"I can explain everything. I just need you to give me the chance."

"And why should I?" My voice rises.

"Because I love you." The instant those three words leave his mouth I swear it feels like the floor has opened up and swallows me whole. "I'm in love with you. And I know I don't deserve your forgiveness but I'm hoping you'll give it to me. Because I don't want to live without you in my life."

My heart thunders loudly against my ribcage.

"Can I please come in?" He presses one hand to the frame of the door.

"Okay," I agree, stepping aside so he can freely enter the apartment.

Shutting the door, I turn to find him standing directly in front of me.

"Since the moment we met I've been trying to fight this thing between us. I don't know if it's because I wasn't ready to love someone again or because I was afraid too. But I fell in love just the same. I don't think I realized just how deep I was in it until the day of your accident. The thought of losing you, it crippled me, and I panicked."

"Because you were afraid you would lose me just like you lost her."

"I've spent the last three years trying to piece my life back together, but nothing has worked. I felt empty and no matter what I did that feeling never went away. Until you. You brought light back into my life. You made me laugh again. You made me *feel* again. You were the missing piece I had been searching for. I just didn't know it at the time."

"You went to California." It's a statement, not a question.

"I did."

"Why?"

"To say goodbye." Tears form behind his eyes but not a single one falls. "After Finley died, Claire gave me a note she had left for me." He reaches around and pulls a folded piece of paper from his pocket. "I think this will explain everything." He slides the note into my hand.

I unfold it with shaky fingers, my heart beating so hard I can barely hear myself think over the loud strum pulsing in my ears.

And before I even read the first word, I know what a monumental moment this is. Because he's sharing her with me.

He's letting me in. And that means more than any words he could ever say.

My dearest Abel,

I've written this letter so many times in my head that it almost feels rehearsed as I put it on paper for you now. There are so many things I want to say and yet there aren't nearly enough words to do it.

First, I want you to know how much I love you. Because of you my life ended with happiness and love, which is much different than the way it began. Thank you for that.

I never admitted this to you, but I fell in love with you the very first night we met. How could I not? You took one look at me and I felt my entire world shift. We only spent ten hours together. Thirty-six thousand seconds. Six hundred minutes. However you break it down, those ten hours changed everything. You changed everything.

I've told you before that I was grateful to the cancer because it brought me to you. No matter how much I wish our ending had been different, I wouldn't change one single thing about our story. Because it was the perfect story. Maybe it didn't end in the traditional version of happily ever after, but I think we came pretty close.

I left Claire with instructions to leave you with half of my ashes. I want you to take me with you, Abel. Keep me close. And when you're ready, I want you to let me go. You'll know when the time is right. And when that time comes, take me to the beach where you asked me to be your wife and sprinkle me into the water that once danced around our feet. Let me go, Abel. Let me go, and live. Live your life fully, fearlessly, and without limit. Live for us both. And never forget how much I love you.

Until we meet again,
Just Finley

Tears are falling down my cheeks by the time I reach the end. But my tears aren't just for Abel. They're for Finley too. Because she loved him. She loved him like I love him. And she was forced to let him go.

"You took her with you…" I say, piecing it together.

"I did." He nods, taking the letter back. He folds it slowly and then slides it back into his pocket. "It took me three years, but I finally did what she asked me to do. I let her go."

"Abel…"

"I will always love her," he continues without letting me say more. "There isn't a day that will pass when I won't think about her and wish our ending could have been different. But I realized something very important these last few days. It's okay to love you both."

"Of course it is." I step closer, my good hand going to his chest.

"I know I've made a mess of things. And I know I hurt you." He reaches up and cups my cheek. "But this was something I needed to do, and I needed to do it before I told you how I feel. Because I want you to know that I mean it. I'm in love with you, Peyton. I'm so in love with you…"

"I love you too," I cut him off. "I have from the beginning. That's why I agreed to a casual relationship even though that's not what I wanted. I wanted you. I wanted you so badly I was willing to take any little piece of you that you were willing to give me."

"I'm yours." It's his turn to interrupt me. "You don't just get a piece of me, Peyton. You get all of me." He pulls me close, his mouth hovering right above mine. "That is, if you still want me."

"I do," I sob, fresh tears pooling in my eyes.

"Then I'm yours." He presses his lips to mine and it feels like time slows down around us. Like suddenly we're the only two people in the world.

The moment is full of unspoken words, yet his touch says it all. I am his. And now, he is mine...

Epilogue
Abel

Two years later...

"You ready?" I smile at Claire, who looks stunning in her floor length wedding dress. Her hair is tied up and hidden beneath a sheer white vail. She's breathtaking, just like her sister was on our wedding day.

"I'm so nervous," she admits, her hand shaking as she slides her arm through mine

The wedding party has all filed into the church. Now, all that's left is for me to walk the bride down the aisle and give her away to one of my best friends.

Nick isn't who I would have chosen for her, but he's turned out to be exactly what she needed. I've never seen either of them so happy and it warms my heart to know I was here to witness it all. That I was the person she chose to share this incredible moment with.

I know Finley's here with us now, smiling down on her sister and the happiness she's found. I feel her everywhere. Always. But sometimes, like right now, the feeling is more pronounced, her presence more known.

"Don't be." I slide my hand on top of hers. "Just focus on Nick."

She nods once before the double doors in front of us open and everyone inside the church stands. I smile down at Claire, then turn my focus forward as we slowly make our way down the aisle.

When we reach the alter, my gaze slides to the left where Peyton is standing among the small line of bridesmaids. She looks so beautiful. Her round belly pronounced in her soft pink dress. I can barely tear my eyes away from her.

She gives me a knowing smile and winks before turning her attention to the minister as he begins to speak.

Once my duties are complete and Claire joins Nick, I shift to the side and take my place next to Aaron as one of the groomsmen.

The ceremony goes by in a blur. As much as I try to keep my focus on the bride and groom, I find my mind wandering back to six months ago when it was Peyton and I standing in front of all our family and friends pledging our love to one another.

It feels like only yesterday, yet so much has happened since then. We bought a house. I bought a bar, which I play at often. And in just four months' time, we will be welcoming our first child into the world. A daughter that we plan to name Aurora Finley, after the two loved ones that we lost.

My life is fuller than it's ever been, and I know that I have both Finley *and* Peyton to thank for that. They got me here. And while it was a long and painful road, I can honestly say that I know I'm where I was always meant to be.

Peyton

"Look how happy they are." I gesture to where Nick and Claire are dancing a few feet from Abel and me.

Abel's gaze follows mine and I feel him nod as we continue our slow sway to the music.

"And what about you?" he questions, pulling my eyes to him.

"What about me?" I question.

"Are you happy?"

"Happier than I've ever been," I answer truthfully.

Sure, we've had our ups and downs and little hiccups along the way, but we've come out of each one that much stronger.

Abel is my rock and I am his.

We understand each other on a level I'm not sure others would be able to. We're there for each other. And we never take a single moment we have together for granted. Because we both know firsthand that tomorrow is not a guarantee.

"And how's our little princess this evening?" He looks down at my belly for a brief moment.

"Moving around a lot. I swear I can feel her more and more every day."

"Just wait, before long we'll be able to see her foot through your belly." He smiles excitedly.

"Have you been watching more pregnancy videos on YouTube?" I arch a brow at him.

"Noooo…" He drags out purposefully.

"Abel." I laugh.

"What? I can't help it." He chuckles.

"Just like you couldn't help yourself from reading every pregnancy and childbirth book you could find. And how did that turn out for you?" I ask, already knowing that it only served to freak him out.

He spent weeks obsessing over my every move, convinced that if I so much as lifted a basket of laundry I was putting myself and the baby at risk. Thankfully, our doctor was able to put his mind at ease at least a little bit. He still freaks out every now and again but it's not as constant as it was before.

I try to be patient with him because I know he's just scared. Scared that something will happen to the baby. Scared that something will happen to me. Unfortunately, I don't think that fear will ever leave him. It's a part of who he is now. Another part of him that I love.

"You may have a point," he finally agrees, leaning forward to lay a light kiss to my mouth.

Even after all this time I still get that familiar fluttery feeling in my chest when he kisses me.

"Your parents are in this room," I remind him when he moves in to deepen the kiss.

"And?" he murmurs against my lips.

"I really don't think your mother wants to see us making out on the dance floor." I giggle, pulling my face back.

"She'll look away." He pulls me back in, kissing me harder.

"Get a room," Aaron grumbles, followed by Henna's soft laugh.

Well, at least that means they're getting along today. They've been on again, off again for the last year. Eventually they will figure their shit out. Until then, we've all had to get used to their rollercoaster of a relationship.

"Abel." I finally manage to break free enough to say his name.

"Okay. Okay." He pulls back, a wide, dimple filled smile lighting up his handsome face. "I can't help it. You just look incredible in this dress." He slides his hand across my hip.

"So incredible that you want to take it off me?" I tease, pressing my body firmer against his.

"Say that again and we're getting the hell out of here, middle of the reception or not," he warns, a playful spark in his eye.

"You can't leave. You still have to give your toast," I remind him. "Have you figured out what you're going to say yet?"

"I have a few ideas." He shrugs.

"Well you better nail those down because I think you're up," I say right as the song ends. Nick and Claire exit the dance floor, followed by the rest of the wedding party.

Pressing up, I gently kiss his jaw before turning and heading back to the wedding party table. Instead of following me, Abel heads to the DJ booth to retrieve a microphone.

After clicking it on, he taps it a couple of times to make sure it's working. For someone who makes a living performing in front of people, you'd think this would be no problem for him, but I know how nervous he's been about giving this toast.

I think it's because he wants to get it right for Claire.

"Hey everyone." He gives an awkward wave and a few people chuckle. "So, when Nick first asked me if I would give this toast, I told him no. I said no, not because I didn't want to do it, but because I didn't know how to. Nick's easy." He points to his friend and they share a little laugh. "We've been friends since we were teenagers and somehow, he still manages to get me into trouble all these years later." Various laughter filters through the room. "You know I love you, man and I'm so happy for you." He shifts, now addressing the room again. "See, that was easy." More laughter. "But Claire." His gaze slides to her and something passes between them. I can feel it, as if it's ricocheting off the walls and hitting everyone in the room.

In that moment I know they're thinking of Finley, and my heart aches for them both.

I once wondered how I could be with Abel knowing I was always going to be his second choice. But it's no longer her or me/me or her. It's us. She is his past and I am his future. And like him, she is also a part of me. Of my life, of my past, and of my future. My hand slides across my stomach and I can't help but smile feeling the bump where our daughter is growing inside of me.

"Claire isn't so easy," Abel continues after a long pause. "You see, Claire and I have been through a lot together. I would even go as far as to say that if it wasn't for her, I wouldn't be standing here today. She is selfless and beautiful, and she loves with her whole heart. She is everything that is good in this world, and for the life of me I can't figure out how she ended up with this guy." He breaks the heaviness with a little joke, jabbing his thumb in Nick's direction. "But in all seriousness, Claire," he speaks directly to her now. "I love you. You are my best friend. You brought me back from my lowest and lit the way to another path. You gave me my happily ever after." His gaze shifts to me and goosebumps erupt down my arms. "Now, you get to have yours." He raises his glass, as he turns back to Claire. "I know you wish your sister was here, and so do I. But she's always with you. And I will be too. I love you both. To Nick and Claire."

"To Nick and Claire," everyone chimes in, lifting their own glasses.

By the time he returns to the table I've managed to blot my cheeks dry, but he knows the moment he sits down next to me that I've been crying. I can't help it. Watching him up there, watching him so vulnerable and open, it got to me.

"Hey." He slides in close. "You okay?"

"Stupid pregnancy hormones," I grumble, fresh tears forming out of nowhere.

"Babe." He grins, taking my face in his hands.

"You said I was your happily ever after," I blubber like a baby.

"Because you are." He drags the pads of his thumbs under my eyes, wiping away the tears. "You gave me a reason to look forward to tomorrow instead of fearing it." His hands slide from my face before one finds its way to my belly. "And I can't wait to see what an incredible future it will be." He leans forward, pressing a light kiss to my lips before murmuring, "And they both lived happily ever after."

And they did...

The End

Acknowledgments

Thank you so much for taking the time to read WHAT COMES AFTER. After reading Ten Hours, I know everyone was really hoping for Abel's happily ever after and I hope you love the one he got. I know I did.

***To everyone who helped make this book possible**- thank you.*
*My editor **Rose**, for being a master with a red pen.*
*My friend and teaser extraordinaire, **Angel**- at this point I've run out of things to say other than I love you and thank you!*
***Melissa Gill**- for designing the PERFECT cover for Abel and Peyton.*
*My book besties **Joni** and **Jackie** (who talks in cursive when she's drunk).*
*My friend and fellow author, **Alex Grayson.***
*My agent- **Two Daisy Media.***
*My **husband** and **children** for always supporting my dreams and pushing me to be the best version of myself.*
*My **family** and **friends**- your support means more than you will ever know.*
*To my **readers**- thank you. If I could hug each and every single one of you in person I would. It's because of you that I'm able to live my dream and I will forever be grateful. From the bottom of my heart- thank you.*

XOXO

-Melissa

57459885R00151

Made in the USA
Middletown, DE
04 August 2019